Also by Beth Rinyu

The Exception to the Rule

An Unplanned Lesson

An Unplanned Life (the sequel to *An Unplanned Lesson*)

For updates, visit Beth Rinyu's author page:
www.facebook.com/BethRinyu

Drowning in Love

Beth Rinyu

ISBN-13: 9780615843490
ISBN-10: 0615843492

Hugs and Kisses to...

My Mom, Joanne Kruplo and Sarah Guernsey for pre-reading and giving me great feedback. Janet Halasz for looking over my manuscript one last time, making sure that it's in the best possible shape for you guys to read. Stephanie Lane for allowing me to tell her the plot of each story as I'm writing it even though she wants to be surprised - she knows I can't keep a secret. Sandi Lynn for always being there to listen to me vent, while offering great advice. Katrina Tingle for finding all of those great character inspiration photos. If anyone from Hollywood is reading this, she's your girl for a casting director! To all of the awesome book bloggers who spread the word about my books. And my readers who have read and enjoyed my first two books and have taken this journey with me from start to finish of this book. I know that Travis & Mia will be in good hands with you guys. As long as I know there is at least one person getting enjoyment from my books, I will keep writing…. you guys are the best!
And as always….my husband and kids for allowing me to ignore them while I wrote this story; for some reason I don't think that they minded.

Dedication...

This book is dedicated to my Grandmom Marion. Mia is a lot like she was....caring, kind and always allowing everyone into her huge heart.

Drowning in Love

Prologue

Mia...

What defines the perfect life? Well, I wasn't quite sure, but I was fairly certain that mine was pretty close to it. I was marrying my high school sweetheart in just a few short months. Together, we had pursued our dream of living in New York City in our tiny Greenwich Village apartment. But to me, it didn't matter where we lived – as long as I was with Eric Callahan, I was happy. I first met Eric in the fifth grade. I was the new girl and couldn't help but notice the cute boy with the big brown doe eyes who sat in the front of the class because of his constant chattering. I was told to stay away from him because he belonged to Tiffany Bennet, the most popular and mean-spirited girl in the fifth grade. All of the boys liked her, probably because she had something that most ten-year-old girls lack: boobs. So, being the new girl and wanting to fit in, I kept my distance. All throughout middle school, I crushed on him from afar, and even though Tiffany had long since moved on to someone new, I still never had the guts to tell him how I felt. It wasn't until Mrs. McVay's tenth grade biology class that I finally got the nerve to talk to him. Eric and I were partnered up during the frog dissection unit. Since I was totally grossed out by the whole thing, Eric just took charge and did everything. Ever since that day, that's how it's been. Eric was my best friend, my finder of lost things, my foot warmer on a cold winter night, keeper of my heart, and my soul mate. He was a New York City Police officer, and I had followed my love of cosmetology and was working at a very upscale New York City Salon. I had never been happier. But sometimes *happiness can be taken away in the blink of an eye, leaving you scared, alone, and wondering how you will ever pick up the pieces of what was once a fairy tale life.*

I stepped out of the shower into the tiny steam-ridden bathroom, while Eric stood at the bathroom sink, shaving and wiping the condensation from the mirror.

"Sorry," I said as I wrapped myself in the towel and hugged him from behind.

He turned around with his half shaven face and hugged me back. "That's okay, but only because you're so cute."

"Can you believe that in a little less than three months, I will no longer be Mia Taylor?"

He kissed me on the forehead. "I can't wait. All of these overtime shifts will have paid off when I'm sitting on a beach in Aruba with Mrs. Mia Callahan."

I smiled, just thinking about our honeymoon. "I wish we could both call out today and stay in bed and practice for that honeymoon." My towel fell off when I lifted my arms and wrapped them around his neck.

He looked down at my naked body. "You're killing me, Mia." He glanced at his watch. "Ten minutes?"

"I'll take it!" I grabbed his hand and led him into the bedroom.

***

I got through the workday with ease and stopped off at the store. I called Eric once I was home. It was six o'clock and he was working until seven. "I'm cooking your favorite tonight, eggplant parm, so don't eat anything."

"Okay."

"You will be home on time, right?"

"Yup, and you know I want to pick up where we left off this morning."

I giggled. "Eric....is Ian right there with you?" Ian was Eric's partner.

"Yeah. He doesn't pay attention to anything, though." He was silent for a moment as I heard a call coming over the radio. "Aww, damn. I may be just a little late."

"Ugh....Okay, I'll keep it warm for you. I love you and be careful."

"Always, and I love you too."

I hated his crazy schedule. He had been working so hard, picking up every overtime shift that he could get to pay for our wedding and honeymoon. We just had to get through the next three days and then we were on vacation for a whole week. We didn't have any plans other than finalizing the wedding details and just taking time to slow down and relax. After two hours of slicing, breading, frying, and baking, I was finally taking the eggplant from the oven when I heard a knock on my door. Eric must have forgotten his key *again*. His timing was perfect. I opened the door and instead of seeing Eric on the other side, it was two police officers I didn't know.

"Mia Taylor?"

"Yes?" I felt my heart drop to my knees. Somehow, I knew; they didn't need to say anything – I just knew.

"Mia, there's been a shooting....." Those were the last words I heard before I totally blacked out.

I was sitting on my couch; I didn't even know how I got there. The female police officer handed me a glass of water as she held a cold rag on my head. "Are you okay?" I couldn't answer. I was in shock. She took my hand and rubbed it gently.

"I need to go see him." My voice was shaking.

"Okay, are you sure you're okay? Do you need us to call you an ambulance to have you checked out?" the male police officer asked.

"No, I just need to see Eric; he needs me." I began to cry.

The female police officer placed her hand on my shoulder. "We'll take you to the hospital, Mia."

"Has anyone notified his parents?" I asked.

"Yes, they're on their way."

I threw on my flip-flops and followed them out the door.

When we arrived at the hospital, the male police officer checked in with the nurse. Eric was still in surgery. I took a seat in the waiting area. The female police officer, who had finally introduced herself as Judy, took a seat next to me.

"Mia, is there anyone that you would like me to call, to be here with you?" I knew that I had to break the news to my mother. Since I probably wouldn't even be able to get the words out without breaking down, I gave Judy her phone number so she could handle it.

I pulled my legs up onto the chair and wrapped my arms around them. I rested my head on my knees and thought back to this morning. We were talking about our wedding, our honeymoon, our life together as husband and wife. Never in a million years did I imagine that I'd be sitting in a hospital while he was fighting to make that life happen.

"Is Ian okay?" I asked, finally lifting my head from my knees.

"He's okay. He's in a state of shock. He's not handling this too well," Judy said.

Of course, he wasn't handling this well. He and Eric were super close. They had been partners since Eric had joined the force. He thought of Eric as a younger brother.

My tears began to fall once again when I saw Eric's parents. His mother's eyes were swollen and I could tell that she was feeling the same way that I was.

"Mia!" The tears rolled down her face. She wrapped her arms around me and we both broke down together. Eric's mom and dad were like a second set of parents to me. Eric's father was always such a big strong-looking man, but tonight he seemed as fragile as glass as he hugged me tightly.

We sat together in silence, waiting for Eric's doctor to appear and tell us that everything was going to be okay. Unfortunately, the news that he had to deliver was the opposite of what we wanted to hear. Eric was shot in the jaw. The bullet had lodged in his shoulder and torn through two main arteries in his neck, which had severely affected his blood flow. His brain was greatly affected by the lack of oxygen. There were a few more tests they wanted to do, but right now, the prognosis seemed grim.

My mother and stepfather appeared right when I needed them most. "Mom!" I cried.

"Oh, Mia!" She hugged me tightly. I felt like a little kid again as I curled up in her arms. My stepfather took the empty seat on the other side of me and gently rubbed my back. Once I felt calm enough to speak, I gave them an update on Eric.

"But it's okay; he's going to pull through this and everything is going to be okay, I just know it," I said.

"Mia, they have him in a room. Would you like to go see him?" Eric's father asked.

I nodded and stood up on my shaky legs. I followed Eric's father down the hallway and into Eric's room. He led me in and then immediately walked out to give me some privacy.

Eric was hooked up to every machine imaginable with a tube down his throat. It pained me just to look at him. I took his hand in mine as the tears rolled down my face.

"This wasn't supposed to happen, Eric. You can't leave me. I won't be able to live in a world without you." The haunting rhythm of the beeping machines was a painful reminder that this was the only thing keeping him alive. "I can't say goodbye to you, I just can't. You have to pull through this. We have so many things that we have planned in life and if you think I'm going to let you back out of them because of this, you're wrong. Please, Eric . . . please." I buried my face into his chest and began to sob.

I still had my head buried in his chest and was clutching his hand tightly when his father walked back in the room.

"Mia." His tone was gentle.

I lifted my head and smiled through my tear-filled eyes. "He's going to be okay; you don't have to worry," I said.

He closed his eyes as if my words pained him. He took my hand and helped me up, leading me back into the waiting area to my parents.

"Mia, why don't you let us take you home to get some sleep and we'll come back first thing in the morning?" my stepfather gently asked.

"No. If he wakes up, I need to be here."

"Mia, sweetie, it's after midnight. You need to go home and get some rest," my mother said.

"Mom, he is going to wake up. You know that, right? He would never leave me." I could feel the hysteria in my voice as I tried not only to convince my mother but also myself of that fact.

Her eyes filled up with tears. She didn't respond. She just pulled me to her and kissed me on the head.

I said my goodbyes to Eric's parents. They were sticking around for a little while longer and then staying at Eric's aunt's apartment in the city.

"Promise me that you will call me if anything happens?" I asked.

"I promise," Eric's mother answered

I hugged her tightly. "I'll see you tomorrow," I said. It was now just a waiting game – the longest wait of my life.

***

Three days passed and the test results were not what anyone had hoped for. Eric had no brain activity whatsoever. But I was still holding out hope. Eric was still here physically and that was all that mattered. I could still feel the warmth of his skin and kiss his lips, so to me he was still alive. I had hunkered down in his room for the past seventy-two hours, only leaving when the nurses would come in and tell me that visiting hours were over. I would talk to him just as if he were there listening to me. I talked about our wedding, our honeymoon, and what our life together would be like after we were married.

I was in my usual spot, sitting in the chair right along Eric's bedside with his hand in mine, when his dad walked into the room.

"I was just telling Eric that once we have kids we really need to move back home, away from the city. That would be better for you guys too, because then you would get to see your grandkids all the time," I said.

Eric's dad looked at me sympathetically. "Mia, we've made the decision. Eric wouldn't want to be kept alive this way."

I shook my head in disbelief. "No, no, no!" I shouted. "Please, don't! He's alive, he's breathing. Please don't take him away from me. I will die right along with him. Eric is strong. He's going to wake up; I know it." I was trying to catch my breath. Eric's father looked at me with tear-filled eyes as the nurse came running in, hearing my screams.

"Is everything okay?" she asked.

I bent down and hugged Eric. "Please don't let them do this….please. He loves me and I love him. We're going to get married and have kids. Please, I'm begging you."

Eric's father had tears rolling down his face as he looked at me. "I'm sorry, Mia." He put his head down and walked out the door.

I buried my head into Eric's chest and began to sob. "Eric, please wake up, baby. Don't let them do this to you."

The nurse came over and tried to pry me gently away from him, but it was useless. I wasn't budging. She finally gave up and walked out the door, leaving me alone one last time with Eric. I kissed him over and over again. I wanted to taste him on my lips for the rest of my life. I took a deep breath, memorizing every inch of his familiar face. I rested my head on his shoulder and whispered in his ear, "I will love you forever, Eric...."

Chapter 1

Mia...

The steam from my hazelnut coffee rose from my cup and flooded my senses. As I looked out my bedroom window, the gray clouds were now overpowering the bright morning sunshine that was streaming through just an hour ago. It was so reflective of my life. I had never been happier. Until that day it had all changed, one year ago, and the sunny world that I had been living in became filled with clouds. In the blink of an eye, my past, present, and future were taken away. After Eric's death, I hid in my apartment for three long weeks, not wanting to talk to anyone. I was numb. I would wrap myself in his clothes and pretend that he was still there with me. I was living in a fantasy world, but that was the only thing that kept me from going completely insane. My mother and sister did their best to coax me from my depression, but it was of no use. Eventually, I was forced to join the land of the living once again, not by choice, but by duty. I had bills to pay and without Eric around to help with supplementing the income, I was falling behind – big time.

I was a totally different girl than I had been a year ago. The old Mia Taylor was always smiling and carefree. She would spend the majority of her day laughing and just reveling in her perfect life. The new Mia was the complete opposite – an empty shell. Time didn't seem to be healing the wounds; it was just a band aid that could be ripped off at any time and begin to bleed uncontrollably. I took one last sip of my coffee and finished getting dressed. I took a deep breath and kissed the picture of Eric that I had sitting on my nightstand, like I did every day before facing the world and heading out the door.

I dragged myself into Salon JR, putting on my happy face. I had a full schedule today, which meant I would be keeping my mind occupied. I was hoping that this would aid me in forgetting that today was the one-year anniversary of the day that Eric was shot. Although it wasn't the day he died, it was the day I had lost him forever.

I walked in to find Juan, another stylist and part owner of the salon, standing behind the desk. Juan and I had hit it off right away, but over the past year, he had become my rock. He had been the only one that I felt comfortable talking to about Eric. I wasn't afraid to express my feelings to him. He made me laugh – something that didn't come easily these days. I never tired of listening to his countless stories of the arguments that he would get into with his boyfriend Brian, the other owner of the salon. They were perfect for each other; even though they were both in their thirties, they would still bicker like an old married couple.

"Girl, what is going on with that hair?" Juan asked, clearly referring to the messy bun I was sporting today. Normally, I would have my blonde hair either perfectly flat-ironed or in big loose waves. Today, I wasn't in the mood to mess with it, so this was the outcome.

"Deal with it," I said.

"Mmm.....you're never going get back into the dating game with that mess on top of your head."

Juan had been on my case for the past few months about testing the waters again, but I wasn't ready. I wasn't sure if I would ever be ready. I couldn't fathom ever loving someone as much as I loved Eric.

"That's okay. I'm perfectly fine being miserable alone."

"Mia, need I remind you that you just turned twenty-seven? Thirty is just around the corner. I know it's going to be hard at first, but you have to take that first step. You're still alive and you have a life to live whether you want to or not."

If anyone else had said that to me, I would have probably told them to go to hell. But Juan and I had no boundaries. He was allowed to tell me exactly what he thought and vice versa. He picked up the can of hair spray and ran his fingers over my hair, giving it a good spray. "There. That's a little better." Juan was always so into his appearance. He was a walking fashion plate. He had dark brown eyes that matched his closely cropped dark brown curly hair.

My schedule was up on the computer and I had noticed that my first appointment had canceled. *Great. Just when I thought I was going to be too busy to think about anything else today.*

My attention was hastily taken away from the computer screen when I heard Juan mumble under his breath, "Oh, Miss Thing, look at him." I looked up to find a very tall, attractive man, dressed in what looked to be a very expensive suit, approaching the front desk. I kicked Juan under the desk to stop him from his obvious eyeball assault on this man. He pulled it together and put on his best deep voice. "Can I help you, sir?"

"Yes, I wanted to see if you could squeeze me in for a haircut before my ten o'clock meeting."

Juan looked down at the computer screen. "Sure. Mia will be able to do you." Juan must have felt me staring at him. "Oh, I mean she'll be able to fit you in – to, umm, cut your hair. Abby will take you to her chair."

His stare was intense as he fixated his hazel eyes on mine before Abby took him back.

Juan grabbed me by the hand and pulled me over to the make-up artist's station. "What are you doing?" I asked.

"Of all days for you to look like you've just rolled out of bed," he said as he began to powder my face. "And no mascara today? What is up with that? You have these beautiful blue eyes and you do nothing to accent them!"

"Juan, will you -" I stopped talking when he began to attack my lips with lip-gloss. He adjusted my bun the best that he could and gave it another spray with the hair spray. I looked at him and shook my head as I began to walk away.

"Wait, one more thing," he said as he grabbed my arm and pulled me back. He unbuttoned the top button on my blouse. "Work it, girl!"

I buttoned my blouse back up to where I had it. "I'm not working anything except my scissors, cutting his hair!"

"Such a waste of a perfectly beautiful straight guy," I heard him say as I walked away.

I took a deep breath and walked over to my chair. "Hi, I'm Mia." Normally, I didn't get nervous when I was around incredibly handsome men. Because the truth was, I had never really paid attention when I *was* around one. I always had the most handsome guy in the world, so there was no reason for my eyes to wander. But now, since Juan had to bring to my attention just how good looking this man was, I could feel my nerves getting the best of me.

"Hey," he replied as if it was effort to do so.

"So, what did you want done today?"

"Just trim it."

I grabbed my scissors and began to cut his thick brown hair. At first, the silence was a little awkward, but after a few minutes, he began to respond to the endless alerts of text messages coming through on his phone, allowing me to cut his hair in comfortable silence.

I was just about done. All that was left to do was to shave the back of his neck. His phone began to ring and I was surprised when he answered it instead of letting it go to voice mail until we were done. His conversation sounded like it was a bad business deal. He began to move his head, expressing his disdain to the person on the other end. This was making it very difficult for me to finish. I stopped for a few seconds, holding the razor in my hand, waiting for him to hang up. He gave me a look of displeasure and then looked down at his watch, never skipping a beat in his phone conversation.

Well, maybe if you hung up the damn phone and stopped moving your head, I could finish – jerk! I did my best to work with his moving head as his anger continued to build and his head continued to move. Then the caller on the other end of the phone must have said something that really irked him. He jerked his head just as I was gliding the straight-edged razor over the back of his neck. I panicked as I watched the blood begin to roll down his neck. I hurried up and grabbed the towel, trying to control the bleeding, but it was too late – the collar on the crisp white shirt that he had on under that expensive suit was stained with blood.

He stopped his phone conversation for a brief second when he looked up and saw the blood on the towel.

"I'm sorry," I whispered.

He abruptly hung up the phone. "Are you an idiot or something? I have to be at a meeting in twenty minutes!"

I felt my anger growing. I was the type of person who always stood up for myself. I never allowed anyone to talk to me that way, customer or not. "I'm sorry, but maybe if you weren't moving your head all over the place, then this wouldn't have happened!" My voice was growing louder.

"Oh, well, sorry. I guess I didn't realize that they gave me the most inexperienced person to cut my hair!" he shouted.

My jaw dropped. Luckily, Juan came running over just in the nick of time to stop what was about to come from my mouth.

"Oh, what happened?" Juan asked, trying to play peacekeeper.

"I'll tell you what happened. This incompetent doesn't know what the hell she's doing when it comes to cutting hair!" His voice carried so everyone in the salon could hear what was going on.

I was fuming and I was about to let him know it. "You know what –"

"Mia, I'll finish up here." Juan shot me a look as if he were trying to tell me to stop.

I stood there silently as I bit my lip, trying to control myself from what I wanted to say. "Mia, I got it," Juan repeated. I gave the man sitting in my chair one last look of displeasure and stormed into the break room, ignoring the stares of the clients, who had heard what had just transpired.

I stayed in the break room until Juan came back to tell me that he was gone. "Well, I guess you won't be going out on any dates with him," Juan joked.

I didn't find it humorous at all. My blood was still boiling over that jerk. "He was a complete asshole!"

"Yeah, I guess he was," Juan finally admitted.

"I am so glad that tomorrow is Sunday. I need a break." Even though that break would mean how I spent most Sundays for the past two months: going to my client Charlotte Montgomery's home and doing her hair. Mrs. Montgomery had been my client in the salon since I had first gone to work there. She was well into her eighties, very wealthy, and very demanding. Most of the staff at the salon didn't care for her, but she and I had hit it off immediately. I was the only person she would allow to touch her hair when she would come for her weekly appointments. She had recently undergone surgery and was still recovering, so I had made arrangements to go to her posh penthouse on the Upper East Side every Sunday and do her hair. I actually enjoyed the few hours that I would spend there each week. It was nice to see how the other half lived. She would always have a nice spread, which would include an array of elaborate breakfast items. She had several maids and a cook. I felt like I was in a different world when I entered her home.

"Are you going to the Ice Queen's tomorrow?" Juan asked.

"Juan, that's not nice; she really isn't bad."

"Well, she's been hogging you every Sunday morning for the past two months. I miss our Sunday breakfast dates," Juan whined.

"Well, you do have a boyfriend that you can go on those breakfast dates with, you know."

"Yeah, but he's no fun. I like it when it's just us girls!" We both began to laugh. I shook my head and went back out to the front to greet my next client, hoping that the next one would be a little bit nicer than the last.

Chapter 2

Mia...

I was glad to enter the confines of my tiny little apartment after a very long and tiring day of feeling like I couldn't please any of my clients. I poured myself a glass of wine and dumped the vegetable lo mein that I had picked up on my way home onto a plate. I had found that I was able to muddle through the daytime and put on a happy face; it was the nights that I was having the hardest time coping with. Sure, I was used to not having Eric around on the nights that he had to work, but I knew I would be able to hug him and kiss him when he returned home in the morning. Going to bed alone and knowing that the man you love wouldn't be walking through that door ever again wasn't easy.

I was feeling unusually low tonight. I wasn't sure if it was because of the fact that tonight was the one-year anniversary of that dreaded day or because of that jerk I had encountered at the salon today. I took a sip of wine and a few bites of my food before becoming disinterested in both. I walked over to the tiny closet that contained mine and Eric's clothes. After a whole year, I was finally able to start slowly getting rid of his things, but there were a couple of items that I refused to part with. I pulled out his black hoodie. It was his favorite sweatshirt and even though it was old and worn, he had refused to part with it – and now, so did I. If I breathed in really hard, I could swear that it still smelled like him. At least that was what I told myself. I lay down on the couch and hugged the sweatshirt tightly. I closed my eyes, imagining that I was wrapped in his arms, and fell into a deep sleep.

I jumped from the couch the next morning, trying to figure out where I was. Once I awoke a little, I looked at the clock. *Shit, 8:45.* I had to be at Mrs. Montgomery's by ten o'clock. I got up, took a quick shower, and dressed. I chugged down a cup of coffee and got on my way.

I got out of the taxi and was greeted by John, the doorman for Mrs. Montgomery's upscale apartment building.

"Hey, Mia, how are you?" John said as he held the door open for me. John was a middle-aged, chubby guy who always had a smile on his face, and always managed to put a smile on mine every time I saw him. He had just had his fourth child, a little girl after three boys. He was so proud and would always show me pictures of her.

"I'm good. How's the beautiful little baby doing?" His smile widened.

"Oh, she's perfect, thanks for asking." I smiled back and headed inside. I waited for the elevator door to open and made my way up to Mrs. Montgomery's penthouse. I was greeted by Mrs. Montgomery's maid, Bernice. "Good morning, Mia, Mrs. Montgomery is waiting for you in the dining room.

Mrs. Montgomery was sitting at the large dining room table with a cup of tea in her hand and her head buried in the newspaper. She looked up when she heard me enter. "Oh, Good morning, Mia, dear. Sit down and have a cup of tea with me." I took the seat across from her as Bernice poured the hot water into my teacup. It always felt a little strange to me, having these elaborate breakfasts with Mrs. Montgomery. I wasn't used to having people wait on me. I felt like a little kid again, having a tea party with my stuffed animals. "So how was your week?" Mrs. Montgomery asked as she took a sip of her tea.

I dipped my tea bag in the water. "Okay, I guess. Yesterday was a year ago that –" I took a deep breath and tried to regain my composure.

Mrs. Montgomery placed her hand on mine. "Oh dear, I'm so sorry." Despite what everyone else thought about Mrs. Montgomery, I really liked her. She had been so kind and caring to me after Eric's death and it really had meant a lot to me.

I nodded in appreciation.

"You know, when my husband passed away, I thought my world had ended. It took me a while to live my life again, but I did. I was too old to get back into the dating game and, quite frankly, I really didn't have any interest. But Mia, you are a young beautiful girl; don't let your life pass you by. I'm sure that's not what Eric would have wanted either."

"I know," I whispered. "I just miss him so much." I bit my lip to stop from crying.

Mrs. Montgomery rubbed my hand gently. "Someday, you will meet that someone special who will help take away the pain."

I nodded as I wiped the tears that were beginning to flow from my eyes.

The rest of the morning was spent coloring and cutting Mrs. Montgomery's hair. She told me all about her latest purchases that she had made online while I put the final curls in her hair. We were deep in conversation when Mrs. Montgomery looked up at the person who had just entered her kitchen.

"Travis!" she stood up and threw her arms around a very familiar-looking man. I stared at him closely and realized it was the same arrogant man that had screamed his head off at me in the salon yesterday. But instead of being dressed in his overpriced suit, he was wearing a casual pair of sweats and a grey tee shirt.

"Mia, this is my grandson." I could feel my face turning red as he gazed at me. I had heard all about Mrs. Montgomery's grandson. He was an Olympic swimmer who had won multiple gold medals and Mrs. Montgomery adored him. There was no doubt at all that he was handsome. His body was the definition of perfection. If only Juan could see the way his muscles rippled through the t-shirt that he was wearing right now, he would for sure be having a full-blown heart attack.

"Charlotte, I'm sorry to interrupt, but there's a Tom Kellerman on the phone for you," Bernice interrupted.

"Oh, yes, I have to take this call. I'll be right back." Mrs. Montgomery walked out of the kitchen, leaving me feeling awkward and alone with her grandson. I began to pack up my stuff, trying my best to ignore his gaze.

I finally looked up at him. He narrowed his eyes as if he were confused by my presence. "Are you -"

"The girl that you humiliated in front of all of her co-workers and clients yesterday? Yes, that would be me."

"What are you doing here?" His tone was much softer than it had been yesterday.

"Your grandmother has been a client of mine for the past three years. I've been coming here to do her hair for her while she's recovering from her surgery."

There was a softness in his eyes that was non-existent yesterday.

"Obviously, she doesn't think I'm incompetent. But then again, she isn't stupid enough to move her head around when I'm using a straight-edge razor." I couldn't resist getting in that dig.

"Look, I'm really sorry about that. I was just having a really bad -"

"No need to apologize."

"I'm Travis Montgomery." He extended his hand to me. I hesitantly took his hand in mine and shook it. "I'm sorry, what was your name again?"

"Mia Taylor."

I hurried up and wrapped the cord around my curling iron and threw the rest of the items in my bag. I could still hear Mrs. Montgomery on the phone and was beginning to feel extremely uncomfortable being left alone with her grandson.

"Well, I really have to run. Would you mind telling your grandmother that I had to get going?"

"Sure, no problem. Again, I'm really sorry about yesterday."

"Okay - whatever." I looked up at him briefly and headed out the door.

I stood waiting for the elevator. *God he was gorgeous! Too bad he's an arrogant jerk and not to mention totally out of my league.* But that didn't mean I couldn't imagine what it must feel like to have those muscular arms wrapped around me. I stepped into the elevator. *Must stop thinking such crazy thoughts!* I said to myself as the elevator door closed behind me.

Chapter 3

Travis...

I watched her walk out the door. I felt like such a jerk. I was really horrible with the way I treated her yesterday. She seemed like a really nice girl and I couldn't help but notice the obvious; she was hot. Yesterday started out bad and just got worse. Unfortunately for her, she had gotten the brunt of it.

My grandmother finished up with her phone call and walked back into the kitchen.

"Oh, did Mia leave?" she asked.

"Yeah, she told me to tell you she had to get going."

"Oh, okay." My grandmother looked disappointed.

"She, umm, seems like a really nice girl," I said, trying to get some more information about her without it looking obvious.

"Oh, she is, dear. They don't get any sweeter than her. She's been through a lot, though, the poor thing."

"Oh, really? Why is that?"

"Well, she – "

"Charlotte, I'm so sorry, but Tom Kellerman says he needs to talk to you again."

"Oh, Travis, I'm so sorry but I have to take this again."

"No problem, I just popped in to say hi. I've got to get going anyway."

"Well, please pop in any time. I love seeing you." She kissed me on the cheek and went off to answer the phone.

I stood in the hallway, waiting for the elevator. I began to think about this Mia girl. According to my grandmother, she was sweet, she seemed wholesome enough, and she certainly was beautiful. Yes, she would be perfect. I pulled out my phone and texted my agent: *I think I found the perfect girl.*

Chapter 4

Mia...

Saturday was the one-year anniversary of the day that Eric was shot, but today was the day - the actual anniversary of Eric's death. I was handling it rather well. It was only 9 a.m. and I had already talked to my sister and was just finishing up with my phone call from my mother.

My mom, my sister Tressa, and I were super close. My mom and dad divorced when I was four years old. Tressa and I did the every other weekend thing with him for about three months, until we started cramping his style with his girlfriend. Soon, those every-other-weekend visits dwindled down to once a month, then four times a year, then never. He moved to California with his girlfriend and married her. Last I had heard, he was divorced once again and on wife number three. He never paid my mother a dime in child support, causing her to have to work two jobs to support us. Tressa and I didn't have much growing up, but we had lots of love. As long as we had each other, the three of us were happy.

My sister was two years older than I was. She was married to a great guy, had an adorable three-year-old little girl who was spoiled immensely by her aunt, and another baby on the way. She and my mother lived about an hour away from me in New Jersey. There were so many times in the past year that I had contemplated packing it in and moving closer to them, but I loved my job in the city and I just wasn't ready to leave my apartment. In a weird way, I felt like Eric was still around as long as I was here.

"Okay, Mom, I will give you a call later this week. Give Gary my love." Gary was my mom's husband; they married several years ago. He was a great guy and I was so happy when my mother found him. If anyone deserved happiness, it was her. He took such good care of her and I took comfort in that. I hung up the phone and quickly finished dressing for work. Even though I knew my feet would be killing me, I decided on my strappy sandals with my black sleeveless dress. They went together perfectly, so I would just have to sacrifice comfort for style. I threw my flip-flops in my bag - just in case.

Thankfully, I was able to hail down a taxi with ease and be on my way to the salon. "Wow, who's this movie star that just entered the building?" Juan joked. He was no doubt referring to the way that I was dressed and the fact that I had spent extra time doing my hair and makeup. I figured if I was going to feel awful all day on the inside, I might as well look good on the outside. I felt like a mess, since it was a hot and humid July day and I was afraid that all of my hard work on my hair got beat up by the humidity. I quickly looked in the mirror and was pleasantly surprised that it hadn't. I got to work right away on my first client. I was so busy all morning that before I knew it, it was already 1 p.m. I had a whole twenty minutes before my client's color was done processing; since I was starving, I decided to go back to the break room and eat my lunch.

I kicked off my shoes, opened up the magazine on the table, and began to eat my salad. I was thoroughly engrossed in one of the latest gossip articles when I looked up to see Juan standing over top of me.

"Oh my God, Mia, that hot guy from the other day is here asking for you!" I looked up from my salad at Juan, completely clueless.

"Who?"

"You remember, the one that you maimed. Mrs. Montgomery's grandson – the swimmer." I had filled Juan in that day on the way home from Mrs. Montgomery's about her grandson. I made sure that I had included just how sexy he looked in that form-fitting tee-shirt that he was wearing. I could practically hear him drooling over the phone.

I rolled my eyes. *What the heck was he doing here?* "Oh, jeez, Juan, you didn't tell him I was here, did you?"

"Well, duh, of course I did!" He grabbed my hand and pulled me up from my seat. He handed me a piece of gum and ran his hand through my hair, unable to resist fluffing it out a bit.

I slapped his hand, stuck the piece of gum in my mouth, and reluctantly walked up to the desk.

He was handsome, no doubt about it. He was dressed in another perfectly tailored suit. I did my best not to look obvious as I checked him out.

"Hey, are you here for a matching cut on the other side of your neck?" I joked, trying to hide my nerves.

His grin was a mile wide, exposing his perfect teeth. "Oh, no thanks. I'm all set with that. I actually just came to see you, and to see if you wanted to go out to dinner one night this week. Think of it as a thank you for giving up your Sunday mornings to help out my grandmother."

Juan walked over to the desk, pretending to be engrossed by something on the computer and clearing his throat loudly.

"That's really not necessary." I did my best to ignore Juan kicking me under the desk.

"I know it's not necessary, but I want to. Besides it will allow me to alleviate some of my guilt for acting like such a jerk toward you the other day."

I was silent for a brief moment. "When were you thinking?" *What am I thinking? I don't want to go out with this guy! I don't care that he's totally gorgeous. He was a total jerk to me the other day!*

"Tomorrow night."

"I don't know," I pondered. "I have a lot going on." He didn't need to know that meant picking up takeout and falling asleep on the couch.

"It's just dinner. You need to eat, right?"

He had a point. Dinner with him probably would be better than takeout

"Um, sure, I guess. What time and where?"

"Seven o'clock and I'll pick you up. I just need your address."

"Oh, I could just meet you at the restaurant."

"No, I insist."

I hesitantly wrote down my address and handed him the piece of paper.

"I'll see you tomorrow at seven," he said as he shoved the piece of paper in his pocket and walked out the door.

Juan waited until he was completely out of the door before he stood up and grabbed my hand. "Girl, I got my work cut out for me. I will be doing your hair and makeup before this date tomorrow night!"

I rolled my eyes at him. "Oh my God, Juan, talk about being put on the spot. I don't want to go out with him!"

Juan waved his hand in front of my face. "Hello, are you crazy? That guy looks like a Greek god."

"Wow, I see another celebrity is coming into the salon now," Victor, another stylist at the salon said as he made his way in the door, walking past Travis.

"I know, isn't it great?" Juan said gleefully.

"Why are you so excited, Juan; you hate anything that has to do with sports," Victor said.

"Because our little Mia is going on a date with him tomorrow night!" Juan exclaimed.

"Mia, you're really going on a date with that guy? From what I've read on the internet, he's a real womanizer," Victor said with concern.

"It's not a date. It's a long story," I said, suddenly feeling my salad churning in my stomach.

"Oh, Victor, that's right; you weren't here the other day for Mia's mishap. Come in the back and I'll tell you all about it," Juan said as he and Victor walked off.

What did I just get myself into? I am not ready to start dating, especially not someone of his stature. He's not only out of my league; he's out of my universe. I was going get my feet wet with this dating thing, all right. I just wished it wasn't with someone who had so much experience with water.

Chapter 5

Travis...

I walked out the salon and took a deep breath. Damn, she was gorgeous. I was going to have a hard time keeping my hands to myself around her. But something told me she wasn't like any of the other girls that I had been out with. Somehow, I didn't think that I would be getting laid after just dinner and a few drinks with her. I could tell when she looked at me that she was unfazed by who I was.

I was finally able to flag down a taxi. I gave the driver the address of the restaurant that I needed to be at. I was trying my best to focus on the task at hand and the business luncheon that I had to be at in fifteen minutes. But every time I tried to concentrate, my thoughts kept going back to Mia and that sexy little black dress that she was wearing.

Chapter 6

Mia...

Wednesday had arrived and my nerves were getting the best of me. Juan had gotten tied up with a client, so he wasn't able to do my hair and makeup after all. He made a point of telling me several times throughout the day just how I should style it. I quickly jumped into the shower, threw a few curls in my hair, and applied my make-up as usual. I didn't feel any need to overdo it to try and impress this guy. I wasn't looking to get involved with anyone and I was pretty sure that he wasn't either. I wasn't sure where we were going for dinner and I was hoping that the black capris and black and white striped top that I was wearing weren't too casual.

I buzzed him in and took a deep breath when I heard the knock at my door. The butterflies that were flapping around all day in my stomach erupted as I opened the door. Boy, was he good looking. *Too good looking.* The kind of good looking that immediately led my mind to believe those stories I saw on the internet last night. At the time, I scolded myself for reading them; now, it just made me curious.

I was glad to see that he was dressed casually as well in khaki pants and an olive color polo shirt that made his hazel eyes look green. I was finding myself being very self-conscious in his company as he entered my apartment. I definitely wasn't the type of supermodel girl that he was used to dating and I'm sure my tiny apartment paled in comparison to his.

I noticed him checking me out from head to toe and felt a little awkward. "Are you ready?" I asked.

"Um, yeah," he finally answered, breaking himself from his trance.

We took the short walk to the Italian restaurant that was just a few blocks up the street from me. It was a beautiful, humidity-free, July night. I had never been one that had trouble making conversation – apparently, not even around a gorgeous Olympic superstar. By the time we reached the restaurant, I realized that I had been talking non-stop.

We stopped just before entering. "I'm sorry; I just realized that I was rambling. You could have just told me to shut up."

He smiled and I couldn't help but notice the deep dimple on his left cheek. "No, that's okay. I enjoyed listening to you."

We entered the restaurant and the hostess took us over to a small intimate table that was out of the way. "Have you ever eaten here?" he asked.

"No. I always wanted to try it, though."

"Me neither, and me too." He smiled.

The waitress came over and took our order. While we waited for our dinner, we sipped on wine as he gave me a little insight about himself. I knew that he came from money, just from knowing who his grandmother was. I found out that he was twenty-eight years old, grew up in Connecticut, had a place in the city, and his family had a vacation home in Vermont. Besides swimming, he loved to ski and snowboard.

"Isn't it hard doing all of that training and living your life in the public eye?" I asked, taking another sip of wine.

"You get used to it. After a while you just become numb to both."

"Hmm, I guess. I sure wouldn't want anyone being able to type my name in a search engine and see my whole life story." *Oops, I said too much.*

He smiled and my stomach fluttered. "I see you've been doing your research."

I felt myself blushing just a little. "Well, I had to make sure that I wasn't going out with an axe murderer," I joked.

"Well, seeing how you were the one that almost cut my jugular vein, maybe I should have been the one doing the research on you."

I wasn't sure if it was his adorable dimple when he smiled or the wine that was making me feel very hot, but by now, I was burning up. "Very funny," I said as I rolled my eyes at him, unable to hide my smile.

"So since you know a little about me, tell me something about yourself," he asked just as the waitress placed our food on the table.

I looked down at my plate of pasta primavera, not knowing what to say. I hardly knew this guy and I didn't feel comfortable divulging anything personal to him, especially not the living hell my life had been this past year. "Not much to tell," I said as I moved my food around on my plate.

"Oh, come on, that's not fair. You learned everything that you wanted to know about me with a click of the mouse and I don't get to hear anything about you."

I looked up at him. Despite everything that I had *read* about him, he didn't seem like that cool, callous womanizer that all of the gossip websites portrayed him as. There was something in his eyes that made me believe that maybe there was more to him deep down inside. I took another sip of wine and took a deep breath. "Well, I'm twenty-seven, I've worked at the salon for the past three years, and that's really all there is to tell."

"Oh, I think there may be more to you than that."

I shrugged my shoulders.

"Are you seeing anyone?"

Drowning in Love

I shook my head.

"So, how come a beautiful girl like you doesn't have a boyfriend?"

I looked down quickly, trying to contain the tears that were beginning to burn my eyes. He must have sensed my anguish. "Oh, I'm sorry, I didn't mean to-"

I looked back up. I knew my eyes were filled with tears and it was obvious that he had seen it also as he looked at me sympathetically. "No, it's okay. I had a boyfriend; well actually, a fiancée." I looked away briefly before biting my lip. "And he," I paused. "He died." I was finally able to get the words out.

"Oh God, I'm such an idiot for asking you that. I'm so sorry," he said.

"That's okay, you didn't know." There was an awkward silence, making me feel compelled to continue. "Eric was a police officer. He got called to a robbery in progress and, well…" I couldn't finish.

"I'm really sorry. When did it happen?"

"He died a year ago yesterday." I looked up at him sadly.

He looked as if he was gathering his thoughts, trying to think of something to comfort me.

"I'm slowly getting over it," I said, trying to put his mind at ease.

He nodded. "So how's your dinner?" he asked.

I twirled the angel hair around my fork and took a bite. "Really good," I said, grateful for the change of subject.

He smiled and I felt the pain from just seconds ago washing away.

The rest of our dinner was filled with happy conversation. I found myself laughing a lot more than I had this past year. Strangely, I was completely at ease with him. Of course, the four glasses of wine might have had something to do with it.

By the time the check came, I was feeling a little dizzy; I was a lightweight when it came to drinking and had completely overdone it. I got up from the table and tried my best to balance my shaky legs.

"Are you okay?" Travis asked.

"Yeah, usually one glass of wine is my quota."

He began to chuckle. "Oh, a girl who can't handle her alcohol."

"I haven't gotten that bad yet, have I?" I grinned.

He grabbed my arm and guided me through the maze of tables. As we made our exit, I noticed a few people looking up from their meals, probably recognizing who he was. I imagined the headlines on the internet: *Travis Montgomery with His Cheap Drunken Date.*

We took the short walk back to my apartment and stopped at the front porch of my apartment building. "Well, thank you very much for dinner and –" I stopped for a second when I felt the light headiness taking over and my dinner churning in my stomach. I did my best to try and contain it, but it was of no use. The pasta primavera that was just my dinner a short time ago was resurfacing along with the four glasses of wine that I shouldn't have drunk. As hard as I tried to contain it, I knew that it wasn't possible. I hung my head over the railing of my porch and let it all come out – not exactly a glamorous moment. He held my hair back for me until I finished. I was embarrassed to lift my head and face him again.

"Umm, you can just go," I said with my head still hanging over the railing.

"No, it's okay," he said in a very caring tone.

I finally lifted my head. "Oh my God, this is so embarrassing."

"It's okay; I've been there before."

My head was pounding; I felt like such an idiot. I knew I couldn't handle more than one glass of wine, so why did I have to push it? He grasped my elbow and helped me walk up the stairs and into my apartment. I sat down on the couch and rubbed my temples.

"I'm so sorry," I said.

"What's there to be sorry about? It's not a big deal." He must have sensed that I had a pounding headache by the way I was rubbing my head.

"Did you need me to get you some aspirin before I go?"

I nodded and pointed to which cabinet it was in. He walked over to the couch with two aspirins and a glass of water.

He sat down next to me. "Are you going to be okay?"

"Yeah, I'll be fine."

"Well, I had a lot of fun tonight."

I began to giggle, even though my head felt like it was going to explode. "Well, I guess I gave you something to always remember it by."

He got up from the couch. I started to get up to walk him to the door. "No; don't get up. I can see my way out." I didn't listen – I figured that was the least I could do after the way that I had ended the night.

"Thanks so much for dinner. It was really good, even if I did…" I couldn't finish. I covered my face with my hands. "I can't believe I did that. I'm such an idiot."

"Well, I don't think you did it on purpose, so quit worrying about it."

He was halfway out the door when he turned and asked, "Hey, can I get your phone number?"

I was a little taken aback; I thought that after what had just happened, he would be running for the hills. "Um, yeah, sure." I gave him my number as he programmed it into his phone.

"Great, thanks."

"You're welcome." I stood there, shocked, as I watched him walk away.

I closed the door behind me and flopped down onto the couch. I took my ringing cell phone from the coffee table and answered it when I saw that it was Juan.

"Yes, Juan?" I answered, rubbing my temples.

"Well, how did it go?"

"It went great until – I puked my guts up right in front of him," I moaned.

"What?" Juan screamed into the phone.

I held the phone away from my ear. His piercing screaming on the other end was only intensifying my headache.

"Juan, tone it down; my head is pounding."

"Well, what happened, Mia?" I gave him a complete breakdown of the evening. "Mia, you know that you can't handle more than one glass of wine. Why would you do that?"

"I know; I guess I was just nervous and needed something to relax me a little."

"So I'm taking it that there wasn't a good night kiss involved. Oh God, Mia, please tell me that you didn't kiss him after you puked."

"What? No! He did ask for my phone number, though."

"Wow, either he's a glutton for punishment or he really likes you."

"Ha, ha, very funny. I have to go to bed now, unless you want me cutting more customers tomorrow."

"All right, see you tomorrow, baby cakes!"

"Good night, Juan."

I brushed my teeth, quickly changed into my pajamas, and lay down in my bed. My mind began to wander, the way it always did right before I fell asleep. Juan was right. *Why would Travis Montgomery want my phone number? He could probably have any girl that he wanted. He probably just asked for it to make me feel better about my embarrassment from tonight. Yes, I'm sure that's why.* I closed my eyes and drifted off to sleep, putting any more thoughts of tonight and Travis Montgomery out of my mind.

Chapter 7

Travis...

I got into the cab, feeling really bad about how the night ended. Surprisingly, I had really enjoyed hanging out with her. She was so different from all of the other women I was around. She was able to carry on a conversation. She had her own opinions on things and wasn't afraid to express them and she actually ate. Most of the girls that I took out to dinner would just move the food around on their plate for fear of gaining a pound. There was definitely something about this girl that made me feel drawn to her, even though that wasn't how I was supposed be feeling. She was just a means to an end for me. I tried to remind myself of that, but wasn't having much success. I felt really bad when she told me about her fiancé. I could see the pain in her eyes. It was so apparent how much she had loved him.

The ringing of my cell phone startled me. I looked down and rolled my eyes when I saw the name Chloe. Chloe was my agent and the biggest pain in the ass ever.

"Yeah, Chloe."

"Well, how did it go? Did you ask her to go to the EFE party?"

"No, I didn't get a chance."

"You didn't get a chance? Travis, what are you waiting for?"

"I will, Chloe. Just chill out. I got to go."

"Okay, but don't-"

I hung up the phone before she could finish. I scrolled down to Mia's name in my list of contacts and smiled. Mia Taylor – there was just something about her. She had me intrigued and I definitely wanted to get to know her better.

***

"Travis, that was really good." Jackie said as I got up and dressed. I had just returned to New York after being in Chicago for three days. I found myself thinking about Mia a lot and I didn't know why. I was tempted to text her a few times, but then decided against it. I needed to get this girl out of my head, so the best way I knew how was to have sex. I called Jackie on the way home from the airport and ended up at her place. I liked Jackie because she didn't expect anything else from me. She knew that the extent of our relationship was casual sex. Most of the women I was with knew that I wasn't looking for a relationship, but there were a few who had become somewhat stalker-like after I had slept with them. I knew that I didn't ever have to worry about that with Jackie. "Don't be such a stranger," she said as she walked me to the door.

I stepped outside of her apartment building, realizing that the thoughts of Mia were still just as strong. *What the fuck? I never let a woman rent space in my head like this.* This was my lifestyle; sleeping with any woman I wanted, whenever I wanted. Not pining over just one girl and having my thoughts consumed with her. I decided that I would go with my second best option to clear my head – a good run. I got into the cab and headed home to change, but not before leaving Mia a message, asking her to go to dinner.

Chapter 8

Mia...

By the time Saturday had arrived, I was just about over my humiliation with Travis Montgomery. I hadn't heard from him, which was just as well. Obviously, his request for my phone number was just as I thought; a kind gesture to make me feel better about myself.

I had just finished up with my last client for the day. Brian, Juan's boyfriend, was pacing the floors in the salon, waiting for Juan to finish up. Juan was taking his time on purpose to prolong having to spend the night at dinner with Brian's parents. "Juan, let's go; there's no need to stock any more of that shampoo on the shelves. There's plenty there!"

"Calm down, Brian, and let me go make myself look presentable. You know that bitch sister-in-law of yours is going to be there and I can't have her looking better than me."

"Honestly, Mia, if I hadn't invested all of these years in this relationship, I would be back on the market," Brian said as he shook his head.

"I heard that!" Juan shouted. "And you know that could be easily arranged."

I giggled at the two of them; they always knew how to make me smile. Juan came walking up to the desk. "I can't help it if I'm high maintenance."

I shook my head at him. "Yeah, a *little too* high maintenance."

"Hush, you," Juan said. "Call me tomorrow when you get done at the Ice Queen's; I need to go shopping for a suit for this wedding that I have to attend in a few weeks and I need your opinion."

"Juan, you already have three perfectly good suits in the closet. Why are you wasting money on another?" Brian scolded.

"Excuse me, but do I tell you how to spend your money?" He didn't let Brian answer before he continued. "This is between A and B, so see your way out of it," Juan said to Brian as he jerked his head and went sashaying out the door.

I busted out with laughter as Brian looked at me and shook his head. "Good luck with him tonight, Brian; he is in rare form."

"Thanks. I'm going to need it," Brian said before heading out the door.

I quickly looked at the schedule for Tuesday to see what time my first appointment would be coming in. I was so happy to have the next two days off. I sat back and thought about how I would spend my Saturday night. I couldn't take another lonely one of sitting around my apartment watching romantic comedies, which only made me more depressed. So, I decided that I would head to Macy's and check out some bathing suits. My sister was renting a beach house in a couple of weeks down the Jersey shore and had invited me to come down for few days. I wasn't a swimmer at all; in fact, I was scared to death of the water. But I did have to look fashionable while sitting on the beach and working on my tan. The last time I had bought a bathing suit was well over five years ago, so I figured it was time to update. Yes, shopping would be the perfect remedy to beat the Saturday night blues. I said my goodbyes to everyone as I fumbled around my purse for my phone. I finally found it and pulled it out to call my mom. I looked down at the screen to find a missed call and a voicemail from a number that I didn't recognize. I stepped outside of the salon, into the warm muggy July air, and punched in my password. My stomach dropped when I heard the voice on the other end:

"Hey, Mia, it's Travis Montgomery. I know it's kind of late notice, but I just got back in town and wanted to see if you had any dinner plans. Give me a call when you get a chance." A smile stretched across my face. I bit my lip, contemplating what to do. I looked down at the time on my phone; 4 p.m. I hit the call back number with shaky hands. I waited in anticipation for him to answer and was becoming a little disheartened by the third ring.

"Hello." His voice gave my stomach butterflies.

"Hey, Travis, it's Mia." I could hear my voice shaking.

"Hey, Mia, how are you?" He sounded like he was out of breath.

"I'm good. I'm sorry, was this not a good time to call?"

"No, it's fine. I just got done with my run."

Was he nuts, going out for a run today? It felt like it was 100 degrees out. "Well, I was just returning your call."

"Oh, yeah. Did you have plans for dinner?"

"Well, no, not really. I was just planning on doing some shopping, but I can do that tomorrow."

"Okay, so do you want to go out to dinner? No wine," he joked.

"Um, sure. Where were you thinking?"

"It's your choice."

"Hmm…how about Island Burger?"

"Really?" He sounded surprised by my choice.

"Hey, I'm easy to please. Plus, I'm dying for a milkshake."

"Okay, does seven sound good?" he asked.

"Did I mention I'm starving?" I giggled.

"Six?"

"Perfect. I'll meet you there."

"No, I will pick you up."

"Really, I can just-"

He cut me off. "I will pick you up at your apartment at six."

I hung up the phone and smiled. When I got back to my apartment, I stared into my closet, trying to figure out what to wear. I finally put on my casual khaki mini-skirt and white tank top, threw some curls in my hair, applied a fresh coat of make-up, and waited in anticipation for Travis to arrive. My stomach dropped upon hearing the knock on my door. I ran my hand through my hair and fluffed it out one last time before answering. He once again looked incredibly handsome, dressed in jeans and another one of those form-fitting tee shirts that was making it hard for me to keep my eyes from wandering.

"Hey," I said, unable to contain my smile as I opened the door and let him in. "I just have to grab my purse." He waited in the doorway as I found my purse and we headed out the door. I walked toward the curb, waiting to hail a taxi. He waved his hand for me to follow him. "Don't we have –"

"I have my car."

"Oh." I was a little surprised, thinking that it would be much easier just to take a taxi and not have to deal with the hassle of finding parking.

We walked over to his silver Lexus and he opened the door for me as I got in.

He got in and turned the key. "So, I know you said you were in the mood for a milkshake, so do you care if I switch the venue? I know a place that blows Island Burgers' shakes away."

"Sure. Where's that?"

He smiled. "It's a surprise."

He pulled out into the traffic and drove with ease through the busy streets of the city. I found it so easy to keep up the conversation with him. Strangely, it felt like I was talking to a friend that I had known my whole life. I was able to get some more insight into his life. He was an only child who developed his love of swimming at only two years old, finally achieving his lifelong dream of becoming an Olympic swimmer. He had appeared in the last two Olympics. In the first, he received three medals, one of which was gold. In his most recent Olympics, he received seven, all of which were gold. He had decided to call it quits at only twenty-eight years old and focus on something new that would still include swimming. He had a few business ventures that he was involved in, one of which was starting up a swim school for handicapped children. He did a lot of charity work and had a ton of endorsements with major corporations from all over the world. He still competed from time to time and was a stickler for keeping himself in the same shape that he was while in the Olympics. I felt a little guilty for not really paying much attention to the Olympics; I had heard his name mentioned before, but never paid much attention to the man that was behind it. I wasn't into sports, especially not swimming. I had a strong fear of the water that stemmed from my childhood. During one of our scarce childhood visits with my dad, I almost drowned in his girlfriend's pool. My father had left my sister and me in the care of his girlfriend's ten-year-old niece, while he and his girlfriend went in the house to "grab a bite to eat" – or, in other words, have a quickie. My sister and I were playing kickball and when I ran to get the ball, I lost my footing and fell into the pool. I had never seen my mom angrier than that day. If she could have ripped my dad's eyes out, I think she would have. I never stepped foot into a pool, or any body of water for that matter, since then.

"So, you won't even give me a hint as to where we are going?"

He smiled and shook his head.

"Okay, you're not some crazy kidnapper who's going to take me to the middle of the woods and kill me, are you?" I joked.

He laughed. "Now, that's not one of things that you read about me on the internet, was it?"

"Actually, that was probably the only thing that those crazy websites haven't said about you." I giggled.

"Well then, you're safe. Don't you know that everything they print on those websites is true?" he joked.

"I sure hope not, for your sake."

"Why? What do they say?"

"You mean you don't know?"

"Mia, when I told you that night that you get used to living your life under a microscope, I meant it. The first rule is, never read anything about yourself on the internet."

"Hmm...I guess that's good advice, but I think I would be dying, knowing that people were talking about my personal life all around the world. I would have to know what they were saying, truth or not."

"That's because you're a woman."

"Hey, what's that supposed to mean?"

"Well, women tend to care more about other people's perception of them than men do."

I shrugged my shoulders. "I don't know, maybe."

We finally pulled into the parking lot of what looked to be a hole in the wall diner in the middle of nowhere. "Where the heck are we?" I asked.

"The middle of the woods. I have to give you your last request of a milkshake before I murder you," he laughed.

"Okay, so we just drove an hour to a diner. When there are probably about one hundred of them in walking distance to my apartment."

"Oh no, Mia, this isn't just a diner. This is *the diner*. You'll see what I'm talking about."

We got out of the car and walked inside. It was decorated in 1950's décor and I wasn't sure if was meant to look that way or if it really hadn't been updated since then. I looked around – it was packed!

"Well, either you're right or this is the only restaurant out here in the boondocks."

I could immediately see the eyes of the customers focusing on Travis. This was making me feel a little uncomfortable, being with him. I hated having any attention placed upon me. We followed the hostess to the only empty booth and it was just a matter of seconds before he was approached by a middle-aged woman and her two sons.

"I'm so sorry to bother you, Mr. Montgomery, but my boys are huge fans of yours. Would you mind signing this?"

He smiled at her and her boys. "Sure, no problem." He took the piece of paper and the pen that she was holding and signed his name. He shook both of the boy's hands.

"How old are you guys?"

"I'm thirteen, and he's ten," the older boy said, pointing to his brother. I watched as they both looked at him with admiration.

"Do you guys like to swim?"

"Yeah, a lot," the younger boy finally spoke up.

I propped my elbow on the table and rested my head on my hand. I couldn't believe the enjoyment that I was getting over watching him interact with these two boys.

Okay, maybe Travis Montgomery was a womanizer and not boyfriend material, but a friendship – yeah, I could definitely see that happening.

Chapter 9

Mia...

Travis walked me to the front porch of my apartment building. I really had a great time and was so glad that I had agreed to go out with him. I had caught a glimpse of the old Mia tonight, the one who loved to laugh and actually got enjoyment out of life. He was so easy to talk to and I found that I wanted to continue to build upon this relationship. I actually wanted to be his friend. Yes, he was gorgeous and I certainly was attracted to him, but I had read all about his "love 'em and leave 'em" reputation and I didn't want that. I actually wanted more. If it meant just being friends – hanging out once in a while and being able to feel again – then I was willing to overlook that perfect body, that adorable dimple in his cheek, his cleft chin, his beautiful hazel eyes that changed colors, and those flawlessly full lips that looked just perfect for kissing. But somehow, I didn't think that was what he was looking for. I had a feeling that he was expecting more.

"So, was that shake worth the drive?"

"Mmm hmm. I had a really good time tonight, thanks."

He was silent for a brief second. He smiled and took my hand in his. "I did too, Mia." He kissed me gently on the cheek and stared into my eyes as if he were waiting for me to make the first move and kiss him on the lips.

Well, it's now or never, Mia. Let him know how you feel from the get go and if he doesn't want to be just friends, then you can both just move on.

"Look, Travis, I really think you're an awesome guy and I really and truly love spending time with you. But the only thing I have to offer you is friendship. I just hope that we can continue to hang out together as friends."

He looked at me as if he were surprised. I could tell that he wasn't used to being rejected by women. He seemed to be deep in thought before he nodded. "Okay, I would love to consider you a friend."

I smiled at him and began to giggle. "So, I guess this means that I'll never hear from you again, right?"

"No, actually, just the opposite. I have this event that I have to go to next Saturday night and I really wanted to bring just a *friend*. But the problem is all of my friends are guys, up until now."

I raised my eyebrow at him and smiled. "Well, I don't know. That would mean I would have to rearrange my busy Saturday night of watching romantic comedies and eating bad takeout to fit you in."

He shook his head and chuckled at me.

"Yeah, I think that can be arranged. Assuming I'm the friend that you're planning on asking."

"Well, since you're my only female *friend*, I guess you will have to do," he joked.

"Okay, I need details. What time, where, and most importantly, what should I wear?"

"Seven o'clock, the Ritz Carlton, and formal."

He reached into his wallet, pulled out a business card, and handed it to me. I looked it over to find it was from a personal shopper from Bloomingdales. "What's this for?"

"Take this card with you, have her help you with a dress, and they'll bill it to my account."

I handed the card back to him. "Thanks, but I can pick out and pay for my own dress just fine."

"Mia, I'm not going to make you spend all that money on a dress when I'm the one that asked you to go with me."

"Travis, if I couldn't afford a dress, I wouldn't have agreed to go. And besides, my friend Juan is my personal shopper. He would kill me if I bought a dress without getting his okay first."

"Mia, at least let me –"

I put my hand up to stop him. "That's enough or I will just have to cancel out on you," I joked.

"Wow, you are really different. If I had given any other girl free reign at Bloomingdales, they'd be beating down the door to get in."

"That's right, Travis Montgomery, Mia Taylor is an original and don't you ever forget it." I giggled. "Besides, *friends* don't take advantage of each other's kindness."

A smiled stretched across his face that made me want to kiss him right on his dimpled cheek. *Friends shouldn't be thinking such thoughts either!* I thought to myself.

"I like you, Mia."

"Well, good, because despite my first impression of you, you're not so bad yourself."

He took a step off the porch. "Well, goodnight."

"Good night and thanks for dinner," I said.

"No problem; you're a cheap date."

I playfully smacked his shoulder. "I am not; just easy to please."

"I can see that." He smiled again. *Oh, what the hell!* I leaned down from the step that I was standing on above him and quickly brushed his cheek with my lips. "See you Saturday."

"See ya, Mia," he said as he stood there waiting for me to enter my apartment building.

I closed the door behind me and stood against it for a few seconds, trying to gather my thoughts. Travis Montgomery, Olympic superstar, who could have any girl that he wanted, just asked me to be his date for a very important event of his. I just didn't get – at all. But, I wasn't going to overthink it; instead, I was going to enjoy this new friendship that had just begun.

I couldn't dial Juan's number fast enough as I walked up the stairs to my apartment. It went to voicemail after the fourth ring and then I remembered he was out to dinner with Brian's family. I left him a message, telling him all about my night.

I entered my apartment and quickly changed into my pajamas. I was so excited but I didn't know why. It wasn't like we were dating or anything. Maybe it was because for the first time in a long time, I didn't actually feel numb. I felt like I was starting to break free from this yearlong fog that I been encased in. I ran to my ringing phone that was on the kitchen counter, thinking it was Juan, but equally as pleased to see that it was my sister.

"Hey, Tress, what's going on, girl?"

"Besides the fact that I feel like an overheated cow, not much at all."

"You are not a cow; you're pregnant with my beautiful niece number two."

"Oh my God, Mia, wait until you see me. I really popped!"

"That's awesome!"

"Oh, that's easy for you to say. You're not the one walking around with a watermelon in your stomach in this heat."

"Oh, stop complaining. Do you realize how blessed you are?"

"I know. I'm sorry. I'm just miserable right now. But why the heck do you sound so upbeat?"

"Well, I have a new friend."

"Oh, is this friend a male?"

"Yup."

"Is he straight?"

"Yup." I giggled.

"Oh, do tell," Tressa said as if she were intrigued.

"Well, really, he is *just a friend*. I made that clear to him."

"Oh my God, Mia, will you just tell me all about him? The suspense is killing me!"

I went on to tell my sister the whole story, starting right from the awkward day that I had first cut Travis' hair. When I told her his name, I waited in angst for her reaction.

"Why does that name sound so familiar?" She paused for a moment and then gasped. "Oh my God, Mia. Is it that swimmer guy?"

"Mmm hmm."

"Holy shit!"

"Well, relax, because really, we are just friends. That is it."

"Mia, how are you going to be able to control yourself around a body like that? My God, I remember watching him in the Olympics and drooling over the sight of him."

I laughed a genuine laugh, one that hadn't escaped my insides in over a year. "That is exactly why I just want to be friends with him. I know all about his reputation with women. But I really enjoy his company, so I figure if we don't start anything physical, then things won't get complicated. Besides, I'm not ready to start dating anyone just yet."

"Mee, Mee, it's been a year. I don't think Eric would be upset with you if you started living your life again. I'm sure that's what he would have wanted," Tressa said gently.

"I know, but the last thing I need to do is to start a relationship with someone who has reputation for *not having* relationships," I joked. "So I will just admire that perfect body from afar while I enjoy his company."

"Well, you have better self-control than me, that's for sure. I would be ripping his clothes off – if I wasn't married, of course," she joked.

We finished up our conversation and I took my phone over to the couch with me as I began to flip through the channels to find something to watch. I looked down at my vibrating phone on the coffee table. A smile stretched across my face when I read the text message:

Just wanted to let you know I really enjoyed your company tonight – friend. See you Saturday.

Yup, Travis was just a friend. A friend that gave me butterflies in my stomach, but nonetheless *just a friend*.

Chapter 10

Mia...

The week flew by. Juan and I spent three very long nights shopping after work to find the perfect dress. We finally compromised on a floor-length sleeveless dress with a draped cowl neckline. I preferred it in black, but Juan insisted that I go with a color called "spring green," insisting that it would accent my blue eyes and sun-tanned skin. I finally gave in, admitting that his fashion sense was a little better than mine.

Saturday had arrived. I rushed home from work and took a shower. Juan did my hair in perfectly formed loose curls. I wanted to apply my own make-up, but he had insisted on doing it. I finished dressing while Juan waited out on the couch for the final product.

He stood up when I walked out of the bedroom and put his hand on his cheek. "Oh my God, Mia! If only I were straight." We both began to laugh. "You look like a princess. You are going to be the most beautiful girl there."

"Aww, you are too sweet." I looked in the mirror, happy that I had listened to Juan and had gone with his color choice. My skin was glowing. By the time Juan left, I found myself sitting around, trying to keep my mind occupied. My nerves were finally getting the best of me. I waited anxiously for Travis to make his way up the stairs after I buzzed him in. I took a deep breath as I turned the handle on my door to let him in.

A full-fledged grin appeared on his face as I opened the door. "Mia, wow, you look beautiful. I mean, you always look beautiful, but tonight…" His eyes widened and he shook his head.

"So, do you approve of this dress?"

"Hell, yeah."

"Told you my personal shopper is better than yours," I joked.

"I can see that."

"Well, you don't look so bad yourself." Boy, was that an understatement! He looked absolutely delicious, wearing a black tux. His short brown hair was perfectly tousled on top and his hazel eyes were once again favoring the shade of green. He still towered over me, even with the three-inch heels that I was wearing. I grabbed my hundred-dollar micro mini purse that Juan insisted I buy and we headed out the door.

I wasn't sure if he was driving or if we were taking a taxi. He took me a little off guard when he took my hand in his and walked me over to the limo that was parked a little ways down the street from my apartment building.

"A limo?" I asked, looking at him a little shocked. I wasn't used to all of this and I was a little uncomfortable. I was just an ordinary girl and I didn't intend on changing that for anyone. But maybe, for just one night, it would be fun to pretend to be living a fairy tale.

The limo driver opened the door for me as I got inside. Travis got in after me and took the seat across from me. "Wow, is this your usual form of transportation?"

"Well, I figured that you wouldn't want take a dirty old taxi in that beautiful dress of yours, and this way I don't have to worry about driving in case I decide to drink."

I nodded and looked around the inside of the huge limo. The only other time I had been inside of a limo was for my sister's wedding, and that one was nowhere as big as this one.

I fixed my eyes back on Travis, who was gazing intently at me, making me feel a little uncomfortable. "What's the matter?" I asked.

He gave me a half smile. "You."

"What are you talking about?"

"It doesn't take much to impress you, does it?"

I smiled back. "No, not really. So, whose party is this, anyway?"

"It's for a company called EFE. I have an endorsement with them."

"Oh," I said, looking out the window, pretending like I had a clue as to what he was talking about.

We pulled up to the hotel and my nerves began to take over. I didn't know what to expect. I certainly didn't lack self-confidence and I was comfortable in most social situations. I just wasn't sure what type of people I would be encountering tonight.

Travis got out of the limo first and took my hand to help me out. He again took my hand as we entered the hotel. My eyes were bombarded by the flashes of the cameras snapping pictures of the two of us. We entered the elegant ballroom that was already filled with people. I looked at some of the elaborate gowns that some of the women were wearing and I was beginning to feel a little inadequate.

"You're the most beautiful woman here," Travis whispered in my ear, making me feel a little bit better and at the same time a little uncomfortable. Somehow, that statement didn't sound like something that *just a friend* would say.

"Hey Travis, there you are," a tall blonde woman said as she approached us. She looked me over, up and down, and nodded at Travis as if she approved.

"Chloe, this is Mia."

She extended her hand to me. "Nice to meet you, Mia, I'm Travis' agent."

"Nice to meet you, too," I said as I shook her hand back.

The night progressed very well and for the most part everyone was very friendly. Travis stayed by my side for most of the night, except for the few times that Chloe would pull him off to the side for a private conversation. I looked at Travis a little strangely when he wrapped his arm around me as he introduced me to the president of EFE. I quickly removed myself from his arms after the man had walked away. I didn't want him to start thinking that I was going back on my plan of friendship only. "Do you want a glass of wine?" Travis asked.

"Oh, no, that's okay. Don't want to have a repeat performance from the most embarrassing night of my life."

He laughed. "I thought you said you could handle just *one* glass."

"Yeah, but I'd rather not." I didn't want to take a chance of doing anything that might cloud my judgment and have me waking up in his bed tomorrow morning.

"Okay then. Do you want to dance?"

"Um, sure, why not?"

He wrapped his arms around my waist, keeping a comfortable distance between the two of us. As much as I hated to admit it, it felt wonderful having his strong, muscular arms wrapped around me. My sister was right; this friendship thing was going to be a lot harder than I thought. As the music played, he moved his hands up the small of my back and pulled me closer. I was beginning to re-think my whole *just friends* plan. The music ended just in time. He still had his arms wrapped tightly around me and was staring down into my eyes. My knees were weak as I looked up at him, trying my best to avoid the awkwardness of the moment. I cleared my throat and looked away briefly. "Well, I think we should get going. I have to be at your grandmother's early tomorrow."

He was still staring at me silently with a hint of frustration on his face before he nodded. "Okay," he finally responded.

We were heading out the door when Chloe pulled him off to the side again. I watched as she high-fived him and began to laugh. I silently wondered what they were talking about, but then quickly dismissed that thought, not really caring about any of his business-related stuff.

The limo ride home was mostly silent. I stared out the window as I started to come to the realization that this "just friends" deal with Travis wasn't going to work. I knew exactly what he wanted and I wasn't willing to be his next one-night fling. He closed the privacy divider and climbed over to my side of the seat. Something told me my resistance was about to be put to the test – *God give me strength.*

He took my hand in his. "Thanks for coming with me tonight."

"Sure, no problem."

He leaned in and brushed his lips on mine. I looked up at him and bit my lip. Within a matter of seconds, he had his tongue halfway down my throat and his hands were exploring my body. I responded back just as eagerly, but only for a brief second before I finally came to my senses. "Travis, no!" I pushed him away. I could tell by the look on his face that he wasn't used to hearing that word.

"Mia, I know that you're just as attracted me as I am to you, so why are you fighting it?"

"Because, I told you, Travis. I really enjoy hanging out with you and I don't want to ruin it by crossing that line. I should have never come here with you tonight. I feel like I just led you on and that was so wrong of me." The limo had just pulled up to my apartment and I wasted no time getting out, not even waiting for the limo driver to open the door.

"Mia, wait."

"No, Travis, I have to go!" I quickly closed the door and got into my apartment building as fast as I could. I entered my apartment, kicked off my shoes, and sat down on the couch.

What the hell was I thinking? A guy like him would never want to be just friends with any girl, especially not me. I felt so foolish for even entertaining such an idea. I wanted to call Juan or even my sister, but it was after midnight, so I put those ideas to rest. I changed into my pajamas. I tossed and turned endlessly, trying my best to fall asleep and not deal with this until tomorrow or hopefully, after my hasty departure tonight – never.

Chapter 11

Travis...

What the hell did I just do? This wasn't supposed to be part of the plan. I should have never tried that with her. I couldn't behave the same way with Mia that I normally did with other women. She was different. But she just looked so damn beautiful tonight that I couldn't resist. I ran my hand through my hair, contemplating what to do. She was really serious about this friendship thing, but something deep down inside was telling me that she wanted me just as much as I wanted her. I closed my eyes and thought back to just a little while ago when I had her in my arms on the dance floor. Her skin was so soft and she smelled so good that she was driving me crazy. I knew she sensed it and I was hoping to get the same reaction from her, but instead, she asked to leave. Whatever it was that we had, I knew that I wasn't ready to lose it. As sexually frustrated as she got me, I really enjoyed spending time with her and I wasn't ready for it to end. I was willing to play this friendship game with her for however long she wanted. At least I knew where to find her tomorrow and I would make a point of being there bright and early.

Chapter 12

Mia...

I arrived at Mrs. Montgomery's for my usual Sunday morning routine of doing her hair. I hadn't told her anything about my get-togethers with Travis and I was most certain that Travis didn't either, since she had never mentioned anything to me. I was giving her one last spritz of hair spray when I heard someone clearing their throat loudly. I turned around to find Travis standing in the doorway. He was wearing athletic shorts and a tee-shirt, looking like he had just gotten done going for a run. "Travis! What a pleasant surprise," Mrs. Montgomery said as she got up to give him a hug. He smiled at me, making my knees go weak. I gave him a quick smile back and began to pack up my things. "Are you hungry, dear? I could have Bernice make you some breakfast."

"No, actually, I just stopped by to see if Mia wanted to have coffee with me."

"Oh." Mrs. Montgomery looked a little shocked before a huge smile stretched across her face. She turned around and looked at me, waiting for my response.

"Well, actually, I have to meet my friend Juan in a little bit to go shopping."

"We won't be long, I promise."

I looked at Mrs. Montgomery, who had a pleading look on her face. "Okay, as long as I'm done in time to meet him." A look of relief flashed over Mrs. Montgomery's face. I grabbed my bag, said my goodbyes to Mrs. Montgomery, who was all smiles, and followed Travis out the door.

We stood in the hallway and waited for the elevator. "I have to give you credit; that was pretty slick," I said.

"What?"

"Asking me for coffee in front of your grandmother, so I couldn't say 'no.'"

"You could have said 'no.' No one was holding a gun to your head."

We got into the elevator and continued with the conversation. "Look, Travis, I think it's better if you and I just don't have any type of relationship. It's obvious that we can't be just friends."

"No, Mia, you're wrong. We can be friends. Look, I'm sorry for what happened last night. This whole friendship thing with women is new to me. But I really do like you and I have a lot of fun when I'm with you. And I'm not going to lie; I think you're absolutely beautiful."

We stepped off the elevator and out of the apartment building into the warm muggy air. "Travis, why would you want to be friends with me?"

"Why wouldn't I?"

"Because I'm just ordinary. I'm not those supermodels that you're used to being around."

"No, Mia, you're not. You are so much more. Not only are you beautiful, but you also have a great personality, you're smart, and you're funny. So sometimes ordinary is better."

He held the door open for me as we entered the coffee shop that was just up the street. I once again noticed some of the eyes that were fixated on him as we walked in, again making me feel a little uncomfortable. We ordered our coffee and sat down at a small table. "So, Travis, tell me; why did you want to have coffee with me today?"

"Because you're a friend and friends go out for coffee. Plus I wanted to apologize for taking advantage of our friendship with my forwardness in the limo last night."

"Really, you don't have to keep taking me out to dinner or for coffee just to alleviate your own guilt."

He shook his head and smiled at me. "That's not what I'm doing, Mia. I happen to really enjoy hanging out with you."

I shrugged my shoulders and took a sip of my coffee. "Okay, if you say so."

"So, *friend*, I was wondering what your plans are for next Saturday afternoon?"

"I will be sitting on a beach, hopefully working on my tan, if the weather cooperates."

"Oh, you're going on vacation?"

"Well, not exactly. Unless you call shacking up with your pregnant sister, her husband, her three-year-old daughter, and my mom and stepdad in a three-bedroom house at the Jersey shore for a few days a vacation."

He smiled. "So you have a sister?"

I nodded.

"I just realized I really don't know much about you. Do you have any other siblings?"

"Nope, just Tressa. It's been just her and my mom for most of my life." I went on to tell him all about my childhood and how my dad had left when I was just a small child.

"So it sounds like you guys are really close."

"Yeah, we are." I smiled just thinking about the great relationship that I had with my mom and sister.

"When will you be back?"

"Sunday. I was hoping to be coming home on Friday, so I could have a few days to unwind before heading back to work, but I'm at the mercy of my mom and stepdad. That's one of the disadvantages of living in the city and not having a car."

He was silent for a moment as if he were deep in thought. "Well, then, how about if I pick you up on Friday? That way, you have your few days to unwind."

"What? Are you crazy? I'm not going to have you drive all the way down there just to pick me up!"

"Mia, my motive isn't completely unselfish. If you're home by Friday, then you will be able to come to the party with me on Saturday afternoon."

"What party?"

"It's for another company that I have an endorsement with. I don't really want to go, but I have to. So, I figured if I took someone fun along, it might not be half bad."

"Hmm...well –" He looked absolutely adorable with a pleading look on his face that made it impossible for me to say 'no.' "Fine," I finally answered.

"Oh, one other thing, you don't get seasick, do you?"

"No, why?"

"Because it's on a boat. It's a lot more casual than last night."

"Oh, well, it's not like you haven't seen me puke my guts up before, so if I do, I'll feel a lot more comfortable this time," I joked.

He laughed as we got up from the table to exit. I waited as he was stopped by a man who had recognized him and began to strike up a conversation. He was finally able to break free and we headed out the door. We agreed that he would pick me up at noon and I would text him the address of my sister's beach house once I found it out myself.

"Are you sure, you want to do this?"

"Absolutely." His smile widened.

"Okay, suit yourself." He flagged down a cab for me and opened the door as I got in.

"See ya Friday, Mia," he said before closing the door.

Travis Montgomery was going to drive three hours out of his way just so I could go to a party with him. I still didn't get it, but I couldn't help but smile anyway.

Chapter 13

Mia...

"Oh my God, Mia. You couldn't have waited until after I had the baby to bring him around. I look like a cow!" My sister scolded me as she nervously ran the brush through her hair.

My mother and sister were acting like the president was coming to pick me up. By the time Friday had arrived, they were both a bundle of nerves.

"Tressa, will you just relax? You look beautiful, and why are you so worried about impressing him? You're married, girl!"

"Mia, I may be married, but I'm not blind and he is hot!" She sat down on the bed and handed me the brush. I plugged in my curling iron, waiting for it to heat up. I ran the brush through her blonde hair, which was the same exact shade as mine. My sister and I looked a lot alike except for our eyes; hers were more grayish than blue. We resembled my mother. Her hair was a little darker than ours, but her eyes were bright blue. I threw some curls in Tressa's hair and pulled the top back into a clip.

"There, you look beautiful."

She rolled her eyes at me.

"Aunt Mee-Mee. Mee Mom said that Trabis is here," my adorable niece Paige said as she walked into the room, clutching to her baby doll.

"Thank you, baby girl," I said as I bent down and kissed her on the head. I walked into the living room where Travis was being ogled over by my mom, my stepdad, and my brother-in-law.

"Hey," I said as a smile stretched across my face at the sight of him. He smiled back and I got butterflies. "Well, I see you met everyone already." My sister cleared her throat loudly. "Oh, I'm sorry, not everyone. Travis, this is my sister, Tressa."

He held out his hand to my sister and she looked like she was going to pass out. "It's nice to meet you, Tressa."

"Yeah, you too," she said shyly.

I felt my niece tugging on my leg. I picked her up. "Oh, and how can I forget, this is my beautiful niece, Paige." She gave Travis a shy little smile before burying her face in my shoulder.

"Sweetie, I was just telling Travis that we're planning on having a cookout tonight and would really love you guys to stay for dinner," my mom said.

"Oh no, Mom, it's a long drive –"

"It's okay," Travis interrupted. I raised my eyebrow at him. "Really, it's fine," he said.

"Okay, then I guess we'll stay," I said.

"Great!" My mother's grin was a mile wide. "Come on, Gary, we have to go to the food store," my mother said to my stepdad.

I waited until everyone cleared the room. "Are you really sure that you don't have anything better to do today than to spend the day with my family?"

"No, I don't." He flashed me that gorgeous smile.

"All righty then."

"Aunt Mee Mee, can we go see the horsies again?" Paige asked as she came walking into the living room. The horsies that she was referring to were on the merry-go-round. We had spent last night on the boardwalk and I had ridden the merry-go-round with her more times than I could remember.

"Oh, cutie pie, not today."

She looked up at me sadly. "What does she want?" Travis asked.

"She wants to go on the boardwalk."

"Well, do you want to go?"

"Really?" I asked, a little shocked. Somehow, he didn't strike me as the child friendly type.

"Yeah, why not?" he said.

I asked my sister if it was okay if we took Paige to the boardwalk. She all too willingly obliged. I was happy to be able to give her a little break. I couldn't imagine that chasing around after a three-year-old when you were seven months pregnant was very fun at all.

Paige jumped into her stroller and we began the short walk to the boardwalk. "So, do you like the beach?" Travis asked.

"I do; I just don't swim in the ocean. Let me rephrase that: I don't swim anywhere."

He looked at me as if he were surprised. "Really? Why not?"

I explained to him about my near drowning experience as a child and how I hadn't been swimming ever since.

"You just need to overcome that fear, Mia, and you will be swimming in no time."

"No thanks." I smiled.

We finally reached the boardwalk. The smell of cotton candy, sausage, peppers, and onions, suntan oil, and salt air immediately made me smile. My mother would scrape together money every year to make sure that my sister and I would get to visit this magical place at least once every summer growing up. So the memories of this place were strong and happy for me. I looked down at Paige, who was sound asleep in her stroller, grasping tightly to her baby doll. "Well, she's passed out," I said. Travis smiled as he looked down at Paige. We walked up and down the boardwalk. I took in all of the familiar sounds of voices coming over the loud speakers, trying to entice us to play their games. The screams of individuals who were brave enough to ride the roller coaster merged with those of the pesky sea gulls flying overhead.

Travis stopped off to play a basketball game. "You know, the hoop is smaller than the ball, so it's impossible to win," I said.

"Nothing's impossible, Mia."

"Okay, smarty pants. Make it in the hoop then," I joked.

The man handed Travis three basketballs. He took the first shot and it rebounded out of the basket. The second shot followed suit. He carefully concentrated on the third shot, looking like he was deep under pressure. I looked on and laughed at him. He finally released the ball, took his best shot, and missed again.

"Ah…nothing's impossible, huh?" I teased.

"No, I'm just out of practice." He laughed.

The man working behind the game looked at Travis. "Hey, are you Trav-"

"Nope." Travis cut him off mid-sentence.

I began to smirk as we walked away. "Why did you lie to that guy?"

"Because I have a reputation to protect. I can't let everyone know that I suck at basketball." We both began to laugh.

I was having a great time with Travis as we walked up and down the boardwalk. I wasn't even feeling uncomfortable with some of the awkward stares that he was receiving from a few people who must have recognized him. I learned a little more about him as well. He attended New York University and had a degree in Sports Management. His parents still lived in their Connecticut home, which he had grown up in. His mother was an elementary school principal and his dad was a cardiologist. His childhood seemed so different from mine. He attended private schools, lived in a big house in an affluent community, and had the best of everything. Not that I didn't have the best of everything; just not material things. But I couldn't have asked for any more love and support than my mother had given to my sister and me while we were growing up. I knew that was why I didn't have a strong need for material things in adulthood, because my mother helped me realize that wasn't what mattered in life.

Paige was still sound asleep. We took a break and sat on a bench looking out onto the ocean. The warm breeze, the salt air, and the familiar sound of seagulls flying overhead put my mind at such ease. There was no place else on earth that I would have rather been at that particular moment. "How could you not like the ocean?" Travis asked as he stared off.

"It's not that I don't like it. I just don't like swimming in it."

"That's because you haven't been to the *right* ocean."

I giggled. "An ocean is an ocean."

"Have you ever been to an island?"

I shook my head.

"Well, if you had, then you would probably change your mind. Saint Lucia has some of the most beautiful beaches around."

"I have no doubt that it's beautiful, Travis, but it still doesn't change the fact that there are a million little creatures swimming around with you out there. Not to mention waves!"

He shook his head. "Not in Saint Lucia; the water is so calm it's like being in a pool."

"A pool with sharks, piranhas, barracudas, and God knows what else."

He laughed. "I'm going to make a swimmer out you yet, Mia."

"Try as you might, but it will never happen." I smiled.

His smile back took my breath away, making me think that maybe I could trust him enough to help me overcome my fears in more ways than one.

Chapter 14

Mia...

We took the short walk back. Paige had finally woken up just in time to ride the merry-go-round - four times. She too was now a fan of Travis'. She took to him instantly and I was surprised with how good he was with her as well.

My sister was sitting on the front porch, reading a book. Paige jumped out of her stroller and went running to her. "Mommy, I went on the horsies and Aunt Mee Mee and Trabis gave me cotton candy."

My sister raised her eyebrow at me. "I'm sorry, but she wanted it." Paige ran inside to go find my mother. My sister got up to chase after her. "Let me go wash her hands before she makes a sticky mess out of everything, thanks to you." She smacked me lightly on the head with her book.

Travis and I sat on the swing on the front porch. It was a beautiful sunny day with a light breeze. "So are you bored to tears yet?" I asked.

"No, not at all. Why would you think that?"

"I don't know; my family isn't exactly exciting."

"I don't know, from what I've seen so far, your family seems great."

"Oh, yeah they are, just not very exciting." I laughed.

He smiled that butterflies-in-my-stomach smile again and without even realizing what I was doing, my hand was on top of his. He looked down, smiled again, and wrapped his hand in mine. There was a comfortable silence between us as we glided back and forth, hand in hand.

My mother poked her head out the front door. "Oh, there you are. Why don't you guys come and join us in the backyard?" I didn't want to get up; I felt so relaxed, but I didn't want to seem unsociable, so Travis and I followed her back.

It was a great night. Any time spent with my family was great, but tonight seemed to be more special. Travis fit right in with everyone and I noticed that the nervousness that my mother and sister had been feeling earlier in the day about meeting him had completely washed away. Travis just had a way of making people feel comfortable in his presence. I was shocked when my brother-in-law and stepfather started talking about Travis' intense workout routine.

"Get out! You swim ten miles a day?" I asked as my jaw dropped.

"No, not every day. I have to change it up with weight training."

"But wait, you didn't get my question. You actually swim ten miles at one time?"

He laughed. "Yeah," he answered as if it weren't a big deal.

"Wow!" I shook my head in amazement.

"Mia, thank God you never aspired to be an Olympic hopeful," my brother-in-law said as he laughed at my reaction.

"Haha, very funny, Shane." I playfully smacked him on the arm.

"So, do you think you're going to compete in the next Olympics?" my stepfather asked.

"No, I think I'm done with that."

My sister came walking out with Paige in her arms. "Give Aunt Mee Mee a kiss goodnight." She put Paige down and she climbed on my lap. "Night night, Aunt Mee Mee." She wrapped her arms around my neck and kissed me on the cheek.

"Good night, baby girl. I love you so much and I will see you again really soon."

She climbed off my lap, turned around, and looked at Travis. She smiled at him and said, "Bye, Trabis, thank you for taking me to the horsies."

My sister and I looked at one another and giggled. Travis' smile was a mile wide. "You're welcome, Paige, anytime." She smiled again and ran off to my mother. I looked down at my watch to see that it was already nine o'clock. Even though I didn't want this most perfect night to end, I knew that it had to. We had a long drive ahead and since Travis had mentioned earlier that he had been up since 5 a.m. doing his workout, I figured the sooner we left, the better.

After a half-hour long goodbye on my mom's and sister's parts, we were finally headed home. The long drive home was filled with conversation, something that I never had a hard time keeping up with Travis. About a half hour to go in the drive, I began to feel myself becoming sleepy. I rested my elbow on the car door and placed my head in my hand. The next thing I knew, Travis was gently nudging me. I opened my eyes, trying to figure out where I was and was a little embarrassed once I had finally figured it out.

"I'm sorry," I said.

Travis chuckled. "What are you sorry about?"

"For falling asleep."

"That's okay; you were tired."

He got out of the car, took my bags out of his trunk, and carried them up the stairs for me. I opened up the door and he took a step in, placing the bags down on the floor. "Thanks for driving all that way," I said.

"Thanks for agreeing to go with me tomorrow," he answered.

"I had a really good –" we both began to say at the same time, causing us both to laugh.

"Well, I'll see you tomorrow, Mia."

"Okay," I said, looking deeply into his eyes. I stood on my tippy toes and placed a soft gentle kiss on his cheek. "Good night, Travis."

He took a deep breath. "Good night, Mia," he whispered before walking out the door.

I closed the door and smiled. Today was a great day, not only because I spent time with my family, but because of Travis.

I shook my head to try and dismiss any more thoughts of him for the night. I pulled my cell phone from my purse and texted Juan: *The bitch is back in town.* I changed into my pajamas and grabbed my vibrating phone from the table to read Juan's response: *There's only one bitch in this town and that would be me. You are junior bitch, remember? And this bitch will be over bright and early with coffee so we can catch up! Goodnight, baby cakes xo*

I smiled at his response. I was truly blessed to have such great people that I cared about so much in my life – I couldn't help but think, was Travis Montgomery becoming one of them?

Chapter 15

Travis...

I headed down the steps and to my car. There was something about her that made me feel so different. She had a way about her. She didn't care about who I was, and I liked that. Most women that I knew were consumed with Travis Montgomery, the Olympic gold medalist, which I never cared about because I was only interested in one thing from them. But Mia looked beyond that. She actually wanted to get to know me as a person. I had never cared about getting to know any girl before or meeting their family. I only cared about getting them in bed. Mia was so different. I wanted to know more about her. I really enjoyed seeing the layers of personality peeling back. Not that I didn't want to have sex with her. I probably wanted her more than any other girl I had ever met. She was the complete package; she was beautiful, funny, and had a great personality. I laughed to myself, remembering how she referred to herself as ordinary. She was far from it; in fact, she was the most extraordinary girl I had ever met.

Chapter 16

Mia...

"Rise and shine, Petunia." The sound of Juan's voice made me sit up in bed.

"Geez, Juan, you just gave me a heart attack," I said as I rubbed my eyes.

"See what happens when you give me a key to your place, I can pop in at any time so you better be on your best behavior at all times."

I shook my head at him and got out of bed. I went into the bathroom and threw some cold water on my face before sitting down to the coffee and bagels that he had brought over. "So how was the beach?"

"Oh, I had a great time!"

"And?"

"And, what?"

"What's going on with that beautiful man that has been showing so much interest in you?" I couldn't help but smile, thinking about Travis. Juan, who knew me so well, was able to read the expression on my face right away. "Spill your guts, Mia!"

I told him how Travis drove down to my sister's beach house to pick me up, about the great day that we had spent together yesterday, and that I was spending this afternoon with him.

Juan shook his head and smiled. "How long are you going to make this poor guy wait before you sleep with him?"

I ripped a piece of my bagel apart and stuck it in my mouth. "I'm not going to sleep with him."

"Oh, Mia, come on. You are insane! He is totally gorgeous!"

"I am aware of that. But I see more to him than a beautiful face, a perfect body, and a gold medalist. I really like the person he is inside and if I sleep with him, I will just be another one on his list and he'll move on to the next."

"You don't know that, Mia. It sounds like he really likes you."

I shrugged my shoulders. "So tell me what I have to look forward to when I come back on Tuesday?" I asked, trying to shift the subject.

Juan waved his hand in front of me. "Oh, girl....." He filled me in on all of the drama and gossip that I had missed in the week that I had been off. I was thankful to be off the subject of Travis. I didn't want to think about a choice that I didn't want to make, but that I knew was inevitable. I was too happy reveling in the present and the perfect relationship that was beginning to form.

***

Travis was at my apartment by one o'clock. The cab dropped us off in front of the harbor. The bright sunny morning had now turned into an overcast, chilly afternoon. We boarded the high-end yacht and I was in a complete state of awe. I felt like I had to lift my jaw from my knees as I took everything in. I never imagined that a boat could be this big and elegant.

"Are you okay?" Travis asked.

"Yeah, just a little shocked. This boat is beautiful!"

Travis nodded in agreement.

"Who owns this?" I asked.

"I'm not really sure, I'm thinking one of the presidents of the company."

Travis introduced me to over a dozen people throughout the afternoon. I found that he was focusing his constant attention on me, almost seeming bothered when someone would come over to talk with him. I looked out of the corner of my eye and watched as a very tall and very beautiful brunette approached us. She was dressed casually in capris and a halter top, which she had no business wearing with the size of her chest. I quickly looked down at my chest and couldn't help but think, *my bra must look like a training bra compared to hers.*

"Travis! I haven't seen you in a while." She wrapped her arms around his neck. I looked away, reminding myself that we were just friends.

"Are you going to be around later tonight? I would love to catch up - if you know what I mean?" she said in a very sexy voice.

Travis removed her arms from his neck. "No, actually I'm not."

"Oh?" She looked at him like she was disappointed.

He quickly turned his attention to me. "Kelly, this is Mia."

"Oh." She sounded surprised as she finally noticed me standing there. She looked me over, up and down, and raised her eyebrow. "And she is?" she asked Travis rather sarcastically.

I hated when people would refer to me in conversation as if I weren't even standing there. "*She* would be a friend of Travis,'" I answered back just as snidely. I could see Travis smirking at my sarcasm.

"Well, Travis has a female friend; that's a first."

"Well, you know what they say, there's a first for everything," I said with a smile.

"Hmm, well it was good seeing you again, Travis. Call me sometime," she said, giving me a fake smile before walking away.

I looked up at Travis. He was smiling and shaking his head. "Sorry, sometimes the inner bitch comes out in me every now and then," I joked.

I quietly excused myself as two men approached Travis and began to strike up a conversation with him. I stood by the railing of the boat, looking out onto the water. The clouds and cool breeze were making the hair on my goose-bumped arms stand at attention. I silently scolded myself for not remembering to bring a jacket to throw over the sleeveless shirt that I was wearing. I thought back to the last time I had been on a boat. Eric and I were taking a fall foliage tour of the Hudson Valley. I closed my eyes, feeling that dull ache in my chest whenever I thought of him.

It was a bright, crisp October day. Eric placed his arm around me as we looked out onto the river taking in the beautiful pallet of colors surrounding us.

"I think we should get married in the fall, what do you think?" Eric asked.

"Sounds perfect. Then we can have our first baby a year from that and then a second one in three more years."

He shook his head and smiled.

"Well, I want some time to be able to enjoy the first one."

He wrapped his arms around me and pulled me closer. "You're quite the little planner, aren't you?"

"Yup, I am, especially when it comes to planning out the rest of my life with you."

He smiled and kissed me softly on the lips. "I love you so much, Mia."

"I love you too, Eric – forever."

I quickly rubbed the tear that was flowing down my face as I heard Travis approaching.

"Hey, are you okay?" he asked.

"Yeah, just thinking of old memories."

He looked at me sympathetically. "Old memories are good, Mia, but don't let them stop you from making new ones."

I nodded, wiping away another tear that escaped my eye. I crossed my arms in an effort to keep warm.

"Are you cold?" he asked.

"A little."

He stood behind me and took me totally off guard when he wrapped his muscular arms tightly around me and pulled me close. I bit my lip, wondering if I should break free. Instead, I leaned my head back on his chest and closed my eyes. I felt his lips kissing the top of my head – Suddenly, I wasn't cold anymore.

Chapter 17

Mia...

On the way back to my apartment, Travis received a text from his friend, asking if we wanted to join him and his wife for a drink before they headed out to a business dinner. Since I had no other plans for my big Saturday night, I agreed. We entered the restaurant and Travis immediately spotted his friends, sitting in the bar area. "Mia, this is Mike and Stacy."

"Hey, Mia." His friend Mike extended his hand to me.

"Hi, Mia! It's so nice to meet you!" Stacy said as she jumped up from her seat, shaking my hand and giving Travis a hug.

They were an adorable couple, looking almost more like they were brother and sister than husband and wife. They both had dark hair and dark eyes. Stacy's hair was cut into a cute pixie-style cut that was perfect for her petite frame.

Mike pulled the bar stool out for me to have a seat while Travis stood alongside of me.

"So, Mia, Travis says you're a hairstylist?" Stacy said.

I nodded.

"That's got to be a tough job, on your feet all day, trying to please everyone."

"Yeah, it is, but it's rewarding in its own way."

"Well, I imagine it's a lot more exciting than having a boring old office job like I do." She smiled.

I smiled back. "Yeah, I have some days that are more exciting than others."

Drowning in Love

Travis handed me a glass of wine, while he and Mike ended up in a deep conversation with the bartender. I didn't mind, though. I was finding that I really was enjoying Stacy's company.

"So are you and Travis dating?"

"Oh no, we're just friends." She raised her eyebrows at me as if she were surprised. "I really like hanging out with Travis and I don't want to ruin that by – well, you know."

She smiled as if she finally got my point. "Well, I've known Travis since college and I have never heard him *gush* over a woman the way he has about you these past few weeks - just sayin'!" She laughed.

I smiled and felt myself blushing at her words. "Well, he's a pretty great guy too."

I looked up and suddenly saw two guys standing beside us. "Hello, ladies, we were wondering if we could buy you two beautiful women a drink," one of them said.

"Oh, no thanks, I don't think my husband would appreciate that too much," Stacy said.

He turned his attention to me. "Well, what about you? Is a guy lucky enough to have a beautiful woman like you for his wife?"

"Umm, no, but I'm good." I lifted up my glass of wine.

"Ah, come on, just one drink." He was persistent as he moved closer and placed his hand on my thigh, making me feel very uncomfortable.

I noticed Travis, out of the corner of my eye, stopping mid-conversation with Mike and the bartender when he noticed the man speaking to me. Within seconds, he was by my side. "Mia, is everything okay?"

He wrapped his arm around my waist. I smiled in appreciation. "Yeah, everything is fine. I was just telling this gentleman here that I didn't need another drink."

The man looked at me and nodded. "You really shouldn't leave a beautiful woman like her unattended," he said to Travis.

"And you better just keep moving on before I kick your ass," Travis said, causing both Stacy and me to look at him with surprise.

The man stood there for a second, glaring at Travis as if he were challenging him. "Do you not fuckin' understand English?" Travis raised his voice. Stacy's eyes widened, while I bit my lip and held my breath, hoping that the man would just walk away. The last thing I wanted was for Travis to get in a fight with someone over me. I was finally able to breathe again when the man gave me one last glance and moved on.

"Travis, thanks, but I had that all under control." I looked down, noticing that his hand was still wrapped tightly around my waist. I could tell that he was bothered by what had just taken place.

"I should have fuckin' kicked his ass – Fuckin' asshole."

"Travis, calm down!" Stacy said.

He finally released his grip from my waist and stared at me with an intense look in his eyes.

"Yo, Travis, come here for a sec," Mike yelled over.

He slowly walked away like he was afraid to leave my side. The whole time, Stacy stared at him and shook her head.

"Wow! What the hell was that? I've never seen him behave that way," Stacy said.

I shrugged my shoulders. I didn't know how to answer that one. She knew him better than I did.

"Well, if he's that overprotective of you as a friend, I would sure hate to see what he would have done to the guy if you were his girlfriend." She shook her head and smiled.

I smiled back; I was a little taken off guard by Travis' behavior myself. I appreciated him rushing to my side to help, but on the same note, that *wasn't* how just a friend would act. I knew deep down inside that with the time we were spending together, we were slowly becoming more than just friends – like it or not.

We finished up our drinks and were readying to leave. "I wish we could be having dinner with you guys, instead of Mike's stuffy old co-workers," Stacy said.

I smiled. "It was really nice meeting you guys."

They both smiled back at me. "You too, Mia. Hopefully we'll see you around a lot more." Mike looked over at Travis and raised his eyebrow. Mike shook my hand, and Stacy gave me and Travis each a quick hug.

Travis and I headed out the door and waited for a cab. "You know I had that situation with that guy all under control earlier, right?"

He looked angered by the mere mention of it. "Yeah, well, I was just making sure."

"Well, thanks for looking out for me."

He nodded as a smile finally appeared on his face. "Anytime."

I smiled back as my stomach twisted and turned in a very good way. My heart was feeling things that I'd never experienced, but I knew one thing was for sure; it was so not the way it should be feeling for just a friend.

***

Travis walked me into my apartment. He was leaving for Arizona in the morning for some special swim meet. He explained it all in detail to me, but I didn't really understand it. Then he was headed up to his family's vacation home in Vermont to go fishing and unwind for a few days. I was actually getting disheartened, knowing that I wouldn't be seeing him for a while.

"Well, thanks for a great time," I said.

"You're welcome."

I wasn't ready for our time together to end, so I decided to be bold. "Are you up for pizza and a movie?"

He smiled. "Sure."

I closed the door behind us, more than happy to be having his company for the evening.

It was a great night. We ordered pizza and watched a movie on-demand. My stomach muscles hurt from laughter at both the movie and the conversation. I actually found myself getting saddened when he looked down at his watch, realizing that it was getting late.

"I have to get going; my flight leaves at six a.m."

I nodded as he moved closer and brushed his lips on mine. He was staring into my eyes as our lips parted. He took my face in his hands and began to kiss me deeper, this time exploring my mouth with his tongue. I couldn't resist any longer. I knew that I wanted him just as badly. I wrapped my arms around him and lay down on the couch, pulling him toward me as our tongues continued to collide. He moved my hair out of the way and began to kiss my neck, sending shivers through my body. His hand moved up my shirt and under my bra. My insides were yearning for him as he began to unbutton my pants. I was hoping that I was just imagining the voice that I was hearing - but I wasn't.

"Oh, Brian, honestly –" Juan stopped himself mid-sentence. I jumped up, buttoned my pants, and adjusted my shirt as Juan mouthed the words "I'm sorry" to me.

Travis sat up, looking a little frustrated as he ran his hand through his hair.

"Oh my goodness, we're really sorry. We just got done with dinner and I wanted to drop off some of this key lime pie that we had for dessert. I'll just leave it in the fridge and we'll be on our way."

I introduced Travis to Brian and reintroduced him to Juan. I walked them both to the door.

"Continue on where you left off and I want details," Juan whispered. I pushed him out the door as Brian followed behind him, laughing.

"Kick his ass, Mia," Brian said.

"I just might." I shook my head and smiled.

I closed the door behind them just as Travis stood up. "I really have to get going."

"Oh, okay." I was hoping that I was hiding the disappointment in my voice.

I knew that the moment had passed anyway; no chance in trying to relive it - thanks to Juan! "Have a safe trip," I said as I walked him to the door.

"I will." He smiled at me, making me detest Juan at that particular moment for stopping what could be happening right now. He gave me a quick kiss on the cheek before walking out the door. I closed the door behind me, leaning my back up against it. "Damn it, Juan," I said underneath my breath. It was probably just as well anyway. I would have just been regretting it in the morning, no doubt. I was still leaning up against the door and I jumped when I heard someone knocking. Foolishly, I opened it up without looking to see who it was. I smiled when I saw that it was Travis.

"Hey, Mia, do you want to come to Vermont with me next weekend?" I knew that really meant, *Do you want to come to Vermont, so we can sleep together next weekend?*

I took a deep breath before answering, "Sure, that would be great."

Chapter 18

Mia...

I begged Juan not to schedule any more appointments after my 1 p.m. on Saturday so that we could leave for Vermont at a reasonable time. He abided by my wishes since I think he was more excited about the possibility of me having sex than I was. I brought my bag with me to work. Travis was picking me up from the salon at two and we were leaving right from there. I felt a little guilty about not telling my mom that I was going, but I made sure that I told my sister, just in case there was an emergency. She, of course, was elated. I was thankful that Mrs. Montgomery was now recovered and had just been in the salon on Thursday to get her hair done. I wouldn't want to have to explain to her why I would have been missing our Sunday appointment. My stomach was churning, the closer that it got to two o'clock. I had actually missed not seeing Travis for a week and I was totally surprised that he actually called me twice while he was away.

My last client was gone for the day and I sat around, waiting anxiously. "Mia, are you waxed down there?" Juan asked.

"What!" I smacked him on the arm.

"Well, if I can't ask you, then who can? I'm sorry. I just want you to be prepared. I know it's been a while and you may be out of practice."

I put my hand over my ears. "Oh my God, I'm not having this conversation with you!"

I looked up at Travis as he walked through the door and a smile stretched across my face. "Hey," I greeted him.

"Hello," he responded as he took off his sunglasses and smiled. He was dressed in tan shorts and a black polo shirt, and to say that he looked absolutely beautiful was an understatement. He grabbed my bag for me as we headed out the door.

Juan grabbed my arm, pulled me back, and whispered in my ear, "If you do not take advantage of that hot body in every single way imaginable, I will kill you - lucky bitch!" I smiled and gave him a kiss on the cheek. "I will live vicariously through you," he shouted. Thankfully, Travis was already out on the busy street and couldn't hear him.

The drive to Vermont was long, but very entertaining. Travis and I talked and laughed nonstop the whole time. Four hours later, we were pulling into the driveway of an elaborate log cabin-style home surrounded by mountains. I got out of the car and looked around at the beauty surrounding me. Travis grabbed the bags from the trunk and we headed inside. My jaw dropped when I walked inside. It was open and airy with a cathedral ceiling and skylights throughout. The upstairs looked over the enormous great room, which had a huge fireplace. "Oh my God, Travis, this is beautiful." He smiled at my enthusiasm.

"Are you hungry?" he asked.

"Starving!"

He opened up the fridge, which was stocked with food. "How did all the food get in there?" I asked.

"The food store delivers. I arranged for the cleaning lady to let them in today."

"Oh." I smiled at his ability to plan things out.

"I'm guessing since you've eaten a burger before that you're not a vegetarian?"

"Never!" I laughed.

"Okay, good." He pulled out two filet mignons from the fridge.

"You can cook?"

"Yes, I can cook." He chuckled.

He threw the filet mignons on the grill while I helped prepare the salad. We sat down to dinner just as the sun was beginning to set over the mountain range. I stopped eating for a second to look out the window and take in the beauty right in front of my eyes.

"Did you bring your bathing suit?" he asked as we finished eating.

"Yes, but I don't know why you insisted. I told you I'm not swimming, especially not in a dirty old lake."

He shook his head and laughed at me. "Just got get it on."

"What, are you crazy? If you think I'm going swimming *in a lake* in total darkness, you are completely insane! Don't you ever watch horror movies?"

"Mia, you are too funny." He laughed. "Trust me; I'm not going to put your life in danger with a crazed madman lurking in the woods."

I rolled my eyes at him. "Fine." He grabbed my bag and led me up the stairs to a huge bedroom lined along the walls with windows. "You want me to get changed in here? There aren't any curtains up, anyone could see me."

He began to laugh hysterically. "Mia, you're not in the city anymore; the nearest neighbor is two miles up the road. So, the only eyes that may get a peek of you are the wolves and bears. Oh, and I forgot there's been rumors that there's some lions running around too."

"Ha, ha, make fun of me." I smirked at him.

"The bathroom is right in there, if it makes you feel better." He stood staring at me for a brief second.

"Okay, be gone with you," I said as I pushed him out the door and closed it behind him. I pulled my bathing suit from the bag along with my toothbrush and toothpaste. I changed into my navy blue two-piece, feeling a little inadequate as I looked at myself in the full-length mirror. I was thankful for the extra padding in the top. I clearly was not blessed in that area and from the women on the internet that I had seen Travis with, he was used to women who were. I brushed my teeth, pulled my hair in a ponytail, and took a deep breath. I threw my tank top on over my bathing suit, so I didn't feel like I was walking around half-naked.

I walked down the steps and stopped dead in my tracks at the sight of Travis standing in the kitchen, shirtless in just his swim trunks. He had his back turned toward me as he was texting, allowing me to stare comfortably at the perfection standing before me. He placed his phone down on the counter when he turned around and saw me. He handed me a towel and led me through the house into the garage and through another door. "Where the heck are you taking me?"

We walked into a dark room. The strong smell of chlorine immediately hit me in the face. He flicked on the lights and my jaw dropped when I saw the huge swimming pool. "Wow!"

He laughed at my reaction. "Now you don't have to worry about any killers lurking in the woods." He took my towel from my hand and placed it on the table. I sat down at the ledge of the pool and stuck my feet in the water while he immediately dove in.

"Come on, Mia, come in."

I shook my head. "No thanks. I'll just watch you."

"Ah, come on, don't be chicken." He pulled himself out of the pool and sat down beside me. "There's nothing to be afraid of; I'm not going to let anything happen to you. Trust me." He slid back down into the pool and wrapped his arms around my waist to try and pull me in. "Fine!" I lifted my tank top over my head, threw it off to the side, and slid down into the water.

I was comfortable as long as I was in the low end where I could touch the bottom. I felt my nerves getting the best of me once he began to pull me into the deeper end.

"It's okay," he said, seemingly sensing my nervousness. He made sure that he held on tightly to me, taking me even deeper. I wrapped my arms around his neck.

"Travis, that's far enough."

"Mia, there's nothing to be afraid of. I'm not going to let you drown, I promise." I pulled myself closer to him as we floated around. I was beginning to relax a little. "See, I told you, there's nothing to be afraid of."

"Yeah, this isn't really that bad. Just don't let go of me!"

We floated around the perimeter of the pool, ending back in the low end. I was just about to release my arms from around his neck when he looked deeply into my eyes as the water cascaded over our shoulders. He leaned in and kissed me. I closed my eyes and savored the touch of his lips on mine as our tongues began to explore each other's mouths. His hands emerged from underneath the water. He began to move them up and down my body and removed my bathing suit top. My insides were aching for him.

His tongue cascaded down my neck, finding its way to my breasts. He removed my bathing suit bottoms and placed them on the ledge of the pool. His hand trailed back under the water, stopping between my legs, beginning a delightful assault on my body. I closed my eyes and leaned my head back. It had been so long since I felt so alive as his fingers moved around inside of me. I pulled him closer to me, yearning to feel his body against mine. I grazed my lips along his chest. He tilted my head to him, leaned down again, and kissed me with a sense of urgency. He wrapped his arms around me tightly as his lips remained locked on mine and his tongue continued to explore my mouth.

"Mia, you have no clue what you are doing to me right now," he whispered in my ear. "I want you so fuckin' bad. Please tell me it's what you want too."

It was what I wanted, more than anything. But I was a little apprehensive. I was sure I wasn't as experienced at this whole sex thing like the women he was usually with.

I nodded.

"Say it, Mia, tell me that you want me inside of you." His voice sounded so sexy and demanding.

"I want you, Travis. I want to feel you inside of me."

With just those words, he was set over the edge. He quickly removed his bathing suit. Even though I was nervous, my insides were longing for him. "Are you on birth control?" I nodded. I didn't know why I was; I hadn't had sex in over a year. But I had just never stopped taking it.

"Travis, I've never been with anyone else but Eric. I'm scared that I'm not going to be any good at this."

He looked at me and smiled as if he was surprised. "It will be fine, I promise."

He lifted me up and pulled me toward him, leaning me against the wall of the pool as he entered me. I bit my lip as my body adjusted to him. He looked down at me as the water beads dripped from his hair. "Are you okay?"

"I'm fine." I pulled him closer and kissed him as he began to move about inside of me.

"Oh my God, Mia, you feel so good." The water lapped over our shoulders. "I want to make you feel good, Mia, just relax." I couldn't believe how my body was reacting to him. I had never felt so at ease and I had never wanted anything more. My insides became more awakened with each move that he made. After a few minutes, I was able to relax completely as I met him with each movement that he made. He lifted me up and wrapped my legs around him, taking himself deeper inside of me. I closed my eyes and enjoyed every single second.

My arms were wrapped around him as I rested my head on his shoulder. "Look at me," he whispered in my ear. I lifted my head to meet his gaze. "Does this feel good for you?" I nodded, not wanting to be broken from my state of ecstasy. "I want you to look at me. I want to see how good this feels for you," he demanded. My eyes remained locked on his as I took in every pleasurable second of him. I couldn't contain it anymore. I let out a light cry as I felt my body begin to awaken from its long slumber and totally melt around him. He moved in and out of me, which only intensified the feeling.

"Oh, Travis." I ran my hand through his wet hair and rested my head on his shoulder as he continued to take me with each move.

His breathing became more intense. He buried his head into my neck as he let out a light groan, finding his own release. My trembling legs were still wrapped around him as he pulled me toward him and kissed me. Travis and I had crossed that line. We were no longer *just friends*. Everything was blurred. I only hoped that I wasn't now just one of his latest conquests.

Chapter 19

Travis...

I held Mia tightly in my arms and kissed her on the head as she slept. I had never felt the way that I was feeling right now with any woman after sex. Maybe that's because that's all I viewed it as with every other woman. Mia was so different. The look in her eyes when she told me that she had never been with another guy but her fiancé just made me want her more. This was not part of my plan; I wasn't supposed to be having feelings for her, but I did and they were so strong that I couldn't fight them even if I had tried.

She opened her eyes and smiled. "Hey," she whispered in a very sleepy voice as she looked up at me and squeezed me tightly.

I couldn't resist kissing her soft lips. I couldn't resist making love to her once again.

Chapter 20

Mia....

I awoke the next morning with Travis' arms wrapped tightly around me. We were up half the night with another round of intense lovemaking. My body was in a complete state of euphoria. I had worried about having sex with someone again after Eric. Eric and I were each other's one and only and I didn't know what it would be like with someone else. But Travis put me at such ease. He was so gentle and caring and at the same time intense and demanding, but in a very good way.

He kissed me softly on the head. "Good morning."

I rested my head on his chest and traced my finger up and down his stomach. "Good morning." He must have sensed the apprehension in my voice.

"Hey, what's wrong?" He pulled me toward him. I shook my head. "Mia, I can tell that something is bothering you."

"I just don't want to ruin our friendship, Travis."

"Oh, baby, we didn't ruin anything. If anything, we just made it stronger."

"Are you sure?"

"Mia, I told you before, I love being around you and I meant it. I have never met anyone like you before in my life. So if you think that my feelings are going to change just because we *finally* slept together, you're wrong."

"I'm sorry, Travis, I just –"

"You are so different, Mia; you make me feel things that I've never felt before with anyone."

I closed my eyes and hugged him tightly. I was still feeling a little apprehensive, but I also knew that there was nowhere else in the world that I wanted to be more than in his arms at that particular moment.

Travis cooked a delicious breakfast before we headed out for the day. I had never been fishing and was actually excited to try it. We walked a little bit to a beautiful lake that was surrounded by trees that provided shade from the warm summer day.

We sat down on a log as Travis showed me how to bait the hook. "Um, I'll let you do that." I laughed. I placed my pole into the water and waited. "How long before we catch something?"

"Mia, you have to have patience when you're fishing." He chuckled.

"Oh, that stinks!"

He laughed even harder. "You are too much."

I wasn't the outdoorsy type, but I was having a great time being here with him.

"You never went fishing as a kid?" he asked.

"No, my mom is a lot like me. We're not 'country' girls." I laughed. "I guess that's what happens when you don't have a dad in your life; you don't get to experience these manly things."

"Does it bother you? Not seeing your dad?"

I bit my lip and looked away. "It did for a while, but not anymore. I consider my stepdad as my father now. I am so thankful to have him. He's my own Mike Brady."

His grin was a mile wide. "Wow, are you a Brady Bunch fan?"

"I am!" I smiled back. "I can name the episode within a matter of minutes of it coming on."

"Oh, Mia, you will never know more about the Brady Bunch than I do."

"Oh yeah, try me!"

We spent the rest of the afternoon quizzing each other on Brady Bunch trivia. My stomach flipped when he placed his hand in mine.

"You know part of the reason that we haven't caught anything is probably because we haven't stopped talking. I forgot to mention, you're supposed to be quiet when you fish."

"Well, then, maybe we should stop talking."

"Yeah, maybe," he said as he moved closer to me. I placed the pole down when his lips touched mine. I was unable to control myself as I began to kiss him harder. I couldn't believe how much I wanted him again. I was beginning to feel like I couldn't get enough of him.

He released his lips from mine. "Mia, I think we better get going before this goes any further. Remember, in those horror movies the couple always gets murdered when they're having sex in the woods."

I giggled and brushed my thumb along his cheek. "Okay, but only if you promise that we can pick up right where we left off once we're safely inside."

I had never seen his dimples looking deeper. "Absolutely."

***

I was feeling totally bummed on Monday night when Travis dropped me off. It had been one of the best weekends of my life. I had never imagined that I could be this happy again. He walked me up the stairs to my apartment. I opened the door and we stepped inside.

I dropped my bag on the floor and wrapped my arms around him. "I really had a great time. Thank you so much for inviting me."

He kissed me on the lips and hugged me tightly. "Thank you for coming." I was so happy, I wanted to cry. He pressed his forehead against mine. "I'll see you this week, Mia."

"Okay," I whispered. He rubbed his hand gently over my cheek and kissed me softly on the lips before exiting. I closed the door and locked it. I slid down to the ground with my back up against the door. I couldn't stop smiling. It didn't even matter anymore about not knowing what I was headed for. My feelings for him were strong, I couldn't deny that and even if I tried to fight it, I knew I wouldn't be able to.

I sighed, thinking about coming back to reality. I walked into my bedroom to prepare my clothes for the workday tomorrow. I felt heaviness in my chest when I looked at the picture of Eric on my dresser. I picked it up and kissed it.

I sat down on my bed and held it close to my heart. "I don't know if I should be talking to you about this or not. But I felt like you should be the first to know. I'm starting to feel again. I'm happy, Eric, but I feel guilty about being happy. I don't want you to think that this means I don't love you or that I will ever forget about you because you will always live on in my heart, just not in my life." The tears rolled down my face. "I will always love you – forever." I placed the picture on my nightstand and just stared at it for a few more minutes. My ringing cell phone broke me from my trance.

I wiped the tears from my eyes upon seeing that it was my mother.

"Hey, Mom!" I tried to sound as upbeat as possible.

"Hello, Missy, do you have anything that you'd like to share with me?"

Big mouth Tressa! "I don't know, do I?" I tried not to laugh.

"Spill it, Mia!"

My mother and I had a sisterly relationship. I felt like I could talk to her about anything, but sex was where I drew the line. "I went to Vermont for a couple of days with Travis, which I know that *big mouth* already told you."

"I can't believe you didn't tell me," my mother said, sounding a little like her feelings were hurt.

"I'm sorry, Mom. I just was feeling a little guilty over the whole thing to begin with."

"What? Why?"

"I just feel like I'm betraying Eric."

"Oh, Mia, sweetie. Don't feel that way. You're moving on with your life and there's nothing wrong with that. It's perfectly normal."

"I know." Sometimes just hearing my mom reaffirm what I already knew deep down inside was all I needed.

"So, tell me all about it."

I couldn't stop smiling as I told my mother all about the past few days, making sure that I left out some details, which I was sure she had already surmised.

"I'm so happy for you, Mia. He seems like a really nice guy."

"He really is."

We chatted for a while longer before saying our goodbyes. I hung up with her and the doubt that I was trying to ignore slowly came creeping in. *What if this weekend was just a fling to him?* I was hoping that my heart could handle the rejection if it was.

My doubt was quickly washed away when I picked up my phone to find a text from Travis: *I just wanted to thank you again for a great weekend. Can't wait to see you again.*

Chapter 21

Travis...

I couldn't believe what a great time I had. For the first time in my life, I wasn't focused just on the physical aspect of it, although it was good; in fact, it was great! Sex with Mia was so much more than I had imagined. She was so innocent, so different from any other woman I had ever been with. I could still see a little apprehension on her face over us sleeping together. She was doubting herself and our relationship. I wished that she had more confidence in herself and in us. But given my reputation, she had good reason to doubt. I was hoping that the text that I had just sent would alleviate that doubt and put her worries to rest. This was really a first for me, something I had never experienced before. I was falling hard for a woman. Mia was no longer part of any plan. She was still the perfect girl – the perfect girl for me.

Chapter 22

Mia...

The months passed and Travis and I grew closer by the day, allowing me to erase any uneasiness that I had about his feelings for me. My world seemed to be happy once again. I was meeting Eric's parents for lunch. They had retired down to Florida and were up visiting Eric's brother. I still kept in touch with them through emails and an occasional phone call, but I hadn't seen them in well over a year. So to say I was excited about our lunch date was an understatement. I walked into the restaurant and immediately saw Eric's mother, smiling and waving her hand at me. My smile became a mile wide.

"Hey, guys!"

They both got up and hugged me. Eric's mom hugged me for a little while longer before placing her hand on my shoulders, looking me over and smiling. "Mia, you look wonderful, honey."

"Thanks."

I sat down and jumped into conversation right away, filling them in on the last few months of my life.

"And who is this special guy?" Eric's mother asked with a huge grin.

"His name is Travis Montgomery."

"The Olympic swimmer?" Eric's dad asked with surprise.

"Yup!"

"Oh, Mia, we're so happy for you!" Eric's mom exclaimed.

"Thanks." I bit my lip and tried to fight the tears, thinking about Eric and how these wonderful people would have been my mother- and father-in-law right now.

"Mia, what's wrong?" Eric's mother asked.

"Nothing; it just seems weird talking to you guys about another man."

She looked at me sympathetically. "Oh, Mia, you know that this is what he would have wanted for you."

"I hope so," I said as I looked down at the table. "So, tell me all about Florida?" I said, trying to switch the topic.

Eric's mom began to tell me all about their house in Florida. She complained about the heat, the bugs, and her bouts of homesickness. Eric's dad was just the opposite; he was enjoying his time in the warm weather on the golf course all day.

"So did Patrick and Jessica have the baby yet?" Patrick was Eric's older brother; the two of us had always been super close when Eric and I were together. He was like an older brother to me as well.

Eric's mother looked at me sadly. "Yes they did. A little girl; she had to have emergency open heart surgery."

"Oh my God." My heart sank.

"She's still in the hospital, but she's holding her own."

"I'm so sorry." I felt sick to my stomach.

"To make matters worse, Patrick was just laid off and his health benefits run out the end of the month. My sister and I are trying to put together a fundraiser to help them out."

I felt just horrible. I wanted to help them out in the worst way possible.

"Well, would it help at all if I asked Travis if he could attend this fundraiser?"

Eric's father's eyes had a glimmer of hope as he gazed at me. "Mia, that would be wonderful. Do you think he would mind doing it?"

"No, I really don't think he would have a problem with it as long as he doesn't have anything already scheduled. Do you have a date?"

"Well, we were thinking about the tenth of November, but we'd be willing to change it to accommodate his schedule," Eric's mother said.

"Perfect! I will let him know and then I will let you guys know if he's okay with that date."

"Mia, you haven't changed a bit. You're still an angel." Eric's mother smiled with tear-filled eyes as she reached over the table and grabbed both of my hands.

***

I finished up lunch and called Travis. He was just getting done with his run. Since he was still at the park, I told him to wait for me there. It was a beautiful October day and I wanted to spend it outdoors. I got out of the cab and spotted him sitting on the bench, waiting for me. He got up and wrapped his arms around me. "You're all sweaty," I said.

"Well, since you wouldn't let me run home and shower first, this is what you get."

"I don't care; you're still just as cute, sweaty or not. Here, I got you something to replace all of those calories that you just burned off." I stuck the open bag that contained his favorite, a peanut butter fudge brownie, under his nose. We both sat down on the bench as I broke off a piece of the brownie and fed it to him.

"Oh, Mia, you know the way to my heart."

I kissed him gently on the lips. "You taste like peanut butter." I giggled. "Hey, Travis, did you have any plans on November tenth?"

"I don't think so." He pulled out his phone and opened his calendar. "No, nothing. Why, what's up?"

I explained to him everything that was discussed at lunch with Eric's parents. I knew that he probably would be more than willing to help, but at the same time, I didn't want him to think that I was taking advantage of his stature.

"Yeah, that's fine," he said as if it were no big deal.

I smiled and broke off another piece of brownie. "Just for that, you get another piece," I said as I stuck the brownie in his mouth. He laughed and pulled me to him. He pressed his sweaty forehead onto mine. "You are the best boyfriend in the world, you know that?" I said as I kissed him softly on the lips. He smiled and kissed me with a lot more passion. I had my arms wrapped around his neck as our lips slowly disengaged. "I think I may just have to show you just how much I appreciate you."

"That's sounds good to me," he said as he quickly stood up. He pulled me up from the bench and wrapped his arm around me.

"After you take a shower of course." I laughed.

He pulled me close once again, giving me another kiss, just as a photographer snapped our picture.

I stood on my tippy toes and whispered in his ear, "I think we're going to look hot in that picture!"

"Baby, you always look hot."

"And you just won another bite of your brownie." I laughed as we walked off hand in hand.

Chapter 23

Mia...

It was a beautiful crisp early November afternoon. I had just returned from an overnight visit at my sister's. She had given birth two months ago to another beautiful baby girl, whom I couldn't get enough of. I took an early train home so I would be able to meet up with Travis. He had just returned from Colorado. He had been there for the past four days for some advertising promotion and to do some snowboarding. I found that I missed him like crazy when he was away. I pulled my ringing phone from my purse as I stepped off the train. Somehow, the name "Travis" displaying on my phone always made me smile.

"Hey, you!" I answered.

"Are you home yet?" he asked.

"Just getting off the train and getting ready to grab a cab."

"Good, tell the driver to drop you off at my place."

"Okay." I smiled upon thinking that in a few short minutes I would be able to hug him.

I quickly got out of the cab and took the elevator up his apartment. Travis lived in an upscale apartment on the Upper West Side, which was about four times the size of mine. I knocked lightly as Travis answered the door. I was surprised to find Chloe, his agent, there when I entered. Travis immediately wrapped his arms around me and kissed me on the lips.

"Hi, Mia," Chloe said in a very monotone manner.

"Oh, hi," I replied, trying my best to be cordial. There was just something about her that I did not like.

"I'm sorry, I had just stopped by to tie up some business deals with Travis. I'll be on my way now."

She was almost to the door when she turned back around. "Oh, Travis, don't make any plans for the tenth; there's a big sponsor dinner that you need to attend."

"No, I can't do the tenth."

"Why not?" I could tell she wasn't pleased one bit.

"Because, I promised Mia I would attend a fundraiser for her."

"Oh and let me guess, you're not getting paid for this fundraiser, are you?"

I never wanted to smack someone as much as I wanted to smack her right now. I knew that I should probably keep my mouth shut and mind my own business but I couldn't. "No, Chloe, he's not getting paid. Some people actually do things out of the goodness of their heart instead of worrying about the money." The words were out before I could even stop them.

"Oh, I'm sorry; are you his agent now?"

"Good-bye, Chloe," Travis said, trying to break up what was just about to begin.

We both ignored him. "No, I'm not, but that doesn't mean that you control him just because you are."

"Well, it doesn't mean you control him either, just because he's fucking you. If that were the case, then half the female population would have rights to him." She laughed.

You fuckin' bitch! The words were just about to leave my lips, but I stopped myself, seeing the anger that had flashed over Travis' face. "You know what, Chloe, why don't you just shut the hell up? Mia isn't my agent. She's my girlfriend and that means a hell of a lot more to me. Now you've discussed

~ 114 ~

everything business related with me that you needed to, so just leave."

"Whatever," she said, chuckling. "Keep thinking with your dick instead of your brain, Travis, and see how far that gets you."

"Go to hell, Chloe," Travis snapped.

"Fine, just remember that you have an appointment with EFE tomorrow. Do you think you could tear yourself away from Mia long enough to attend?" she asked, seeming unfazed by any of it. "Nice seeing you again, Mia," she said snidely as she flashed me a sarcastic smile before walking out the door.

"Why do you let her act that way?" I asked.

"What are you talking about?"

"The stuff she says to you, it's just wrong. She works for you, not vice-versa."

"She's harmless. All you have to do is tell to shut up and she backs off."

"Well, I don't like her," I pouted.

I really tried not to give much thought to Chloe up until now. The few times that I had encountered her, she always seemed a little standoffish to me and sometimes a little too touchy-feely with Travis. He always made a point of making me feel as if I had nothing to worry about by making sure that he was extra affectionate with me whenever she was around.

He wrapped his arms around me.

"Can we please stop talking about her? I missed my girl these past few days," he said as he placed his lips on mine.

"I missed you too," I said as I ran my fingers through his hair. "Somebody needs a haircut."

"My hairdresser is off today." He smiled.

"I think she could make an exception for a very handsome guy. But not without a price."

"Oh, yeah, how much is it going to cost me?"

I bit my lip and smirked at him. I took his hand and pulled him toward his bedroom.

"Ah, that's my favorite form of payment." He lifted me into his arms and kissed me on the neck as he carried off to his bedroom.

***

The last remnants of daylight were creeping through Travis' bedroom window as I lay in his bed, wrapped up in his arms.

"You do realize that we spent all of this beautiful afternoon in bed?"

He turned on his side and pulled me closer. "And, what's wrong with that? I can't think of anyplace else that I'd rather have been."

"Me neither," I said as I nuzzled into his bare chest.

"Hey, Mia?"

"Yeah."

"I love you."

I looked up at him, speechless. He gazed at me through his long, dark lashes. "You don't have to say it back. I just wanted you to know how I feel."

I bit my lip to stop the tears of joy that were forming in my eyes. "I know I don't have to say it back, but I want to. I love you too, Travis."

Travis Montgomery loved me and I loved him back. Life was definitely looking up!

Chapter 24

Travis...

Mia was so excited to introduce me to everyone at the fundraiser. I was amazed at how many people had showed up. I signed my name so many times that my hand was numb. I could tell right away how much Mia had meant to this family. But then again, Mia meant a lot to anyone that she encountered. She just had a way about her that made you instantly fall in love with her.

"You are just so popular," Mia said as she stood on her tippy toes and kissed me. "Do you want something to drink?"

"Sure."

"Okay, I'll be right back."

I watched as she walked away. She was just so damn cute, always worrying about taking care of everyone else.

"Hey, Travis." Eric's brother Patrick broke me from my trance. "I just want to thank you again, for coming out to this. You have no idea how much this means to me and my wife."

"No problem."

Patrick looked over at Mia. "She's a great girl. After my brother died, she was pretty messed up. I was really worried about her. She didn't handle it well at all. So, to see her this happy again is a beautiful thing. She loves with all her heart. Just please take good care of her; she deserves nothing but the best."

"I plan on it."

He smiled at me and placed his hand on my shoulder.

"You really are a lucky guy."

Yeah, I was....I really and truly was.

***

We were spending the night at Mia's parents' since the fundraiser was right by their house. Mia's mom was babysitting her nieces so her sister and brother-in-law could meet us out for a few drinks. Mia was so excited for me to spend time with her family. She couldn't wipe the smile off her face.

"You have no idea how happy I am right now!" she said as we walked into the bar. "I'm spending the night with my favorite people." She stopped walking and wrapped her arms around my neck. "But you are my most favorite. Thank you so much for doing that for Eric's family today."

"No problem." I leaned down and kissed her.

"Now, Travis Montgomery, don't be gettin' yourself all hot and bothered; there will be none of that tonight."

"Oh, it's too late for that," I whispered in her ear.

Her mile-wide grin quickly disappeared when I pulled my ringing cell phone from my pocket and the name Chloe displayed on the caller ID. I immediately silenced it, ignoring her call. I wrapped my arm around her, but I could feel her tensing up. We were just about to enter the bar when I took her hand in mine.

"Hey, what's wrong?"

"Nothing." She tried playing it off.

"Mia, come on. Don't be pissed. I didn't answer it."

"Well, I don't see why you would have to again; it isn't like she hasn't called you already at least twenty times today."

"Mia, I'm sorry; she's trying to put together this-"

"She's just trying to be a bitch because she knows that you were doing the fundraiser for me, Travis."

She walked in ahead of me. Her mood had totally shifted from just a few seconds ago. She found her sister and brother-in-law, who were seated at a table in the bar area, and gave them each a hug.

"Hey, Travis!" Tressa wrapped her arms around me while her husband, Shane, shook my hand.

I was just about to sit down when I was approached my two women. "Oh my God! Travis Montgomery!" they both said in unison. "Can we get a picture with you?" the shorter blonde asked.

"Umm, sure," I answered.

She handed Tressa her cell phone to take the picture. Tressa was all smiles as she snapped the picture. Mia, on the other hand, didn't look amused. "Thank you so much!" they said before walking away.

"How exciting, having a *celebrity* boyfriend," Tressa said to Mia.

Mia forced a half smile and raised her eyebrows. Tressa and her husband both excused themselves to use the restroom at the same time. I was grateful because it gave me time to talk to Mia. I sat down next to her and took her hand.

"So, are you going to snap out of it or are you going to let Chloe ruin your night?"

"I'm just sick of sharing my boyfriend with everyone else, Travis. If it's not Chloe, then it's random women throwing themselves at you."

I took her face in my hands. "Mia, you have nothing to worry about; my heart belongs to you completely. I'm not going to let go of your face until you smile." A smile finally stretched across her face. "That's my girl!" I kissed her on the forehead. She took my hand and leaned her head on my shoulder.

"Mia, come and dance with me since your sister is no fun," Mia's brother-in-law, Shane, said as he and Tressa returned to the table. Mia got up and kissed me on the cheek before heading out to the dance floor.

Tressa watched them out on the dance floor and smiled. "Thank you for giving me my sister back, Travis."

I wasn't sure exactly what she meant. She must have sensed my confusion and went on to explain. "A year ago, she was on the verge of losing it. I really thought that she would never allow herself to feel again. She wasn't the same Mia that I knew and loved my whole life and it scared me to death."

I looked at Mia out on the dance floor. "Well, she's really easy to love."

"You know, I never thought she would love anyone as much as Eric, but I see the way she looks at you and I can tell that she loves you so very much and that makes me happy. Just please don't ever break her heart."

"Never," I said as I looked away, feeling a huge stab of guilt.

Mia came walking back to the table with a huge smile on her face. "Tressa, your husband has no rhythm." She giggled as she sat down next to me and wrapped her arm around me. "I'm totally over it now," she whispered in my ear.

She leaned in and kissed me deeply, taking me a little off guard, but I liked it.

"Oh my God, get a room, you two!" Tressa teased.

"It's not me; it's your sister's fault," I said.

"Hey, I can't help it if I have the sexiest man around. Sorry, Shane, but he is!" Mia joked with her brother-in-law.

Even though she was absolutely adorable when she pouted, I was glad to have the old Mia back.

After a few more hours and a lot more drinks, Mia had totally gotten over Chloe. We said our goodbyes to her sister and brother-in-law and got into to my car. "Travis Montgomery, I want to ravish your body right now." She wrapped her hands around my neck and pulled me towards her. She moved her tongue around my mouth, making me want her even more than I already did.

"Mia, remember what you said; there will be none of that."

"There will be none of that once we get to my parents' house, but nobody said anything about here." I knew she had a little too much to drink, which was probably causing her out of character behavior, but I didn't care – I liked it. She unzipped my pants and began to stroke me. She ran her tongue up and down my neck. "Do you like this, Travis? 'Cause it's feeling like you do."

I was so hard and I wanted her more than anything. "Mia, you're driving me fuckin' crazy, baby."

She bit her lip and smiled, making my need for her even stronger. She moved her head down to my lap and ran her tongue up and down my throbbing cock. I had to catch my breath, it felt so good, and she knew it. She continued to tease me with her tongue before finally taking me inside her mouth as she gently glided her lips up and down. I was just about there when I grabbed her hair and pulled her up. "Mia, I want to fuck you so bad."

She smiled and took my face in her hands. "What's stopping you, then?" I climbed over the gearshift and started pulling down her pants. She finished taking them off completely. I stuck my fingers inside of her. She was so wet, so ready. I pulled my pants down and shifted myself into the seat, pulling her on top of me. I slid myself inside of her with ease as she began to move. I placed my hands on her hips and saw the look of pleasure that was washing over her face. I was getting even more turned on just watching her. She leaned her head back and began to move quicker. I moved my hands to her ass and gently lifted her up and down. She felt so good, like her body was made just for me. "Oh my God, Travis, this feels so good!" It was only a matter of seconds before she let out a loud scream and melted around me. Within minutes, she was screaming my name again at the same exact time that I released myself inside of her.

She wrapped her arms around my neck and kissed me on the lips. "You are a bad little girl, Mia."

"Only for you. So I guess that makes me *your* bad little girl." She smiled.

I smiled back. She was just *my girl* plain and simple. She didn't need to be anything else. Just plain old Mia Taylor was all that I would ever need.

Chapter 25

Mia...

"Juan, you have to stop double-booking me when you know I have color to do."

"Mia, I thought people were supposed to get nicer when they're gettin' some, but you just seem to be getting bitchier."

I smacked him in the arm. "I'm not being bitchy; I've just been running around like a crazy person all day!" It was two days before Thanksgiving and everyone needed their hair done – like yesterday! I was a little upset about not spending Thanksgiving with Travis; he was going up to his parents' house in Connecticut and had asked me to go. I knew my mother would go into coronary arrest at the thought of me not spending a holiday with them, so I graciously declined.

I walked over to my chair, where Mrs. Montgomery was waiting for me. "Mia, sweetheart, how are you?" She pulled me to her and placed a kiss on my cheek.

"I'm doing great!" A smiled stretched across my face.

"Well, Travis stopped over yesterday and he's doing great too." She smiled back. She took my hand in hers. "I'm so happy for the two of you, dear."

"Thanks!"

"He told me that he had invited you to my son and daughter-in-law's for Thanksgiving dinner."

"Yeah, he did and unfortunately, I don't think my mother could part with me on a holiday just yet."

"That's understandable. My son and his wife are very anxious to meet you. Travis has never invited a girl over for a holiday before. I told them you were special."

"Aw, thank you, Mrs. Montgomery. Are you going to be spending Thanksgiving with them?"

"Oh no, Christmas is enough. I always spend my Thanksgivings with my sisters; it's been that way for years."

"Sisters are the best, aren't they?"

"Yes, they are, dear." She smiled up at me.

I finished up with Mrs. Montgomery and actually had ten precious minutes to throw a yogurt down my throat. I went into the break room and checked my phone to find a missed call from my mother. She never called me when I was at work, so I figured it was probably important.

She answered after four rings and she sounded like death. "Hey, Mom, are you okay?"

"Oh, Mia, I feel like I'm dying. Both Gary and I have the flu. I'm so sorry, sweetie, I'm not going to be up to cooking Thanksgiving dinner. Tressa is going to go to her in-laws now; she said that you're welcome to come along if you'd like."

"No, that's okay."

"Oh, honey, I'm so sorry."

"Don't be silly, Mom. Just get better."

"Well, where are you going to go?"

"Don't worry about me. I have options." I smiled, thinking about what those options were.

We hung up the phone. She made me promise that I would come down once she was feeling better so we could celebrate Thanksgiving then.

I looked at the clock; my ten minutes were just about up. I quickly typed out a text to Travis: *Change of plans, would you still like me to join you for Thanksgiving?*

I put my phone away, figuring I wouldn't be hearing back from him for a while. I was half out the door and stopped myself dead in my tracks when I heard the beeping of my phone. I ran to my purse and pulled it out. I couldn't stop smiling when I looked down at his reply: *You just made my day, baby.*

***

I spent the night before Thanksgiving at Travis' place. I was a little nervous about meeting his family for the first time. Just from knowing Mrs. Montgomery, I knew that they were in a different social class than I was. I was only hoping that they would be as warm and welcoming as Mrs. Montgomery had been toward me. Travis must have sensed my nervousness as I was finishing getting dressed.

"Hey, what's the matter?" he asked.

"Nothing, just a little nervous about meeting your parents for the first time."

He walked over to me and wrapped his arms around my waist. "Mia, relax, there's nothing to be nervous about. They're going to love you just as much as I do."

I smiled as he kissed me softly on the forehead.

After an hour-long drive, we finally pulled into the long driveway of Travis' parents' Greenwich, Connecticut home. It was an exquisite brick-front Tudor-style home that looked humungous from the outside. I tried my best to calm the butterflies flapping around in my stomach.

Travis again sensed my apprehension. He grabbed my hand and squeezed it tightly as we walked through the front door. The house was just as breathtaking on the inside as it was on the outside. I stood in the foyer and was in shock as my eyes began to take everything in. It looked like it had been professionally decorated. It made me realize the stark differences in our upbringing as I compared the tiny two-bedroom ranch-style home that I had grown up in to this home.

"Travis!" a very attractive older woman exclaimed as she came walking out from the kitchen. She wrapped her arms around him and kissed him on the cheek.

"Mom, this is Mia."

Her smile was a mile wide. She took my hands in hers and kissed me on the cheek. "I cannot tell you what a pleasure it is to finally meet you, Mia. I've heard so much about you from Travis and my mother-in-law and, believe me, you must be pretty special if you rate with her," she joked.

She had the same color eyes as Travis and wore her auburn hair short and stylish. "Thank you, Mrs. Montgomery." I smiled, releasing some of the tension that I was feeling just a few minutes ago.

"Please call me Joanne and this is my husband, Jules."

Travis' dad looked like an older version of Travis with gray hair. He was tall, had the same facial features, including the cleft in his chin. The only difference was he had blue eyes instead of the beautiful hazel shade of Travis' that I had become so fond of. He took my hand and shook it gently, giving me a warm smile. "Nice to meet you, Mia."

"You too, Dr. Montgomery."

"No need for formalities, Mia; just call me 'Jules.'"

I smiled at him, thinking this wasn't so bad after all.

Travis' father helped me take off my coat as his mom wrapped her arm around me and led me into the kitchen. "Come and meet my sister and my niece." Travis gave me a reassuring smile as his mother whisked me away.

All of my doubts were put to rest; by the end of the day, I felt totally comfortable around Travis' entire family. I scolded myself for even having any preconceived notions about them. They made me feel totally warm and welcomed. I actually found myself getting a little disheartened when Travis looked down at his watch.

"It's eight o'clock. Are you ready to get going?"

I shrugged my shoulders. "Sure, if you are."

Travis stood up and announced our departure to everyone. "Oh, I wish you guys could just spend the night."

"We can't. Mia has to work tomorrow and I have an early meeting."

"Honestly, Travis, who schedules meetings for the day after Thanksgiving? Don't they know that everyone is supposed to be out shopping?" his mother asked.

"I didn't; Chloe did."

His mother had a look of disgust on her face at the mention of Chloe's name. She shook her head and shivered at the sound of her name. "Well, that would make perfect sense, then."

I found myself becoming instantly curious as to her obvious unfavorable assessment of Chloe.

"Who's Chloe?" Travis' cousin Brenda asked.

"Just a dreadful woman," his mother answered.

"Mom, just stop." Travis shook his head and raised his eyebrow at her.

She finally changed the subject, even though it appeared that she had much more that she wanted to say. We said our goodbyes and were on our way home. About fifteen minutes into the ride, I could no longer control my curiosity. "How does your mother know Chloe?"

"She met her at a benefit that she attended a while back." I could tell from his vagueness that he didn't really care to talk about it.

I, however, wanted to know more. "So why doesn't your mother like her?"

"She just didn't agree with some of the business choices she was making for me."

"Oh." I nodded, wishing that he would elaborate a little further, but I knew it was of no use as he immediately shifted the subject.

"You're staying over tonight, right?" he asked.

"I wasn't planning on it."

He looked at me sadly. "I have to be at work early tomorrow and that would mean I would have to rush home to get dressed in the morning."

"Mia, I know that you packed at least ten outfits in that bag of yours last night because I saw you trying them all on this morning in your state of panic at meeting my parents," he joked.

"Fine." I smiled, thinking about spending another night with him.

He took my hand and lifted it up to his lips, placing a gentle kiss on it.

We arrived back at his apartment. I was freezing from just coming in from outside. I briskly rubbed my hands together, trying to warm them up.

"Are you cold?" he asked.

"A little."

He walked over to the fireplace and turned it on. He pulled his ringing cell phone from his pocket and rolled his eyes when he looked at the caller ID.

"Yeah, Chloe," he answered, not trying to disguise his annoyance in any way. "Yes, I know; nine o'clock."

He walked over to me, wrapped his arms around me, and began to kiss me on the neck, all the while half listening to what Chloe was saying on the other end of the phone.

"Yeah, I'll see you tomorrow. I have to run." He abruptly hung up the phone and dropped it on the counter, right by where we were standing.

"Let me warm you up some more," he whispered in my ear. He gently grazed my earlobe with his teeth. He didn't miss a beat when he reached back to the counter to silence his ringing cell phone, without even looking to see who it was. I was a little more curious as I peeked over his shoulder, becoming a little annoyed when I saw the name Chloe flashing on the caller ID. I erased any more thoughts of her when Travis kissed me deeply, picked me up, and carried me off into his bedroom.

Chapter 26

Mia...

It was hard to believe that Christmas was only two weeks away. I was attending a Christmas party with Travis, which was being hosted by one of the companies with which he had an endorsement. I placed one last curl in my hair before giving it a final spray of hairspray. I looked at myself in the full-length mirror, quite pleased with the girl looking back at me. I was even more pleased when I thought of the great bargain that I had gotten on the little black dress that I was wearing. I buzzed Travis in and unlocked the door so he could just let himself in while I scoured through my closet for a purse that matched my dress.

I found my purse and turned around to find Travis standing in my bedroom doorway. Just when I thought he couldn't get any more handsome, he was. He was dressed in a perfectly tailored suit and his freshly cut haircut that I had just given him yesterday, looked perfect.

"Oh my God, Mia, you're killing me in that dress."

I was killing him, seriously? He had no clue what he was doing to my insides right now!

He moved closer to me and pulled me to him. He began to kiss me and move his hands up and down my body. "Let's just skip this and spend the night in bed instead," he said with his arms still wrapped tightly around me.

I ran my hand across his cheek and smiled. "Come on, silly, you have to go and then there will time for that after."

"Okay, but I'm just showing my face and leaving."

"Suit yourself." I laughed.

Three hours into the party, I was wishing that I had just taken Travis up on his offer of spending the night in bed. I was feeling very uncomfortable and Travis had been drinking a little more than I cared for. Every time I would turn around, Chloe was handing him a drink. I was really getting annoyed with the way she would pull him off to the side for private conversations. She was there with a date and I wondered why she wasn't focusing more of her attention on him instead of Travis. If that weren't enough to push me over the edge, Travis had practically every woman at the party coming up and ogling over him as if I wasn't even there. I had finally had enough of putting on a happy face when inside, I wanted to scream. I was standing alone, waiting for Travis, who was off in conversation at the bar with some man as well as three beautiful women when I was approached by Josh Hamilton, another Olympic swimmer and Travis' main competitor. Travis had introduced me to him briefly in the beginning of the party when he still had his wits about him, but hurried me along when Josh tried to strike up a conversation with me.

"Hey, Mia, it was really nice to meet you earlier."

"Hey, you too."

"Travis is really lucky; not only did he beat me out of a few gold medals, but he has an absolutely beautiful girlfriend."

"Well, thanks." It was nice to have someone to talk to since Travis didn't even know that I existed tonight. Josh was staring at me and I couldn't help but notice just how handsome he was.

"Where is Travis?" he asked.

"Oh, I don't know; he's off somewhere." I was beyond annoyed with Travis at this point and didn't really care where he was.

"Well, do you think he would mind if I stole you for a dance?"

I shrugged my shoulders. "I don't know if he'll care, but I would love to dance with you."

We headed off to the dance floor. He wrapped his arms around me and we began to move to the music. By the time the music was over, I finally noticed Travis and he didn't look happy.

"Hey, Travis, I was just keeping Mia company while you disappeared."

I could tell that he was even drunker than when I had last seen him, if that was even possible. He quickly wrapped his arm around me and pulled me toward him. "I want to go home and fuck your brains out."

Josh looked at him, taken off guard by his crass statement. I felt my face turning red. "Travis, stop it."

"That's right, Josh, this beautiful woman is all mine, so keep your fuckin' hands off her," Travis slurred.

"Travis!" I shouted.

"It's okay, Mia; he's drunk."

"Don't fuckin' talk about me like I'm not standing here, while you're trying to fuck my girlfriend right in front of me," Travis shouted, causing a group of people to turn around to see what was going on.

"Oh my God, Travis, will you please stop it?" I pleaded.

"Did he tell you that he had a bet going on to see how many chicks he could bang in a week? What was your total, man?"

Josh stood there speechless, looking like he was just as embarrassed as I was right now. "Not cool, bro," Josh said, shaking his head.

"Oh, what's the matter? You don't want Mia knowing?" His arm remained tightly wrapped around me. "If you think you're adding her to your list, you're wrong. She's mine."

"Well, it was nice meeting you, Mia," Josh said as he shook his head at Travis and walked away.

I pulled away from Travis' grip. "Get the hell off of me," I said, trying not to make even more of a scene than the one that Travis had just created.

I made my way through the crowd, trying to escape my embarrassment as Travis followed behind me. "Oh, Mia, come on, baby, don't be pissed." He finally caught up with me and took my hand in his.

"I'm going, Travis!"

"Okay, let's go," he responded as he staggered back and forth with glassy eyes.

We were almost out the door. "Travis!" A very attractive and *very drunk* woman wrapped her arms around him. My jaw dropped and stomached clenched with pure disgust as she pulled him closer and kissed him hard. Travis just stood there, staring at her in his drunkenness, like he was oblivious as to what was going on.

She must have seen the look of shock and disgust on my face. "Oh, I'm sorry; you must be his choice for the night. Well, have fun with him; he's really good!" She flashed me a quick smile before walking away.

"Mia –" Travis went to grab my arm.

I pulled away. "Get the hell away from me, Travis." I did my best to fight the burning in my eyes.

"Who the heck was that?" Chloe asked as she came rushing over with her date following her around like a little puppy dog.

"I don't know. Why don't you ask Travis? That's if he even remembers," I responded.

"Oh, Mia, calm down; he's drunk." She chuckled as if it were no big deal.

"Really, I didn't realize that. Maybe if you weren't shoving alcohol down his throat the whole night, he wouldn't be this way right now." I was pissed, *really pissed,* and I wanted to make sure she knew it.

"Mia, Travis is a big boy. He could have stopped drinking any time he wanted. He has a mind of his own. Something I think he's forgotten since he met you, perfect little princess, Mia. I told you before; don't think you're special just because he's fucking you. You're just one on the list of many. It's only a matter of time before he gets bored with you and moves on to the next. Trust me, you are not his type."

"You fucking bitch! Stay out of mine and Travis' relationship."

She rolled her eyes at me. I wanted to scream my head off, scratch her eyes out, and rip that fake hair out of her head. Instead, I refrained, took a deep breath, and just walked away. She wasn't worth getting myself even more upset. I was angry enough with Travis. I just wanted to go home and forget that this night ever happened.

I looked around; Travis was nowhere to be found, which was just as well. I didn't feel like dealing with him either. I hurriedly made my way out the door. I was fortunate enough to jump into a cab that was just letting someone off. "Mia!" Travis shouted as he pushed his way in, moving closer to me. I gave the cab driver Travis' address. I planned on getting him into bed safely and heading home to my place. There was no way in hell that I was spending the night with him tonight. I was angry at myself for even taking the time to make sure that he made it home okay. I knew that deep down inside it was because I wanted to make sure that no one else was taking him home. I hated myself for having such thoughts. I wanted to be able to trust him. But after what had happened tonight, I was having a really hard time with that.

He moved closer to me and moved his hand under my dress. I quickly removed it and slapped it. "Travis, just stop!"

"Come on, Mia, quit being such a fuckin' bitch." I bit my lip again to stop myself from smacking him. *He's drunk; he doesn't know what he's saying!* I kept repeating those words over and over again in my head. I didn't respond as my mom's advice from a long time ago came flashing to the forefront of my mind – *Never argue with a drunk, it's a hopeless battle.* So I didn't. I just looked out the window and did my best to ignore him until we got to his apartment. I gave Travis a good hard push to get him out of the cab and asked the cab driver to wait for me. He was staggering and even though it killed me to touch him, I wrapped my arm around him and helped him walk in.

Charlie, his doorman, opened the door for us. "Hey, Charlie, do you know how much I love this beautiful girl right here?" Travis slurred.

Charlie gave me a sympathetic smile. "Good luck, Mia."

"Gee, thanks." I shook my head in disgust.

We took the elevator up to Travis' apartment. I did my best to ignore his wandering hands once again. "I want to fuck you right here, Mia." He pushed me up against the wall and kissed me.

"Travis, stop it!" I pushed him away.

"Come on, Mia, let's do it right here, baby."

I was so happy when the elevator finally stopped at his floor. I walked him into his bedroom, took off his shoes, and removed his tie. He lay down on the bed and quickly jumped up to run to the bathroom. I shook my head when I heard the sound of him throwing up. He walked back to the bed silently, looking like he was in pain. It was only a matter of seconds of his head hitting the pillow before he was passed out cold. I covered him with a blanket before heading out the door. I stood, waiting for the elevator. I finally came face to face with what I had most dreaded. Travis' past had collided with our present and it was even more painful than I ever imagined it would be.

Chapter 27

Travis...

I rolled over in my bed; my head was pounding and I felt like absolute shit. I hadn't gotten that drunk in a while and my body was paying the price for it now. I tried my best to remember exactly what had happened last night. I remembered Mia being pissed and, given the fact that she wasn't here right now, she must have been really pissed. I slowly got out of bed and made a cup of coffee in hopes that it would help in making me feel better, but no such luck. I picked up my phone and dialed Mia's number. After four rings, it went to her voice mail – *yeah, she was definitely pissed!* I just wanted to go back to sleep, but I had to go make things right with her so I dragged myself into the shower, ignoring the calls from my bed to get back in it. If it were any other person, I would have said *fuck it I'm going back to bed*, but Mia wasn't just any other person. She was my extraordinary girl who probably wanted to kick my ass and, given the way I was feeling, she probably could right now.

Chapter 28

Mia...

I awoke the next morning, not feeling any better than I had when I went to bed. I called my mom and made plans to spend the afternoon and night with her and my stepdad. I needed to get away from this place for a while. Juan had texted me to tell me he was on his way over with bagels and coffee.

"Good morning, pookie dook," I heard his cheerful voice scream as he entered my apartment.

"Hey," I said as I walked out of my bedroom.

"What the heck is wrong with you?"

We sat down to our bagels and coffee and I unloaded everything that had happened last night on Juan. He listened closely and shook his head. "Who's this Chloe?" he asked.

"She's Travis' agent and she is a total bitch! She just acts so weird with him."

"Weird in what way?"

"I don't know; she's always hanging all over him. She acts like she controls him or something." I told Juan about the comment Travis' mother had made about her on Thanksgiving.

"Well, I'll rip her eyes out if she messes with you," Juan said, taking a sip of his coffee. "This is one bitch she doesn't want to mess with." He snapped his fingers and jerked his head.

I shook my head and laughed. "No, she doesn't!"

We talked for a while and I felt a little better. Juan always had that effect on me. He was the only one that could make me smile when I thought it was impossible. I got up to walk him to the door and looked down at my ringing cell phone – *Travis.* "Are you going to answer it?" Juan asked.

I looked down at the phone again; I wasn't ready to deal with him just yet. "Nope, fuck him!" I smiled.

"That's my girl." Juan gave me a high five. "Make him beg!"

"You are too much, Juan." I shook my head and laughed.

"Hey, it works. After five years, Brian is still crazy over this bitch!" I laughed even harder. "See ya, baby cakes." He gave me a kiss on the cheek and headed on his way.

I picked up my phone from the table; no voicemail, so I just ignored the missed call as if it didn't exist. I jumped in the shower, quickly threw my hair in a ponytail, and put on some makeup.

I cringed when I heard my door buzzing. I knew exactly who it was before I even hit the button. I was hoping not to have to deal with him today, especially not face to face. I stood at my door, prepping myself for him as he made his way up the stairs.

I opened the door and let him in, pulling away as he went to kiss me.

"Okay, I deserve that," he said.

I completely ignored him and went into my bedroom to finish dressing as if he wasn't even there. He followed me in and sat down on my bed.

"Mia, I'm so sorry. I should have never drunk that much last night."

"No, you shouldn't have," I said, finally acknowledging his presence.

"Did you want to do something today?"

I turned around and looked into his bloodshot eyes. He looked so hung over that it was pathetic. "No, I'm going to my parents' and spending the night there."

"Oh." He nodded, looking a little disappointed. He grabbed me by the arm and made me sit down on the bed next to him. "Mia, will you please just talk to me? Look, I know you're pissed and I'm sorry."

"No, Travis; I'm more hurt than pissed. Do you even realize how I felt last night? Between you getting drunk off your ass and acting like a complete jerk and Chloe having her private little powwows with you. But the best part of the night was when that girl kissed you right in front of me like it wasn't a big deal. What hurts even more is I know that she's done a lot more than kiss you before I met you. You go crazy if a guy even looks at me. So just imagine how I felt watching her kiss you."

He sighed and ran his hand through his hair. "I don't know what to say, except I'm very sorry. I can't change the past. But, you are my present and my future. I love you so much, Mia."

As much as I wanted to hug him at that particular moment, I refrained from doing so. I was still upset and wasn't ready to let it go that easy. "Travis, I thought I could deal with your past and your 'ladies' man' reputation, but after coming face to face with it last night, I'm having a really hard time with it."

"Mia, you are the only woman that I want to be with forever. Why the hell don't you get that?" He raised his voice in frustration. He pulled me closer and took me off guard with his kiss. I could still taste the alcohol from last night on him.

I broke free and pushed him away, taking him by surprise. "Stop, just stop!" I shouted. He looked like he was surprised by my rejection. My voice became a little softer. "Travis, I just need some time to think, okay?"

His eyes widened and I could tell that he was starting to get a little panicked. "Mia, what are you saying? Think about what? Please tell me you're not going to end this over one stupid mistake?"

I shook my head. "I don't know what I'm trying to say actually; my head is spinning right now. That's why I just need some time alone. Please, Travis; will you just let me have that?"

He stood up from the bed and nodded. I could see the pain in his eyes and it killed me to see him that way. "Just um… give me a call when you feel up to it."

"Okay," I whispered. I looked away, no longer able to look at the sadness on his face. I waited until I heard my front door close before I buried my face into my pillow, allowing the tears that I had been holding in to flow freely.

Chapter 29

Mia...

My mother and stepdad were waiting for me at the train station. My stepdad grabbed my bag as my mother threw her arms around me as if she hadn't seen me in years. Travis and I had just been down last weekend to celebrate her "belated" Thanksgiving dinner as well as my stepdad's birthday. "Mom, what would you do if I ever moved far away and you only saw me every few months?"

"That will never happen; I won't allow it," she joked as she wrapped her arm around me and we walked to the car. We went out for an early dinner. My mom was off tomorrow and since it was Monday and I was off too, we made plans to do some Christmas shopping before I went home.

The waitress had just brought the food out when my stepdad asked the question that suddenly made me lose my appetite. "Where's Travis today?"

I looked down at my pasta and shrugged my shoulders. "I don't know," I said as I finally looked up, seeing a look of alarm wash over both my mother's and stepfather's faces.

"Oh, honey, is everything okay with you guys?" my mother asked.

"I don't know." I bit my lip and looked down again. I told them about everything that had happened last night. I knew right away that my stepfather thought I was overreacting.

"Mia, he's a guy. Cut him some slack. So what if he got a little drunk?" he said in Travis' defense.

Drowning in Love

"Yes, I know and I could overlook that. It's the women from his past that I'm having a hard time dealing with."

My mother shook her head as if she agreed with me. "Yes, I could see why that would upset you, but he couldn't control her kissing him. It wasn't like he went up to her and kissed her." I looked at her with disapproval for not immediately taking my side like she always would.

"I'm not saying you're wrong. I'm just trying to be impartial," she clarified.

My stepdad had a worried look about it. He and Travis had bonded instantly and I think if we broke up it would probably kill him just as much as it did me.

"Relax, Gary. We didn't break up."

"Phew," he said as he pretended to wipe sweat off his forehead.

My mother playfully smacked him. "I raised my daughter right; if a man does her wrong, she calls him out on it."

I smiled. She was absolutely right and I was so grateful to her for instilling that value in me. I was so thankful when the topic changed and there was no longer anymore mention of Travis' name.

We paid my sister and my nieces a quick visit before heading back to my parents' house. My mother had started a lot of her Christmas baking already, but made sure that she held off on the thumbprint cookies until I was around. I had been helping her with the thumbprint cookies ever since I could remember and no matter how old I got, we didn't break tradition.

"Good night, girls. I have an early day tomorrow." Gary came into the kitchen, giving us both a kiss goodnight.

"Goodnight, Gary," I said as I took a bite from the cookie that we had just taken out of the oven.

He was halfway through the kitchen door when he turned around. "Hey, Mia, remember go easy on him."

I smiled and shook my head at him. "Good night, Gary," I said again, acting as if I was ignoring his request.

My mother and I finished up in the kitchen and brought a plateful of cookies and a cup of tea into the living room. We snuggled under a blanket together and watched TV, finally deciding on the classic movie channel.

"And they lived happily ever after." I giggled as the credits began to roll on the screen.

"Well, what about you? Are you going to allow yourself to live happily ever after?" my mother asked.

I leaned my head on her shoulder as she played with my hair. "I don't know, Mom. I never had to worry about these things with Eric. I always knew where I stood with him."

"Oh, honey, you can't compare this relationship with the one that you had with Eric. You and Eric were each other's past; there was no one else. As you get older, you have to expect and accept each other's past. Mia, you have to have enough faith in yourself and him and realize that maybe you really are all that he needs and wants. Look, I get that you're angry with him for his behavior last night, but, Mia, everybody makes mistakes."

"I know, but it just hurt me so much to see that woman kissing him."

"Well of course it did. You love him; just remember that before you go making any rash decisions. Just remember he's dealing with your past as well."

"What do you mean?" I was in total confusion.

"Mia, I'm sure he worries if he'll live up to Eric too."

She pulled me close and kissed me on the head. "I'm going to bed and you better get going soon too; we have a lot of shopping to do in the morning."

"I am in a few. Goodnight, Mom."

"Good night, sweetheart." She kissed me goodnight and headed off to bed.

I sat on the couch, wrapped in the blanket and staring into space. My mother was right; I loved Travis so much and I didn't want to throw it all away over one little argument. I missed him and I wanted to hear his voice more than anything. I looked at the clock; it was after midnight. I started to type out a text message, but then deleted it. I *needed* to hear his voice. I dialed his number and waited for him to answer.

"Hey, Mia," he answered in his I'm-really-sleeping-but-trying-to-pretend-I'm-awake voice.

"Hey, I'm sorry to be calling you so late."

"No, it's okay."

"I just wanted to let you know that I miss you and I love you and if you ever behave the way that you did last night again, I will have to kill you."

"Oh, baby, I love you too and I'm so sorry."

We talked for a little while longer. "Well, get back to sleep and I'll see you tomorrow?"

"Definitely," he answered.

***

It was exactly 2:15 p.m. when I stepped off the train and entered the cab to head back to my apartment. I wrestled to fit all of the bags from my early morning shopping excursion with my mother, into the cab. Travis had texted me earlier in the day and asked me to let him know when I got home. He was spending most of his day at the gym and the pool. I had texted him back from the train, letting him know that I was on my way.

The cab pulled up to my apartment and I once again wrestled with the bags, this time to get them out. I placed them down on the ground and bent down to rearrange them in hopes of making them a little easier to carry.

"Need some help?"

I looked up into the bright December sunlight, and couldn't contain my smile when I saw Travis standing over top of me.

"Sure," I answered as I stood up. "But no peeking, because Santa may have put a few things for you in there, even though you're on the naughty list."

He lifted his sunglasses on top of his head and pulled me toward him. "I promise, I'll do everything that I can to get off that list," he said, sounding so sexy as he kissed me softly on the lips.

God, I loved him so much!

Chapter 30

Mia...

Travis and I spent the rest of the afternoon together. I went with him and helped him pick out a Christmas tree. I let him talk me into going over to his place for dinner, so we could decorate the tree afterwards. I had really wanted to just stay home and wrap some presents and unwind before going back to work tomorrow, but he always made it so hard for me to resist. I quickly ran home to grab some clothes *just in case* I decided to spend the night, knowing full well that I was going to, while he went home to start dinner.

I was in the hallway locking my apartment door, when my next door neighbor Luis startled me with sound of his voice.

"Oh, Mia, there you are," he said in broken English. I looked over at his pregnant wife, Maria, and smiled down at her swollen belly.

"Hey, how are you feeling, Maria?" Luis translated my question to her in Spanish. She smiled and nodded, responding back to him in Spanish.

"She can't wait to get this over with," he said, chuckling.

I smiled at both of them and couldn't help but feel a little envious. My biological clock was beginning to tick and I was always reminded of it whenever I would see a pregnant woman or was around my nieces. I knew that Travis and I were nowhere near that point in our relationship, but I was hopeful that maybe someday I would have a baby of my own.

"Mia, there was some guy looking for you. He was here last night and just a little while ago after you had left with your boyfriend."

"Hmm…did he say who he was?"

"No, I told him I would give you a message but he said he would just come back."

"What did he look like?"

"He was older, gray hair; that's all I really remember, sorry."

I shrugged my shoulders. "Well, I guess it couldn't have been too important, if he didn't want to a leave a message."

"Mia, you have my cell phone number, well, you know, just in case you need me?"

"Yes, I do and thanks for your concern, but I'm sure it's nothing."

He nodded. We said our goodbyes and I headed down the stairs. I pondered over who this mystery man could be and couldn't think of anyone. It was always in the back of my head that maybe one day, the animal who shot Eric would be set free from prison and come looking for me. But since he got sentenced to life in prison without parole, I knew the chances of that happening were slim to none. I shivered when I thought of his cold, callous eyes on the day of sentencing. I had never been more terrified, yet so fearless as I was on that day, when I had to get up on that stand and speak. It was like I was looking into an empty soul; all I saw were blank eyes looking back at me. I had never loathed someone as much as I loathed him. I wasn't a violent person, but I honestly wished him the worst of everything in prison, so that maybe he could experience one ounce of the hell that he had put me through. I was extra cautious of my surroundings as I stepped out onto the city streets, feeling relieved when I was finally able to hail a cab.

I arrived at Travis' and was greeted by his doorman, Charlie. "Hey, Charlie," I said, feeling a little embarrassed over Travis' behavior in front of him the other night.

"Hello, Mia," he responded back with a smile.

The delicious aroma of dinner wafted through the air as soon as I stepped off the elevator. I knocked lightly on Travis' door; he kissed me on the lips as soon as I entered. "Wow, it smells really good!" I said as I took off my coat and placed it on the chair.

"Do you need some help?"

"Nope, everything will be done in five minutes."

He poured me a glass of wine and sat down next to me at the breakfast counter. "So did you decide if you were going to stay tonight?" he asked with that deep dimpled smile that made it impossible to say "no".

"Hmm....I guess." I smirked.

His smile was a mile wide. "But only because I have a stalker after me," I joked.

I watched as his smile immediately disappeared, making me instantly regret saying anything to him. "What are you talking about?"

I explained to him everything that Luis had told me. "Travis, it's not a big deal."

"Well, until you figure out who it is, you're staying here."

I choked on the sip of wine I had just taken. "What? You can't be serious."

"I'm dead serious, Mia."

"Oh my God, Travis, I'm sure it's –"

"Mia, I'm not arguing with you about it."

I shook my head and took another sip of my wine. *Me and my big mouth!*

Dinner was delicious. I made Travis promise to let me clean up since he cooked. After his third attempt at trying to help me and me resisting, he finally gave up and just sat down in the kitchen, keeping me company. I was in the middle of telling him about my visit with my nieces when his cell phone began to ring. He looked down at it and silenced it.

"Who was that?" I asked.

"Just Chloe, calling me for the hundredth time today to remind me about this meeting tomorrow. Now what where you saying?" he asked, trying to shift the subject.

I put the dishtowel down on the counter and moved closer to him, forgetting all about the story I had just been telling him about my nieces. "I don't like her, Travis."

"Who?"

"Chloe." I went on to tell him about everything that annoyed me about her. Including the little tiff we had gotten into the other night at the Christmas party.

He pulled me down onto his lap. "A lot of people don't like Chloe. She can be very abrupt and a real pain in the ass, but she's one of the best agents around."

I rolled my eyes at him. "If you say so, but if you ask me, she's just like Tiffany Bennet."

"Who?" Travis had a look of confusion on his face.

"Tiffany Bennet. She was the most popular and meanest girl in the fifth grade. She told everyone that I stuffed my bra with tissues, just because she thought I liked Eric." I looked down at my small chest. "Clearly, you can tell that I don't do that, right?" I joked.

Travis laughed and kissed me on the head. "Aw, did you beat her up?"

"No, my mom called her mom and I just got called a tattletale for the rest of the year."

He laughed again, even harder. "Well, maybe you should have your mom call Chloe's mom," he joked.

I lifted my head up and looked at him. "Hell no, I can take her on all by myself." I smiled. He kissed me on the nose and smiled.

"Hey, Mia, I betcha Tiffany Bennet isn't even one quarter as beautiful as you and neither is Chloe, for that matter."

After dinner was cleaned up, we had a great time trimming the tree. After Travis' multiple attempts to try and straighten the tree in the stand and a lot of laughs, we finally settled on it being just a little crooked. It had been a great night.

I curled up next to him in bed as he pulled me closer. "I had fun tonight, thanks!" I said as kissed him on his bare chest.

"So, am I making my way off the naughty list?"

"Almost there." I laughed.

"Well, I guess I'm just going to have to try harder."

He kissed me softly on the head and removed my underwear as his hand wandered down my body. He pulled me on top of him and lifted my nightgown over my head. He had his hands placed on my hips as he examined every inch of my naked body. "How did I get so lucky to get someone so perfect?" He gently traced his fingers over my breast as I looked down at him. "Mia, I can make love to you every day, all day and never get tired of it. I'm so crazy about you." He removed his boxers as I watched the look of pleasure that washed across his face when he entered me. I placed my hands on his shoulders as I moved up and down.

"Oh my God, baby, this feels so good." I smiled at his positive response. He sat up and took himself deeper inside of me. I tilted my head back as he ran his tongue up and down my neck. We moved together in perfect unison. Each movement was more pleasurable than the next. I knew that he was almost ready, just by the way he was responding. I totally relaxed my body and couldn't control the scream that came out of me. I had never felt anything that intense. He only intensified the feeling as he continued his movement.

I buried my face into his shoulder, trying to stifle another scream as he bought me to a second orgasm within minutes of the first. It was only seconds later that he finally released himself inside of me. I still had my legs wrapped around him and my head on his shoulder. I felt so relaxed that I didn't want to move. He kissed me on lips. "Did you enjoy that?" he asked. I nodded, hugged him tightly, and began to cry. "Hey, Mia, what's wrong?" he asked as he wiped away a tear.

"I just never experienced anything like that before. I love you so much, Travis."

He squeezed me tightly. "I love you too, Mia, more than anything in this world, and please don't ever forget it."

"Thank you so much for allowing me to open my heart again. When Eric died, a part of me died along with him. But you – you somehow made that part of me come alive again; something that I never thought would be possible. I don't know how you did it, but you did. I love you so much, Travis, that it scares me."

"Why are you scared, Mia?"

"Because I don't want to ever feel the pain of losing someone that I love so much, ever again."

"Mia, I promise, you will never lose me. You are my girl forever."

I curled up next to him and rested my head on his chest. I was so sleepy.

"Travis?"

"Hmm?"

"Would you still love me even if I did stuff my bra with tissues?"

He began to laugh loudly. "Mia, I would love you no matter what."

"Okay, good night." I yawned. Within minutes, I was drifting off to sleep. I was so at ease. I didn't know if it was from the amazing sex that I had just had or the fact that I was wrapped up in the arms of the man that I loved. Maybe it was a little bit of both, but one thing was for sure, it had everything to do with Travis.

Chapter 31

Travis...

I looked over at her as she slept. She truly was beautiful. A strand of her long blonde hair was draped over her porcelain skin. I watched her breathe, wondering how I had gotten to this place. I didn't fall in love with women; I just fell in love with the idea of having sex with them. But Mia was so different. I was so in love with her, but if she knew the truth, it could destroy us, and the longer I waited, the worse it would be. I just couldn't do it. I couldn't take the chance of losing her. She had become my entire world. I had never felt about anyone the way I had felt about her. She didn't expect anything; she didn't want anything. She loved me for who I was. I couldn't resist running my hand over her warm skin as she briefly opened her tired blue eyes and murmured something incoherent. I pulled her close to me and kissed her softly on her head, breathing in the familiar scent of her shampoo. This girl was worth more to me than any amount of money or all of the medals in the world. I would give up everything to make sure that we were together forever. I tossed and turned, finally giving up on the prospect of any more sleep. My brain was tired from over thinking what could actually happen to us and wishing that I had told her right from the beginning. I needed a good run to clear my head. Everything was going to be fine. Mia would never find out and all that mattered was that I was so in love with her now. I placed a soft kiss on the velvet skin of her bare back, and quietly got out of bed. I looked out my bedroom window at the falling snow and quickly changed. I covered Mia, unable to resist kissing her on the cheek, before heading out into the cold.

Chapter 32

Mia...

The sound of the alarm clock was like nails on a chalkboard. I didn't want to leave the refuge of Travis' nice warm bed. I quickly sat up when I realized he wasn't in it with me. I fumbled for my phone to turn off the alarm clock and rubbed my tired eyes. I slipped my nightgown over my head and stepped onto the cold hardwood floor. I walked into the bathroom, threw some water on my face, and brushed my teeth before heading out into the kitchen. Travis was standing in the kitchen, wrapping up a phone call just as I entered. "Hey, baby, I'm sorry. Did I wake you up?"

"No, my alarm went off." I looked at him, dressed in his sweatpants and running sneakers. He was still wearing his ski cap and I noticed it was wet. When I looked out the window, I saw heavy snow falling down. "Were you out running in this weather?" I asked.

"Yeah, I have a busy day today. I'm not going to be able to hit the gym, so I decided to go for an early morning run."

"You are crazy, you know that?"

"This is the best kind of weather to run in. Besides, I was feeling very inspired after last night."

I smiled and my insides tingled, just thinking about last night. He hugged me as his earlobes brushed against my lips. "Your ears are freezing!"

He bit his lip and whispered in my ear, "Well, I can think of a way to warm them up while inspiring us both for the rest of the day."

"Oh yeah? How's that?" He grabbed my hand and led me into the bathroom. I raised my eyebrows at him and smiled. "Sounds like the perfect form of inspiration to me," I said as we both undressed and stepped into the shower.

The snow was really coming down by the time I got into the salon. I was hoping that maybe it would deter some people from coming out, in hopes of an easier day. No such luck! It was the same old craziness as any other Tuesday. I had just finished up with my last client and realized that I hadn't heard from Travis all day. I knew that he said he was going to be busy all day with meetings. I was a little grateful; it would allow me to sneak out to my apartment without being sequestered to his apartment for house arrest because of my so-called "stalker." I had so much to do at home. I quickly sent him a text to let him know I was done working. I was in the back gathering up all of my things when Brian walked in and startled me.

"Mia, there's some man out at the appointment desk who wants to talk to you. He wouldn't give me his name."

"Okay." I shrugged my shoulders and walked out. I looked at the man standing on the other side of the desk. He was older with gray hair, fitting the description of my "stalker" perfectly. *Well, he can't be too crazy if he's coming to see me in a public place,* I thought to myself as I approached him. As I got up closer, I tried my best to remember where I had recognized him from.

"Hi, can I help you?" I asked.

"Mia Taylor?" he asked in disbelief as his eyes flooded with emotion.

I nodded as I started to become a little uncomfortable.

"God, you are so beautiful," he said as he stared at me.

"I- I'm sorry, but who are you?"

"Mia, sweetheart, I'm your father."

My eyes widened and my jaw dropped. I was speechless. I was finally able to get the words out. "What the hell do you want?"

"Mia, can we just go to the coffee shop next door and talk?"

I shook my head. I had nothing to say to him.

"Mia, please, it won't take long." His request seemed urgent.

"Fine." I finally gave in. I hated that I was such a pushover. We walked over to the coffee shop in silence. We entered and sat down at one of the small tables. "Did you want some coffee?" he asked.

I shook my head. "No, I want to know what's so important that you felt the need to finally get in touch with me after twenty-three years."

He nervously folded the napkin that was on the table. "Mia, I'm dying." I was emotionless as I stared at him intently. "I have terminal cancer."

"Oh, so you felt the need to come here to absolve your guilt before you died?" I knew I sounded heartless, but I was so angry. Angry, over the fact that he never bothered to work things out with my sister and I years ago, but had to come here now to lay this guilt trip on me.

"Mia, I came to tell you I'm sorry. I'm sorry for doing what I did to you and your sister."

"Fine, you said it and now you can go."

He looked at me sadly as I fought with everything inside of me to hold back the tears. He got up from the table and began to walk away.

"Why did you leave us? Why did you make Tressa and me feel like we weren't good enough? What did we do that was so wrong?" I shouted as the tears streamed down my face.

He stopped dead in his tracks, turned around, and sat back down at the table and took my hands in his. "Mia, sweetheart. You girls did nothing wrong. It was me. I was the one who failed you. I was screwed up. I felt like my life had spiraled out of control and there was nothing I could do to stop it. I just thought that you girls would be better off without having someone like me in your life. Then so much time had gone by, I just figured you would resent me."

I shook my head. "Why didn't you let us make that decision?"

"I don't know, Mia. I was wrong and I can't change what I did. I don't expect you to forgive me. I just needed to see you and, hopefully your sister, one last time."

I was looking into the eyes of a man who knew he was dying. He looked so scared, so alone. All of sudden, I was flooded with memories. Not the bad ones that were still fresh in my mind, but the happy ones. Walking to the ice cream shop on warm summer nights with my dad, remembering how he would always let my sister and me get that extra scoop, even though my mom protested. The nights that he would check for monsters under the bed when I was too afraid to go to sleep. I had spent most of my life trying to convince myself why I *shouldn't* love him and I had forgotten about the good times that we had, before he and my mother began to fight like cats and dogs.

He looked so frail and much older than his fifty-two years. Even though I felt like he was a stranger, something about him was familiar. Something that made me realize that deep down inside he was still inside of my heart, tucked away safely in a place that had been under lock and key for the past twenty-three years. Sitting here with him now and looking into his eyes, I suddenly felt the chains being broken from that far-off place. As those guarded walls came crumbling down, I gave him his dying wish - I forgave him.

I had given him my email address, so his wife could email me some pictures that he had wanted me to have of me and him. He gave me his phone number to give to my sister. I warned him that I didn't know if she would call.

We walked out of the coffee shop and stood on the busy street as the cold wet snow began to fall once again. He took my hands in his. "You are a great girl, Mia. Your mother did a wonderful job raising you. I wish you nothing but happiness, the same happiness that you have just given me."

I pulled the sleeve of my coat over my hand and wiped away the tears.

"I may have been a horrible father while I was here. But I promise you, if I'm lucky enough to make it to heaven, I will be watching out for you every single second." The tears flowed down his face as he pulled me close and hugged me tightly. "I love you, Mia."

I swallowed hard at the words I had yearned to hear from him for the past twenty-three years. "I love you too," I whispered. I stood still as I watched him walk away down the dark busy street, until he blended in with the crowd. My tears felt like they were frozen on my face. My father had come back to me, only to leave again forever.

Chapter 33

Mia...

I flopped down on my couch, finally feeling like I was able to breathe for the first time since walking out of that coffee shop. I was numb and it wasn't just from the cold. Every time I thought of the sadness in my father's eyes, my heart would feel like it had dropped into my stomach. I knew that after what he had done to me and my sister, I should have felt nothing for him. But I couldn't; that was not who I was. Once someone had etched a space in my heart, it was impossible for me to feel nothing for them, no matter how much they may have hurt me.

I was hoping to have heard from Travis. I needed to hear his voice to help put me at ease.

I took out my phone and dialed my sister's number. My sister was the opposite of me; she wasn't able to let things go and forgive as easily as I was. I by no means was going to try and force her into doing anything that she didn't want to. I was simply going to deliver the message to her and let her make the decision as to what she wanted to do.

"Hey, Mee Mee." She sounded so upbeat that I felt guilty about what I was about to unload on her.

"Hey, Tress." She immediately picked up on the tone in my voice.

"What's the matter? Please tell me that you and Travis made up?"

"Yeah, Travis and I are fine."

She let out a deep breath. "Tressa, our father came to see me at work today."

She was silent for a brief moment before responding. "What did he want?"

I went on to tell her the reason for his visit and found myself crying once again.

"I don't want his number; I want nothing to do with him, Mia. He died a long time ago to me."

"Okay, he made me promise that I would at least let you know."

She quickly changed the subject, asking me about what was going on with Travis and me. I told her that we had made up and everything was fine. We hung up the phone without any more mention of my father.

Within a matter of minutes, my cell phone began to ring. I got a little disheartened when I looked down and saw that it was my mother instead of Travis.

"Hey, Mom."

"Mia, Tressa just called me. Are you okay?"

"Yeah, I'm fine."

I retold the same story that I just told my sister a few minutes ago.

"Oh, Mia, I'm so sorry that you had to deal with that alone."

"I'm okay." I tried my best to put on a strong front, but I couldn't. I began to sob hysterically. "Oh, Mom, I felt so bad for him. I know I shouldn't have, but I did."

"It's okay, Mia. Don't ever question your feelings, sweetie." She did her best to comfort me. I got up when I heard my buzzer and was filled with happiness at the sound of Travis' voice over the intercom. I opened the door and waited for him to come up as I hung up with my mother.

"Mia, what's the matter?" he asked, no doubt seeing the mess of mascara all over my face.

I couldn't speak. I pulled him close and hugged him tightly. He wrapped his arm around me and walked me over to the couch. He pushed my hair out of my face and wiped my tears away.

"My dad came to see me today." He looked at me sympathetically. "He's dying."

"Oh, Mia, I'm sorry." He pulled me into his chest and kissed the top of my head.

I repeated the entire story for yet a third time. I found that I was just as emotional as I was when telling it for the first time.

"I just wish that he hadn't told me. Sometimes we're better off not knowing certain things."

Travis looked at me almost as if he was taken off guard by what I had just said, before finally speaking. "Mia, you are such a good person. You have the biggest heart of anyone I know. He's the one who missed out all of those years and I'm sure he realized that just by seeing you today."

He held me in his arms until I calmed down. "Were you busy today?" I asked, finally shifting the subject.

"Yeah, sorry I didn't call you; my cell phone battery died."

"You're here and that's all that matters." I kissed him gently on the lips. "Do you need to charge your phone?" I asked.

He nodded and handed me his phone. I plugged it into the charger on my kitchen counter. As soon as the battery started charging up, the endless amounts of beeps came through with all of his messages from the day. He rolled his eyes, trying his best to ignore it.

"Geez, you're one popular guy," I joked.

"Yeah, and I bet all of them are from Chloe."

My smile quickly turned to a frown. He must have seen the unhappiness on my face. "She wants to book me on the Late Show in L.A. I don't want to do it."

"Oh, would she be going along with you?" I said, trying to hide the jealousy in my voice, but failing miserably.

"Mia, our relationship is strictly business. I love you and only you. You are the only woman for me."

"So, why don't you want to go?" I said, trying to sound a little more upbeat.

He shrugged his shoulders. "Why, do you want to come with me?"

"That would be wonderful, but I don't think my job could spare me." I would love to have gone with him, especially if that little bitch was tagging along, but it was hard for me to get any time off from work unless I scheduled it months in advance. "Travis, did you ever sleep with her?"

"Who?"

"Chloe."

He was silent for a brief second. "No," he whispered as he kissed me on the top of my head.

I lifted my head from his shoulder as his phone began to beep once again. "Did I mention that I really dislike her?"

He smiled. "Yeah, you did."

For the first time ever, Travis spent the night at my place. I knew that subconsciously it was because I wasn't ready to sleep in the same bed that Eric and I had once shared with another man, so this was a huge step for me. He pulled me into his warmth as I snuggled closer to him. My lips grazed his neck and I could still smell the faint smell of his familiar cologne. I kissed him softly on his bare chest as my hand trailed underneath the waistband of his boxers. I looked up at him as my tongue made a downward descent on his stomach.

Drowning in Love

The smile on his face made my heart melt and my mind think,
I can't get enough of Travis Montgomery.

Chapter 34

Mia...

Christmas Day was here and I was so happy to be spending it with Travis and my family. We had spent Christmas Eve with Travis' family. I had a wonderful time and really loved being in their company; but I was so looking forward to being at my sister's for Christmas Day. I snapped a million pictures of Paige opening up her presents. This was my favorite part of Christmas, watching her open up her gifts. My sister walked over to clean up the wrapping paper that Paige was getting swallowed in.

"Maybe in a few years, I'll have a niece or nephew that I can spoil," my sister said with a smile. I raised my eyebrows at her and shot her a look of displeasure for saying such a thing in front of Travis. Travis and I talked about a lot of things, but kids were never part of the conversation. It was just too soon to be thinking about that.

"She's kidding, Travis. Don't pass out," I said.

"Why would I pass out? I want kids someday."

"You do?"

"Yeah, especially if it's with you." My stomach did a triple flip.

"Aw," my sister said upon hearing his statement. "Let me take a picture of you guys." I moved closer to Travis as my sister snapped the picture with her phone and immediately sent it to mine.

I was really feeling down by the end of the night. I had a great time and didn't want to leave. My mom tried her best to try and coax me and Travis to stay over her house, but I had to be at work in the morning, so I knew that wasn't an option.

Travis and I arrived back at his place a little after nine. I was exhausted from all of the excitement of the day. I changed into my pajamas and snuggled up with him on the couch, watching TV. He reached behind his back and handed me an envelope and a box. I was a little taken off guard. We had already exchanged presents earlier that morning. I had gotten Travis a new watch and another bottle of his favorite cologne. He had gotten me a beautiful pair of diamond earrings, which I'm sure he spent more on than I cared to know.

"Travis, what is this? We exchanged presents already."

"Just a couple of things I forgot earlier." I shook my head and smiled. I opened the envelope and my eyes widened to find an itinerary for a week-long trip to Saint Lucia, leaving on Valentine's Day. "Oh my God, Travis, This is awesome! I just hope that I can get-"

He stopped me mid-sentence. "It's already taken care of. I talked to Juan, and you have the week off. It's going to be just you and me in paradise, celebrating Valentine's Day for a whole week."

I wrapped my arms around him and hugged him tightly. "That sounds perfect!"

"And I will get you to swim in the ocean."

"We'll just have to see about that one."

He smiled and rubbed his forehead against mine. "Open the box," he said.

"Travis, why did you -"

"Just open it."

I removed the lid to find a necklace with a beautiful gold heart.

"Read the back," he instructed.

I flipped it over. *To Mia, the girl with the heart of gold and my girl forever.* The tears rolled down my face as I ran my thumb over the inscription.

"Okay, if you don't like it, you don't have to wear it, but don't cry about it," he joked.

"I *love* it, Travis. I just never thought I could be this happy again. Thank you so much for this beautiful necklace and for allowing me to open my heart again. I love you so much." I wrapped my arms around him and nuzzled up against him. I had never felt happier than I did right now. I watched the dancing flames in the fireplace while Travis held me tightly in his arms. After living out a yearlong sentence of hell on earth, I had finally made it back to heaven.

***

The week between Christmas and New Year's was always slow at the salon, which I was somewhat grateful for. It allowed me time to catch up with Juan. I felt like I hadn't talked to him in ages with the bedlam of the holidays. The time that we would see each other at work was limited with the mad rush of people needing to get their hair done for the holidays.

"So, how was your Christmas?" I asked.

Juan's smile was a mile wide. "Guess who got a trip to Paris?"

"Oh my God! When are you going?"

"In the spring."

"Ahhh....Paris in the springtime; that's awesome!"

"I know. Brian is now at the top of my list of favorite people – for now." He laughed.

I shook my head and smiled. "What about you? I know you're going to Saint Lucia, but did you get engaged? If you did, I will kill you for not telling before this!"

"No, I didn't get engaged, silly! It's only been five months, Juan!"

"So what! Mia, any fool could see that he's totally in love with you and I'm thinking feel the same way about him."

I smiled. I was completely in love with Travis. And the truth of the matter was, if he asked me to marry him today, I would say "yes." "I do; he makes me smile all day long."

"Mmmm....I bet he does," Juan said as he shook his head.

I laughed as I smacked him in the arm. I showed him the necklace and flipped it over for him to read the back. He fanned his face as if he were trying to stop the tears. "Girl, you're going to make my mascara run," he joked.

"So, what's going on with that bitchy agent of his?"

"Not much. I still don't like her and he's going to L.A. with her next week," I said as if it were no big deal.

"What! Mia, why are you allowing that?"

I laughed at his reaction. "Juan, if I don't have trust in him then what's the point of being in a relationship? Besides, he asked me to go with him."

"Okay, and why aren't you?"

"Um...because I have a job, remember?"

"Oh, Mia, we could probably rearrange your schedule so you could go for a few days."

"Nah, that's okay. Besides, it will give me time to go on a long overdue dinner date with my 'girlfriend.'"

"Name the time and place, baby cakes!" He smacked me on the butt just before my next client came walking in.

Chapter 35

Travis...

I threw the last of my things in my bag. My flight was leaving at 5 a.m. It was New Year's Eve and I was wishing that we didn't make plans to go over my friends Mike's and Stacy's house now. I wasn't going to be seeing Mia for a few days and I wanted to be alone with her. I couldn't believe how much I needed her. It went so far beyond sex. I needed to see her gorgeous face, hear her contagious laugh, and connect with her beautiful soul. This was all so new to me. I never attached emotions to any of the women that I was with. Mia was like an angel who affected everyone that came in contact with her, and the funny part about it was, she was clueless as to how special she was.

I lifted my head to find Mia standing in the bedroom door. I was in awe over how she could make a simple pair of jeans and a sweater look so damn sexy.

"See what happens when you give out the key to your apartment? Anyone can just walk in." She laughed that same laugh that made me want to rip her clothes off and kiss her all over. She sat down on the bed next to me and put her arm around me. "I'm going to miss you." Her soft lips touched mine as she gently moved her tongue inside my mouth. She tasted like her favorite spearmint gum. She had no clue what she did to me, how just a simple kiss from her turned me into a sex-crazed teenager. I pushed her down on the bed and ran my tongue along her neck. She smelled so good, which was only adding to my fire down below.

"Hey, I think maybe we should just get going. The sooner we get there, the sooner we can get back so I can make sure that I give you a proper goodbye." She gave me a sexy grin that made it so hard to abide by her wishes. I found the strength in knowing that we were going to pick up later, right where we had left off. She drove me crazy, but in the best possible way imaginable.

We were the last ones to arrive at Mike's and Stacy's, and I was hoping that it wouldn't appear too rude when we were the first ones to leave. Mike and I had been best friends since college. There wasn't any time since I had known him that he wasn't with Stacy. She went to the same college as we did and they married a few years after graduation. I spent a lot of my down time with the two of them, so I was grateful that Stacy and Mia hit it off right away. They had a lot in common, including sharing one common enemy – Chloe. Chloe never did anything directly to Stacy for her to form an unfavorable opinion, but Stacy would always say there was something about her that she didn't trust.

"Well, it's about time," Stacy said as she made her way through her crowded living room. She gave me and Mia a kiss on the cheek and took our coats.

"Come in the kitchen, you guys." Stacy waved her hand at Mike, motioning for him to wrap up the conversation that he was having.

We followed her into the kitchen as Mike came striding in behind us. "Hey, guys!" He leaned down and gave Mia a kiss.

Stacy was so excited, she looked like she was ready to bust. "Travis, you are our very best friend and we wanted you to know first. "We're going to have a baby!"

"Wow, that's great! Congratulations, guys!" I gave them both a hug. Mike had told me that they had been trying for a while, so this was so nice to hear.

"Oh, my God, that's wonderful news!" Mia's smile was a mile wide, but I could still see a little want in her eyes. I knew that she would make a great mother. She was so kind and caring. It was almost as if that was what she was born to do. I imagined how adorable she would look pregnant. Most of all, I imagined how wonderful it would be to have her be the mother of *my* child.

I knew it was horrible, but I was counting the minutes until we could get out of there. I was tired of talking about swimming, the Olympics, and my medals. I had one thing and one thing only on my mind: Mia. I was just wrapping up a conversation and was headed over to her to see if she was ready. She was talking to some man. I hadn't a clue as to who he was. Stacy stopped me on my way. "Hey, Travis, thanks for coming tonight. I know you have an early flight-" Stacy stopped mid-sentence when she realized I was no longer paying attention. My insides were raging as I saw the man that Mia was talking to with his hand on her ass, pulling her into him. "Travis don't -" Stacy grabbed my arm to try and stop me, but I broke free from her grip.

I rushed over just as Mia was pushing him off of her. "Oh, come on, baby. I will rock your world," he slurred. He was drunk off his ass.

I was so enraged, all I could see was red. "Get your fuckin' hands off her!" I shouted as the room suddenly got quiet.

I had every intention of kicking his ass from one end of the room to the other until Mike came running over and held me back.

. "Travis, it's okay. He's drunk and he's an asshole. He's not worth it." Mia took my hand, calming me down right away.

"Mia, he fuckin'-"

She kissed me on the lips to stop me from talking. "Save that energy for later," she whispered in my ear.

"Travis, thank God!" Stacy said as she saw the guy still in one piece.

"We're going to get going," I said, now feeling like I had the perfect excuse to slip out of there early.

"Mia, I'm sorry, he's just some obnoxious guy that Mike works with. I didn't even want to invite him, but Mike insisted," Stacy said.

"It's not a big deal," Mia responded. I looked at her and shook my head. "What, Travis? Really, it wasn't; he was drunk. If I recall, I remember a certain night when you had a little too much to drink and were just as obnoxious."

"Mia, that's different. I'm your boyfriend." The thought of another man putting his hands on her drove me completely insane.

I was so happy finally to be walking out the door. I grabbed Mia's hand as we walked down the hallway. I was still so pissed off over that fuckin' dickhead guy and Mia's carefree attitude about it. I pushed her up against the wall, just before we got to the stairs and kissed her. "It is a big deal – to me, Mia. I love you and I don't intend to share you with anyone."

She bit her lip and looked up at me with a half grin. "Good, because I don't intend to share you with anyone either, Travis."

Mia had achieved something that no one else was able to do. She completely owned me. My mind, body, heart, and soul belonged to her and the innocence that she possessed made her completely oblivious to it.

Chapter 36

Mia...

I knew that Travis was still bothered by what had happened at the party. So I did my best to take his mind off it when we slipped into his bed for the night. I immediately began to kiss him, starting with his lips, then his neck, trailing little tiny kisses down his stomach. "We have a problem," I said, looking up at him.

"Oh, yeah, what's that?" He looked down at me with a sexy grin.

I snapped the waistband of his boxers against his stomach. "These – they need to come off." I removed them with ease and wrapped my lips around my most favorite part of his body. I took him in and out of my mouth as I teased him with my tongue. He ran his hands through my hair. I could tell that I was driving him crazy and I loved every minute of it.

"Mia, stop. I'm gonna -"

I removed my mouth from him and looked up. "That is the plan, silly."

"Not that way."

"Oh, then how?"

"Inside of you." He pulled me up and quickly hovered over me. "I want to fuck you so bad. I've wanted to fuck you all night – I want to fuck you every second of the day." He was inside of me within a matter of seconds and let out a groan of pleasure. "Baby, I wish you knew how good you feel." He began to move around as I raised my hips to meet him. "Mia, I don't know how long I could last tonight. This feels so damn good." I pulled him closer, enjoying every bit of him. He had no idea what he did to me. Sex with him was unlike anything I had ever known. I felt like I could never get enough of him. Travis made sure that I was satisfied, which didn't take me long, before he finally freed himself into doing what he was trying to hold back.

"Oh my God, Mia," Travis shouted as he buried his face into my hair. I ran my fingers up and down his back while he caught his breath.

He turned on his side and pulled me to him. "I think you're trying to kill me," he joked.

"This is coming from a guy who swims ten miles at once. You shouldn't even be breaking a sweat." I giggled.

"You have more of an effect on me than swimming does."

"Well, I couldn't let you go to L.A. with that little witch without a proper send off."

"Mia, will you stop worrying about her?" he said as he kissed the top of my head.

"Why would I need to worry about her? She has a bad dye job, cheap hair extensions, and fake boobs. Which, I might add, are totally out of proportion with her body."

Travis began to laugh. "Well, not everyone can be as naturally gorgeous as you."

"I know. What can I say?" I laughed.

"One day, Mia."

"One day, what?"

"I'm going to get to see the beautiful babies that we make together."

My stomach fluttered. *A baby with Travis, what a wonderful thought.* I hugged him tightly, wondering how I was going to get through the next five days without him.

Drowning in Love

***

Two more days until Travis came home and my apartment had never been cleaner. In my effort to keep myself busy, I found that coming home and scrubbing my apartment for the past three nights really helped a lot. I had just gotten home from dinner with Juan. Since there was nothing left to clean, I decided to play around on my laptop instead. The late show that Travis was taping was being aired tonight. I was trying desperately to keep my mind occupied so I could stay awake to watch it. I logged on to my email, fifty-seven new messages. I really needed to keep up on checking this more often. I scrolled down through all of them, which were mostly advertisements and junk mail. I immediately clicked on the name Linda Taylor, sent on December 28th.

Dear Mia,

I wanted to let you know that your father passed away peacefully yesterday. He wanted me to make sure that you received the photo that I have attached. You have no idea how much it meant to him to see you one last time. He died a happy man because of you. I know that what he did to you was so very wrong. I met and married your dad a few years ago and I know the guilt of what he did to you and your sister weighed heavily on his mind. He did love you girls, Mia, the best way he knew how. Thank you again for being such a caring, kind, and forgiving person. I wish you nothing but happiness in life and hopefully now you can have a little closure.

Take care ~

Linda

I took a deep breath, trying to hold in the sobs. I clicked on the attachment and the tears rolled down my face. It was a picture of my Dad and me. I must have been about two years old. He was holding me. I had my arms wrapped around his neck with my nose pressing up against his. He didn't even look like the same man I had met in the coffee shop a few weeks ago. He was so young and full of life in this photo.

I felt low, really low, mourning the loss of a man that I never really knew, but my heart was breaking just the same. I dialed my mother's number and gave her the news. She comforted me the best that she could. I didn't want to tell my sister; I was leaving that up to my mother to do. I felt a little bit better by the end of our conversation and with the beep of my phone I was suddenly feeling a lot better, seeing Travis' name coming through on the call waiting. I quickly said my goodbyes to my mother and switched over to Travis.

"Hey, you." I tried sounding as upbeat as possible.

"Hey, baby, what's going on?"

"Not much." I didn't want to tell him right now. I knew that he was going to be taping the show in a little while and I didn't want him being bogged down with my problems.

"Mia, what's wrong?" It amazed me how he could be so in tune to exactly how I was feeling.

"I just found out that my dad passed away about a week ago."

"Oh, Mia, I'm sorry, baby."

"Thanks. So when is my big celebrity boyfriend going into his interview?" I said, shifting to a happier subject.

"In an hour."

"Well, I'm drinking coffee right now to stay up to see you."

He laughed. "I miss you."

I was on emotional overload as his words brought tears to my eyes. "I miss you too -very much. Make sure your hair looks good before you go on; your hairstylist has a reputation to uphold," I joked, trying to lighten my mood.

"I will." He laughed.

"Travis, are you ready?" I rolled my eyes at the sound of Chloe's voice in the background.

"Really? Tell her to go away," I said.

He laughed again. "I love you, Mia."

"I love you too and good luck."

I hung up the phone, feeling a little better just from hearing his voice. I took another sip of coffee, knowing that I would be feeling even better, seeing him on my TV in just about an hour.

Chapter 37

Travis...

The studio was fifteen minutes away from the hotel. I sat in the back of the limo, not paying any mind to Chloe's constant rambling. I wished that I could have been there for Mia tonight. Even though she was trying to disguise it, I knew she was hurting. I thought about all the sadness she had been handed in her life and how she didn't let it break her spirit. She had so much love in her heart and she gave it away so easily to others. I just hoped that love was enough for her to be able to forgive me. I knew I had to tell her once I got back, I had no choice. I knew now more than ever that I wanted to marry her and I didn't want to go into it with any secrets between us.

"Travis?" Chloe waved her hand in front of my face.

"Huh?"

"Did you not hear a word I just said?" she asked.

"Sorry, I'm just out of it."

"Well, I could see that. Just remember you have to nail this interview if you want to pick up endorsements from those other two companies."

"Yeah, whatever." I looked out the window again, thinking about what these endorsements just might cost me.

"Travis, I'm serious. If you blow this, I will kill you."

In that split second, I realized why everyone had such an unfavorable opinion of Chloe; all she cared about was money and power. "Chloe, just shut up."

"What the hell is your problem? What, did little Miss Perfect say something to upset you on the phone?"

"My relationship with Mia is none of your fuckin' business."

"Oh really, I think your relationship with her has everything to do with me and don't you forget it." Her eyes widened. "Are you ready?" she asked with a fake smile that made my skin crawl as the limo pulled up to the studio.

Chapter 38

Mia...

I curled up on my couch with my nice warm blanket, waiting anxiously for Travis to appear on my TV screen. I found myself screaming in anticipation at the commercials. My stomach dropped when the host introduced him. I bit my lip as I watched him walk out onto the stage. He was dressed very casually and looked absolutely gorgeous. I didn't even mind the screams from all the women in the audience. I would be screaming right along with them if I were there. The host went to ask him a question and had to wait until the shrieks were over. "Okay, Travis, I was going to wait to ask you this, but since these women want to rip your clothes off-" he paused again for more screams. "Do you have someone special in your life right now?"

Travis smiled his deep dimple smile. "Yes, very special." The screams from earlier turned to groans.

"Well, you just silenced every single female in this audience."

Travis' smile was contagious; I couldn't wipe mine from my face. "We'll get to the Olympics, swimming, and your medals in a minute. But first we want to hear about the important stuff, like this special girl in your life, right, ladies?" They began to scream again. "So, who is this lucky lady?"

"Uh, you know what, I don't think she would want me mentioning her name on national TV."

"Ah, come on, she's dating Travis Montgomery. I'm sure she doesn't mind if the world knows about it. I will say that your hair is looking really good; do you have a new hairstylist?" he teased, clearly knowing exactly who Travis' "mystery girlfriend" was.

Travis laughed and rubbed the side of his face, like he was a little nervous. "Yes, I have the best hair stylist around."

"All right. One last question and then we'll move onto the stuff we're supposed to be talking about. On a scale from one to ten, how crazy are you for this girl?"

Travis' familiar smile that he had on his face from the time he appeared on my screen suddenly turned serious. "Twenty."

"Aw...." was the only sound that was coming from the audience.

"Really, twenty?" the host said as if he were surprised.

"Yeah, she's really special and she means the world to me."

Another round of "Aws" came from the audience as tears rolled down my face.

The subject finally shifted to swimming. I sat and watched this gorgeous, loving man on my TV screen. *I meant the world to him.* He could have any woman in that audience or probably anywhere, for that matter, and he chose me. I jumped at the ringing of my phone. I looked down to see it was my sister.

"Tressa, what are you still doing up?"

"Um, I have an infant that doesn't sleep, remember?"

I laughed. "Oh yeah, I forgot."

"Oh my God, Mia, I am in tears watching this interview. He is so in love with you. I think I need to start picking out my bridesmaid dress."

"Oh, my God, between you and Juan. You both have me walking down the aisle." I was silent for a moment. I took a deep breath and asked the question that I was going to avoid with her. "Did you hear about Dad?"

"Yeah, I did. Oh, Mia, you have got yourself one good-looking guy who's crazy in love with you, girl!" *Okay, this was her way of saying she didn't want to discuss my dad. So I wasn't going to force her.*

"Yeah, he's pretty cute." I laughed.

We talked for a little while longer before my niece started getting restless for her bottle and we had to hang up. I realized that I was so busy talking to my sister that I missed the end of Travis' interview. I had DVR'd it so I knew I could watch it over again tomorrow, then again and again....

I was so sleepy, I texted Travis before heading into to bed: *I'm going to bed with a smile. I didn't think I could love you anymore than I already did. Get home soon, I want to show you how just how much I do! xoxoxo*

Chapter 39

Travis...

I arrived back to my hotel room. I sat down on the bed and finally checked the twenty plus text messages that had come through on my phone. I ignored them all, only opening the one from Mia. I smiled upon reading it. God, I wish I could be holding her right now. I didn't want to text her back because I knew she was probably sleeping. It was late here and even later in New York. I would call her in the morning, I would much rather hear her voice anyway. I was so tired. I was still on New York time and had some meetings that I had to be up early for. I was just about to climb in bed, when I heard a knock on my door...

Chapter 40

Mia...

I was spending my day off curled up on my couch. It was a freezing cold Monday afternoon and the best place to be was under a blanket and in front of my TV. I was flicking through the channels trying to find something to watch. I was a little surprised when I heard a knock on my door. I wasn't expecting anyone and even if I were, I would have to buzz them in. I figured it was probably my next door neighbor Luis. A smile stretched across my face when I opened the door not to find Luis, but Travis, instead.

"Hey, you, what are doing here? You weren't supposed to be home until tomorrow."

"I got done early." I shut the door as he entered.

I kissed him softly on the lips. "Did you forget that you have a key?"

"No, I wanted to surprise you."

"Well, you did, and it was the best surprise ever!"

He wrapped his arms around me and pulled me into his embrace. His kiss took my breath away. "I missed you so much, Mia." He moved his hands up and down my body. He wasted no time lifting my shirt over my head and removing my jeans. He undid my bra and ran his tongue along my breast. He threw his jacket on the floor and removed his own pants with a sense of urgency. My insides were longing for him.

He picked me up and wrapped my legs around him. He pushed me up against the wall and I felt the fullness of him inside of me. His thrusts seemed urgent, not the tender gentle lovemaking that I was used to with him. "Oh my God, Mia, you feel so fuckin' good, baby." He continued to pound himself into me as I ran my hands through his hair.

"Tell me how this feels for you. Tell me that you like this." I nodded. "Say it, Mia. Tell me I'm the only guy that you will ever let fuck you like this."

I opened my eyes and looked into his. "You are the only man that I will ever need, Travis."

We slid down to the floor. He pinned my arms above my head while he hovered over top of me and continued to move about inside of me. He kissed me deeply. "Mia, I want all of you, baby, and I will give you all of me."

I raised my hips to meet him. "Oh my God, Travis." The intensity of my orgasm was so extreme. He bit his lip and smiled. He continued for a little longer before letting out a loud groan as I felt the warmth of his release inside of me. He rolled over and pulled me close. "Mia, you have no clue what you do to me. I don't ever want to lose you. These past few days have been hell without you."

I leaned my chin on his chest. "Travis, I'm not going anywhere. You're not going to lose me."

He kissed the top of my head. "I love you so much, Mia. I've never felt this way about anyone."

"I love you too, Travis." I hugged him tightly, never wanting to let him go.

We went out to dinner and then back to his place. We made love once again, but this time it was soft and gentle. He played with my hair as I nuzzled closer to him. "There's my old Travis."

He laughed. "I'm sorry, Mia, about earlier. I just missed you so much."

"Don't be sorry. Believe me, my body isn't sorry. It really liked you that way." I giggled.

He shook his head and laughed. He pulled me on top of him. I rested my chin on his chest, staring up at him. "Move in with me, Mia."

"What?" I was a little taken off guard with that statement.

"I want to wake up every day with you in my arms. I want your beautiful face to be the first thing that I see in the morning."

"Travis, I need to think about this." As much as I would have loved to wake up with him every morning as well, the little voice in the back of my mind was stopping me from saying "yes."

"Okay," he answered, looking like he wasn't very happy with my response, making me feel as if I had to justify it.

"Travis, you know that apartments in the city aren't easy to come by, especially in my price range. I'm just not sure that I want to give mine up. I mean, what if things don't work out with-"

He shook his head to stop me before the words could escape my lips. "No, Mia, don't say that. We're going to be together forever, I promise. You work like a dog to afford that tiny little apartment. Come and live here; you won't have to work so hard. Hell, you don't even have to work at all, if you don't want to. Let me take care of you."

I kissed him gently on the lips. "Travis, that is so kind of you and believe me there is nothing in the world that I want more than to wake up with you every morning. But I can't take advantage of your generosity. I actually like working. I'm not saying that I won't consider moving in with you. I'm just asking for time to think about it."

He smiled and kissed me on the forehead. "Okay, take all the time that you need." He wrapped his arms around me tightly. I closed my eyes, feeling so at ease. *Yeah, I could definitely get used to this every night.*

Chapter 41

Travis...

I held her in my arms while she slept. I should have told her tonight. I should have told her on the first day that I had asked her out. I was prolonging the inevitable, but I just couldn't. I missed her so much that my insides had ached for her. I didn't want to ruin this perfect night. I would tell her tomorrow, definitely. I had no choice. Chloe was due back from L.A. soon and I didn't know what she was capable of. The last thing I wanted was for Mia to hear it from her.

I kissed her on the head and watched her sleep. "I love you so much, Mia," I whispered in her ear. I hugged her tightly. I couldn't lose her – I just couldn't.

***

Last night was a turning point for me and Mia. I had to let her know that I meant it when I said we would be together forever and I was going to prove that to her tonight. I carefully scrutinized over every diamond that was shown to me. I wanted to make sure that Mia had nothing but the best, because that's exactly what she deserved.

After about two hours, I finally decided on the three-carat emerald-cut diamond in a platinum setting. "That is an excellent choice, Mr. Montgomery," the lady that had been helping me said. "She's a very lucky lady."

"No, I'm the one that's lucky," I said. The older woman smiled at me as I finished writing out my check. I headed out the door, feeling completely at ease with my choice. I couldn't wait to see the look on her face when she saw this ring. I never wanted anything more. The only question that remained was, do I tell her before or after I ask her to marry me?

Chapter 42

Mia...

I had a little extra time before my first appointment, so I called my sister to get her opinion on Travis' request.

"Well, Mia, I don't know. I mean, you both love one another and he has a point; you're running yourself ragged with work just to afford that little shoebox that you live in."

"Tressa, I don't want to do this because it will be easier on me financially. I want to do this because I know that in my heart that it's truly the right thing."

"Well, Mee Mee, you're the only one that can make that decision."

"I know you're right."

"Can I just tell you how happy I am that you have found someone that you love so much and that loves you back?"

"Thanks." I couldn't contain my smile. I did love Travis very much. I never thought that I would be able to have those feelings for another man after Eric. But Travis helped me to overcome that doubt and I was so happy that he did.

I went through the workday with a little extra spring in my step. I was cooking dinner for Travis at my place tonight and I was counting the minutes until I could see him again. I sent him a text, reminding him about our date. I stopped off at the store on the way home to pick up a few things for our dinner. I was surprised to see Chloe standing in front of my apartment building as I got out of the cab.

"Hey, Chloe, did you need something?" I asked, trying to be cordial, but failing miserably.

"I need to talk to you, Mia." She was very matter of fact.

"Okay, come up." I said half-heartedly as I struggled with my key and the grocery bag that I was holding. We walked up the stairs and into my apartment. I placed the bag of groceries on the counter and removed my coat.

"What's up?" I asked.

"Mia, did Travis tell you that I'm no longer his agent?"

I shook my head. "No, he didn't." I wasn't surprised; Travis usually didn't discuss business with me.

"Well, I'm not. He fired me."

I was starting to feel very uncomfortable. "Oh, I didn't –"

"Look, Mia, I came here to warn you."

"Warn me about what?"

"Travis. Did he tell you that he only started up this whole relationship thing with you to keep his endorsement with EFE?"

I shook my head in disbelief. "Wha –what are you talking about?"

"He was in danger of losing that endorsement because of his bad boy, womanizer reputation. They wanted a *nice guy* to represent their company, a good role model for the teenage boys who buy their products. So Travis and I devised this whole plan. He would start dating a wholesome, all American girl to give EFE what they wanted while the whole time he was fucking me."

My eyes were burning with tears. I shook my head, hoping that I wasn't hearing her correctly. "Mia, he laughed at you for being such a fool and actually buying into his friendship thing and now all of sudden, he's telling everyone how in love he is with you. Don't trust him, Mia."

I looked down at the ground. I didn't want her to see the tears forming in my eyes. "I'm sorry, Mia, for having to tell you this, but obviously we've both been burned by him."

I waited for her to exit before I let the tears flow. I sat down on the couch, put my face in my hands, and began to cry. *How could I have been so stupid to believe that I was actually special?* This was all some sick game to him. I couldn't believe that this was happening. I was numb. I ignored the endless ringing of my cell phone, not even bothering to pick it up to see who it was. All of those times I had seen him and Chloe, having their private little conversations - they were discussing me. I thought back to the night when I had asked him if he had ever slept with Chloe, and how he was hesitant to answer. I should have known then. How could I have believed that he actually fell in love with someone like me? I wasn't special; I was just some stupid girl who believed his sick lies.

My face was buried in my hands when he walked through the door. I couldn't even bring myself to look at him. He sat down next to me on the couch. "Hey, what's wrong?" He went to hug me and I pushed him away.

"Don't touch me. Never touch me again!"

"Mia, what's the matter?" A look of alarm washed over his face.

"This was all some sick game to you? You made me believe that you actually cared about me, like I was special, all so you wouldn't lose some stupid endorsement?"

His eyes began to fill with emotion. "Mia, listen to me." He moved closer to me as I backed away. "I'm not going to lie to you; that's how it first started out, but I swear to God after getting to know you, that all changed."

"You laughed at me with her, Travis? Tell me, was it before or after you fucked her?"

"What? Mia, I haven't slept with her since I met you. I swear to God. I don't know what she told you, but I'm telling you the truth."

I shook my head at him. "Just like you told me the truth when I asked if you ever slept with her at all? I don't believe anything that comes out of your mouth anymore, Travis." He grabbed my arm tightly. "Let go of me, Travis!"

He ignored my request and just moved in closer. "Mia, don't you see what she's trying to do? She's angry because she's jealous of what we have. This is what she wants, Mia, to break us up because she knows I will never feel the same way about her as I do for you."

"Just go, Travis."

"Mia, don't do this."

"I didn't do it; you did. You and that little whore that got so much entertainment out of using me as a pawn to get you what you wanted!"

"Mia, you are the only woman for me. Why can't you see how in love I am with you? Nothing matters anymore. I don't care about any of these stupid endorsements or winning anymore gold medals. All I care about is us."

"You are a liar and a sneak and I will never forgive you for what you've done. I will never believe a word that you say ever again and I can't be with someone like that. I gave my heart and soul to you, Travis, and you took advantage of that, something that I would have never done to you."

"Mia, don't do this to us. You know what we have is special. Don't just walk away from it." I wanted to cry. I wanted to do more than just cry I wanted to break down in his arms and tell him that I forgave him and that I loved him more than anything, but I couldn't. I had lost all trust and respect for him. I looked up at him as he looked into my tear-filled eyes.

I bit my lip and shook my head as the tears flowed down my face. "No, that's where I went wrong. I actually *thought* that it was special, but it wasn't. I was just some stupid, naïve girl who walked right into your trap. Well, now I'm walking out of it. Just answer this question for me please; why did you have to pick me, Travis? After everything I had been through, why did you have to pick me to fall in love with you and have my heart ripped to shreds again?"

He looked away briefly and ran his hand through his hair. "Mia, I'm so sorry, baby."

"Don't call me that."

He looked at me sadly. "Please, will you just give me a chance to explain to you?"

"No, just go, Travis. It's over." My stomach clenched hearing those words come from my mouth.

"Damn you, Mia, you never fuckin' believed in us and now you're willing to throw it all away."

"Don't you dare try to turn this around and make it my fault. I'm not the one who lied, Travis. I'm not the one who used you to get what I wanted. All I did was love with all my heart."

"Mia, I'm begging you."

I looked up at him one last time. "Goodbye, Travis."

He was speechless. He stood up and gazed at me as if I was going to change my mind. I buried my face in my hands again, unable to look at him any longer. I waited until I heard the door slam and I began to sob like a baby.

Chapter 43

Travis...

It felt like I had been kicked in the stomach. The pain in her eyes tore me apart. How could she question my love for her? I sat down on the couch. Everything reminded me of her. I picked up the picture of us that was taken at her sister's house on Christmas. "Mia, baby, I love you. I always loved you." How I wished she could hear me. I needed her to understand that I was lost without her. But it was too late; the look in her eyes told me it was final. I had broken her heart yet again. She didn't deserve it; she had lost so much and was finally able to love again and I had to go and do this to her.

I wondered if it would have made a difference if I had told her instead of that fuckin' bitch Chloe who only embellished it, making it that much worse. I should have been honest with her the night that she had asked me if I had ever slept with Chloe. I should have been honest with her about a lot of things. Chloe was toxic; she didn't care who she hurt to get what she wanted. I could handle her hurting me and spreading my name through the dirt, but I couldn't handle what she had done to Mia. I never gave my one-night stand with Chloe much thought. It had happened months before I had even met Mia; we were both drunk and I really didn't have much memory of it. I thought that she felt the same until the other night in L.A.

I was just getting ready for bed when I heard a knock on my hotel room door. I opened it up to find Chloe with a bottle of champagne. "Well, congratulations, the whole world bought your story and I have two other companies who want you to do advertisements for them! Little Miss Perfect is your golden ticket. But don't worry; we can do a very public break up in a few months. We'll make it look like it's her fault."

She wrapped her arms around my neck and began to kiss me. I pushed her away. "Chloe, what the fuck are you doing?"

"Oh, come on, Travis, we need to celebrate!"

"Chloe, I am totally in love with Mia."

"Oh, Travis please. You may have gotten everyone else to believe that story. But I know better."

"Chloe, I meant what I said tonight. She's my entire world."

"Oh, give me a break, Travis; she's not your type. What, are you going to marry her, have two point five kids, and live happily ever after? You know you will never be satisfied with that life."

"No, Chloe, I will be happy with that life. I love her more than anything and I would give up everything to be with her."

She shook her head and laughed. "Oh, Travis, you stupid man, throwing everything away for sweet, little, innocent Mia. I can't sit around as your agent and watch you give up everything for a girl who's only going to bring you down."

"That's fine, because as of right now, you are no longer my agent."

"What! You just kissed any more endorsements goodbye, Travis, I will make sure of it."

"You do what you got to do, Chloe."

She stared at me briefly before storming out and slamming the door behind her.

I had to come clean with Mia. I had to tell her before she heard it from Chloe. I quickly logged onto my laptop, changing my flight to the soonest one I could get back to New York.

I wished that I could have gone back to twenty-four hours ago and told Mia the minute I had stepped into her apartment. I knew that she would have still been pissed, but at least I could have tried to soften the blow somewhat. Now, it looked like I had something to hide. She actually thought that I had been sleeping with Chloe the entire time I had been with her. I took the little black box out of my coat pocket and opened up the lid. I stared down at the ring that I had planned on giving Mia tonight. It was supposed to be the start of our life together. Now, the only thing I saw when I looked at it was an ending. I was so out of my element with this. I had never agonized over a woman before, because I had never gotten emotionally attached to any of them. I didn't know what to do. So I did the only thing I could think of. I poured myself a shot of Jack, hoping that it would take away this self-inflicted pain.

Chapter 44

Mia...

At what point do we run out of tears? I had cried so much in the past week that I had probably shed ten pounds in water weight. When Eric died, I was devastated, but at least his departure from my life was final. It was so different with Travis; he was still here. I was trying my best to ignore his text messages and his voicemails, which only made me cry even harder at the sound of his voice. I was sick to my stomach over what he had done to me. He played a good game of really making me feel special. I felt like such a fool for actually falling for it. My life would never be the same and I would never trust another man again. Travis had ruined me.

I stepped off the train; my sister and my niece Paige were waiting for me. I smiled for the first time in a week when I saw them. I gave my niece a hug and broke out in tears again; I was still an emotional wreck. My sister looked at me sympathetically, no doubt seeing how swollen my eyes were from all of the crying I had been doing. "Oh, Mee Mee, it's going to be okay, I promise." She wrapped her arm around me tightly as we walked to her car.

We spent the afternoon getting manicures and pedicures. My pain temporarily lifted as I watched my niece's excitement over getting her nails done. "Look at my nails, Aunt Mee Mee," she said as she proudly waved her fingers in front of my face.

"They are beautiful, just like you, Paige."

Drowning in Love

We were heading to my mom's. My sister was meeting her husband there and my mom was making dinner for everyone. We walked in the front door and the delicious aroma of my mom's famous pot roast hit me in the face. I knew she had made it special for me. It was my favorite.

"Mia, sweetie!" She ran to the front door and hugged me tightly. She placed her hands on my face and rubbed her thumbs under my swollen eyes.

My stepfather came out of the kitchen and hugged me tightly as well. "Mia, forget about him," he said, trying to act as if it wasn't a big deal.

"Mia, I have some guy at work that really wants to meet you," my brother-in-law said. My sister was nodding with a huge smile on her face.

"Oh, thanks, Shane, but I'm not ready to meet anyone right now." I was never going to be ready to meet anyone. I was swearing off men. They were of no use to me. They either walked out on me, died on me, or lied to me. I decided that I was going to die a lonely old woman with twenty cats. My sister ran upstairs to my mom's room to get the baby, who had just woken up, while my mother sat down on the couch next to me and admired Paige's fingernails. My sister came back into the living room and placed the baby in my arms. I looked down at her and caressed the velvety skin on her cheek.

"One day, Mia."

"One day, what?"

"I'm going to get to see the beautiful babies that we make together."

I quickly handed the baby off to my mother, trying my best to hold back the tears. I got up from the couch and ran up the stairs into the spare bedroom. I sat on the bed, buried my face in my hands, and let it all come out.

My mother came in and sat down on the bed next to me. She wrapped her arm around me and kissed me on the head. "Shh...." She tried her best to stop my crying.

"He told me he wanted to have a baby with me one day, Mom. He told me he loved me and I believed it. How could he have done this to me?"

"I don't know, Mia. I don't know." She squeezed me tightly and rocked me back and forth until my tears subsided.

"Mia, you will get over this, sweetie. You are strong; you've proven that with Eric."

"I don't know, Mom. It hurts so badly and I still love him so much." I broke down again.

My mother grabbed a tissue from the nightstand and wiped my eyes. "Mia, have you talked to him since that day?"

I shook my head.

"Well, maybe you should hear him out and see what he has to say." I went to interrupt her, but she put her hand up at me. "Wait, just let me finish. Mia, there is no doubt in my mind that he truly does love you. I don't believe for one second that he was lying about that. Yes, he was wrong for what he did, but keep in mind when he agreed to that he didn't know you and once he did, things changed."

"Mom, I asked him if he ever slept with her and he said 'no.' He lied right to my face. Then when I think of all the times she would call him or how they would have their little secret conversations when we would go out, it makes my skin crawl. They were talking about me and how stupid I was for falling into their sick, twisted game; he used me to get what he wanted."

"Mia, why don't you just move back? Get a job here; you can live here until you get yourself together or forever if you want. There's nothing left for you there, except bad memories."

"I still have Juan."

She smiled. "Yes, thank goodness for Juan. He is the only reason that I'm half okay with you staying there."

She hugged me and wiped my eyes again. "Are you feeling a little better?"

I nodded.

"Good, now let's go eat. I put Gary in charge of watching the pot roast while I came up here."

"Oh no, that's not good!" I smiled. My mother shook her head in agreement as we both began to laugh. Yes, I actually made a sound that was very close to a laugh for the first time in a week. It was at teeny tiny step, but at least it was something.

Chapter 45

Mia...

Two week's post Valentine's Day and I had survived it without Travis. He had finally given up with his phone calls and texting as well. Juan once again was my support system, allowing me to tag along with him and Brian on their Valentine's Day date so I wouldn't be alone. I did my best to avoid the internet, television, and gossip magazines, after I *accidently* googled Travis' name on the computer. The headline read: *After Painful Breakup, America's Most Loved Olympian is Back to His Bad Boy Ways.* Underneath was a picture of Travis looking totally wasted with some beautiful woman hanging all over him. I went into the bathroom and threw up after that, vowing to stay as far away as possible from any news from the outside world again.

I was just leaving the opera and heading to dinner with Victor, my co-worker from the salon. He too had just gotten over a bad break up with his boyfriend, leaving him with an extra ticket. This was my life; the only good men I seemed to attract were gay.

"That was really great. Thanks so much for inviting me, Victor," I said in the cab ride over.

"Thanks for coming. It's nice to have someone to commiserate with. Men are dogs!" He laughed.

"Yes, they are. Present company excluded."

He looked around the cab. "I don't see a man anywhere. Oh yeah, the driver." We both began to laugh. Victor was one of those he's-too-good-looking-to-be-straight kind of guys. He was truly gorgeous and probably could have been a model if he had pursued it. Instead, he was chasing his dreams of becoming an actor. I loved hearing his stories about the acting class that he was in enrolled in and some of the famous people he had met because of it. I was so happy that I was beginning to come into the land of the living once again. I still thought about Travis a lot and would have an occasional cry over him, but surprisingly, I was managing. My mother was right; I was strong. Just as long as I didn't hear anything about him or see him – I was strong.

We walked into the restaurant and were seated right away. We both began to laugh when we each caught one another checking out the waiter at the same time. "Girl, he's on my team," Victor joked.

"Yeah, I think you're right." We both began to laugh even louder.

I waited until we placed our drink order before I excused myself to use the ladies' room. I headed to the bathroom, very happy that I had let Victor talk me into coming out with him tonight. I was having a great time. I loved hanging out with my gay friends. If only the straight guys could be like them, then I wouldn't be dealing with any heartache right now.

Chapter 46

Travis...

I was spiraling out of control and I knew it, but I didn't care. Nothing seemed to matter now that Mia was gone. I tried to drink away the pain, but nothing worked. Nothing was taking away the hurt of losing her. Stacy talked me into going out to dinner with her and Mike and her co-worker, Lindsay. I tried my best to pretend that I wanted to be there, even though my mind was a million miles away.

I kept up the conversation as best as I could. But *she* was the only thing I could see when she entered the restaurant. She was wearing the same little black dress that she did the night of my Christmas party, the one that drove me crazy. Her blonde curls were streaming down her face. She looked hot. I totally tuned everything and everyone out as I watched her take a seat in the far off corner. My stomach clenched when I saw that she was with a man. It felt like someone was sticking a knife in my heart every time I would see her laugh at something he would say. I watched as she got up to use the bathroom. Mike finally caught a glimpse of her out of the corner of his eye. I got up from the table and excused myself.

"Travis –" Mike shook his head in disapproval, seemingly knowing exactly what I was planning on doing. I completely ignored him.

I grabbed her arm just as she was about to open the door to the ladies' room.

She gasped as she looked down at her arm and then up at me. I missed those beautiful eyes so much. "Travis, what the hell are you doing?"

I was silent. I didn't know what to say to her. I just looked her over, taking everything about her in and breathing the scent of her favorite perfume. She pulled her arm from my grip and shook her head. She had her hand on the bathroom door, readying to enter again.

"Mia, please, will you just talk to me? I miss you so much, baby."

"Travis, please just stop."

"No, Mia, I can't. I love you so much."

"Really? Because according to all of the gossip rags, you've gotten over me pretty quickly." She looked over to Mike and Stacey and fixated her eyes on Lindsay. "You don't need me, Travis. You have plenty of women willing to keep you warm at night. Don't know if they'll be able to get you endorsements, but then again, that was my job."

"Mia, just stop. I know I should have told –"

"No, Travis, you stop! I don't want to hear anything you have to say. You could have told me the truth at any time, but instead you chose to let me find out from that little bitch."

I could see her eyes filling up with tears and it was tearing me up inside. She was right. I fucked it up; it was all me. I could blame Chloe all that I wanted, but I was the one who chose to hide the truth from her.

I looked over at the table to where her date was sitting, waiting for her. "Who is he?"

"None of your business." I didn't know what was pissing me off more; the sarcastic tone in her voice or the possibility that she may be having sex with someone else besides me. In my mind, she was still mine and the thought of her with another man tore away at my insides.

Beth Rinyu

"Mia, listen to me. You will never mean as much to any other guy as you do to me."

"Well, maybe I don't want to want to mean anything to anybody anymore. Maybe I'll just take a page out of your book, Travis. Fuck him and forget about him. How's that sound?"

I could feel the knife being twisted into my heart even deeper. "No, Mia, that's not who you are."

"Well, maybe I'm a different person because of you. Now, if you'll excuse me, my date is waiting for me." I took a deep breath and watched her walk away. I watched as she said something to her date, before he stood up and they both exited the restaurant.

I walked back over to Mike and Stacy and threw some money on the table. "I'm sorry, but I have to get going." I looked down at Lindsay. "It was, um… really nice meeting you."

I heard Mike's chair sliding across the floor as he got up and came chasing after me. "Bro, she's not coming back. It's over. You need to just face it."

"Yeah, well, maybe I don't want to just face it."

"Travis, what the fuck is wrong with you? You're losing it, man."

I ignored him and walked out into the cold February night. Maybe I was losing it, I didn't know. I had never been in love before and now I knew why.

Chapter 47

Travis...

I shouldn't have been so quick to take Mike and Stacy up on their request to spend a few days in Vermont for my birthday. I knew they were doing it to try and break me from the masochistic state I was in. I figured that maybe a few days away would take my mind off of my fucked up life. But as soon as I stepped foot in that house, I was flooded with memories. Memories of the one person I was trying to forget. The last time I was here, it was with her. There was nothing more that I wished for than to have her here with me now. Stacy went upstairs to take a nap while Mike and I hung out, watching the basketball game. I was on my fourth shot of Jack. I had found that was the only thing that dulled the memories a bit. "Bro, slow down with that; it's only one o'clock," Mike said.

"What are you, holier than thou, now that you're going to be a dad," I said as I lifted the shot glass to my lips and chugged it down.

"No, I'm not. I'm just tired of watching my best friend self-destruct right in front of my eyes."

"Yeah, well, what can I say? This is the only thing that helps me forget about her."

"Jesus Christ, Travis, I never thought I would ever see the day that you would ever let a woman get you this way."

I shook my head, I never thought I would see the day that I would let a woman get me this way either. It had been two weeks since I had seen her in the restaurant with that guy and it was still eating me up inside. The thought of another man touching her made my stomach churn in pure disgust. "You know, I had sex with her for the very first time in this house. I was only the second guy that she ever slept with. She trusted me and I let her down. I was planning on asking her to marry me that night, but instead we broke up."

Mike looked at me in shock. I didn't tell anyone about my engagement plans, not even him. "Travis, when you get back, you need to go see her and talk to her. Tell her how you feel, man."

"I tried. She won't listen to me."

"Make her! Dude, I can't watch you go on like this anymore."

I got up and looked out the window; the snow was starting to fall. I needed to take my mind off Mia. I needed an adrenaline rush.

I turned around to Mike. "Want to go snowboarding."

"It's your birthday, bro. If that's what you want to do, and if it will take you out of your self-pity mode, let's do it!"

Chapter 48

Mia...

I sat on my couch, downing my second glass of wine. Today was Travis' birthday and I couldn't get him off my mind. I pulled him up in my contacts list several times throughout the day, but couldn't bring myself to hit the call button. I kept thinking back to the night that I had run into him in the restaurant and the sadness in his eyes. I missed him so much. My life was empty without him. My head and my heart were in a constant battle since the day I told him goodbye. But tonight, sitting here all alone while wallowing my sorrows into my glass of chardonnay, my heart was crossing the finish line first. I grabbed my phone from my purse and scrolled down to his name. I took a deep breath and finally got up the nerve to hit the call button. After five rings, it went to his voicemail as I tried to quiet the inner-voice inside of me that was saying. *Maybe he's ignoring you on purpose* or *maybe he's out celebrating his birthday with some else*. I composed myself and waited for the beep. "Hey, Travis, it's Mia. I was just calling to wish you a happy birthday and to let you know - I miss you. Anyway, I, umm hope you had a great day." I hung up the phone, instantly regretting my actions. *Sucker, sucker, sucker*! It was written all over my forehead, but I couldn't help it where he was concerned. I missed him like crazy and was still so in love with him. I couldn't deny it anymore.

I arrived at work the next morning to find that my first appointment was a no-show. I took the extra time to check in with my mom and made plans to spend the weekend with her before hanging up. I had never heard back from Travis, making me regret my decision to call him.

I walked out of the break room and was surprised to find Mrs. Montgomery standing behind the appointment desk. She was still my client, after everything that had happened with Travis and me. She would just act normal, like the days before I had met Travis, making sure never to mention his name and neither did I. I quickly rethought the day of the week in my head; it was only Tuesday, not Thursday, which was her normal appointment

"Mrs. Montgomery, you didn't have an appointment today, did you?"

"No, Mia, dear. Would you be able to come outside for a moment?" She had a look of despair on her face.

"Sure." I told Victor where I was going and that I'd be right back.

Her limo driver held the door as we both exited. He opened up the limo door, allowing us both to enter before closing it.

"Mrs. Montgomery, is everything okay?"

She shook her head as she fought the tears. I put my hand on hers to offer her support. There was an agonizing silence as she tried to get her thoughts together.

"Mia, Travis had an accident."

I felt the blood rush from my face. I began to break out in a sweat and tears filled my eyes. All of the painful memories came flashing back as I was suddenly brought back to that day the two police officers were standing at my door, delivering that horrible news about Eric. "What happened?" I whispered.

"He was snowboarding yesterday; he had been drinking and tried doing some crazy jump. He hurt his back – he's paralyzed." She began to burst out in tears.

My stomach clenched. I thought of Travis lying in a hospital bed. I closed my eyes to fight the burning. My head was spinning as I tried my hardest to speak. "Oh my God. What's his prognosis?" My voice was cracking with emotion.

"I talked to my son last night. The doctor said that there's no nerve or spinal cord damage, so his chances of walking again are very good, but he's completely shut down, Mia. Maybe if he saw you, it might give him some initiative."

"I-I don't know. I think it may just make it worse." I couldn't hold back the tears any longer.

Mrs. Montgomery grabbed my hand. "Mia, please. He hasn't been the same since you two broke up. He's become this unhappy, reckless person." She began to break down in tears. "Mia, he's lost without you."

"I just –"

"Please, Mia, tell me you will go see him." She reached in her purse and handed me a folded up piece of paper. "This is where he is at and his room number. Please say that you will, dear."

I nodded as I bit my lip and closed my tear-filled eyes. She hugged me tightly before I stepped out of the limo with my head hanging low.

"What's the matter?" Juan asked as I walked back through the door.

The tears flowed down my face. He wrapped his arm around me and took me in the back. I told him everything, catching my breath a few times in between sobs.

"I was so mean to him, Juan. I should have given him a second chance. It's my fault that this happened."

He hugged me tightly. "Oh, sweetie, it's not your fault at all. You are not responsible for his actions. Don't blame yourself."

"Why did this have to happen? I feel like I have some sort of curse that destroys every man that I love."

"Mia, stop that. You had nothing to do with Eric's death and you had nothing to do with Travis getting hurt."

"I don't know what to do."

"You need to go see him, Mia. Even if he doesn't want to see you, at least he'll know you care."

I nodded as I dabbed my eyes with a tissue, trying my best to pull it together and get through the workday.

By the time I got home, I was spent. I couldn't stop thinking of Travis all day long and each time I did, I would begin to cry. I plopped down on the couch and turned on the TV. I flicked through the channels and came to a stop when I saw Travis' face on the news. I felt like I was dreaming a terrible dream when I heard the newscaster speaking in a very somber tone.

"*Travis Montgomery, America's record medalist, suffered a devastating injury while snowboarding in this popular Vermont Ski resort....*" I quickly turned it off. I couldn't listen; it hurt too much. I did my best not to cry. A million thoughts went through my head. *No wonder he didn't call me back. If only I had called him earlier, then maybe he wouldn't have gone. Maybe this would have never happened.* This was all my fault. He was reckless because of me, because I wouldn't give him a second chance. I wouldn't even hear his side of the story. I had to be there for him. I had to be strong and I had to let him know how much I still cared, whether he wanted me to or not.

****

I walked down the long corridor of the hospital, taking in all the room numbers along the way. I stopped just outside of

Room 205 and took a deep breath. I slowly entered to find Travis sitting up in his bed, watching television. A brief smile that quickly changed to a scowl appeared on his face.

I bit my lip and tried to control my tears as I looked at him. I felt a giant knot forming in the pit of my stomach. This strong, athletic man, now paralyzed. I knew that it was probably killing him inside, having me see him this way. All of the painful memories of seeing Eric lying in his hospital bed quickly came rushing back to me. But Travis was still here. He was still alive and able to hear what I had to say.

"Mia, what are you doing here?" His tone was sharp.

"I wanted to see how you were doing."

He shook his head at me. "Well, now you see."

"I'm sorry, Travis."

"I don't need your pity, Mia."

"I didn't come here to give you pity. I came here to see you."

"Oh, now all of a sudden you care, when before you wouldn't even talk to me?"

"Travis, stop. I didn't come here to fight with you or bring up the past. I came here to be a friend. I want to be here for you, Travis."

"I don't want your friendship, Mia." He looked away.

I sat down on the bed and moved closer to him. "I don't care what you want, Travis, because I'm going to be here for you whether you want me to or not."

"Why? Why do you want to do this for me after what I've done to you?"

"I don't know; I just do. Once I love someone, they remain in my heart forever, no matter what."

His eyes were glassed over and full of emotion as he gazed at me. They weren't those same beautiful color-changing eyes that I had grown so accustomed to looking into. They were different. They were dull and flat and filled with sadness. I gently caressed his face with my hand. "It's going to be okay, Travis," I whispered.

He pulled me into his warm embrace. "I'm scared, Mia. For the first time in my life, I'm scared." The tears were rolling down my face as he hugged me tightly.

I pressed my forehead up to his. "It's okay to be scared, Travis. You will beat this and you walk again, I know you will. Please, let me be here for you."

"Mia, I fucked up my life so bad. First with you and now this." The tears began to form in his eyes and my heart began to break a little bit more, seeing him like this. So scared and alone, it was tearing me up inside. All I wanted to do was take away his pain, but I knew there was nothing that I could say that would make him feel better. All I could do was pull him closer and hug him tightly. I kissed him on the cheek and wiped a tear away that was rolling down his face. "Mia, I don't want to live if it's like this."

"Don't you ever say that, Travis. Do you hear me? You have so many people that love and care about you. You are strong and determined and you will walk again." I ran my hand along his cheek. I couldn't stand the sadness in his eyes. It was as if I was looking at a completely different man than the one I had known just a few short months ago. I had to let him know that his life was worth living. I had to let him know how much I still cared. So I did what my heart was screaming for me to do. I took his face in my hands and kissed him deeply. "I love you, Travis."

His eyes filled with tears once again. "Mia, don't do this because you feel like –"

I put my finger over his lips to stop him from talking. "I think you know me better than that. I don't do or say anything that I don't want to." I leaned my head on his shoulder and intertwined my fingers in his. "You're going to get through this, Travis, and I will be here for you every step of the way."

Chapter 49

Travis...

Mia stayed with me until visiting hours were over. She had no clue how much just seeing her had meant to me. I felt like I was dreaming when I saw her standing in the doorway. She was like an angel, one that I didn't deserve. I needed to get better, for her. I once again screwed up with my own stupidity. I had no business snowboarding that day after all that I drank. I especially had no business trying to do a jump that I knew I wouldn't even be able to land sober. I remember trying to get up after I landed on my back and not being able to move my legs. Mike thought I was joking. I will never forget the look of horror on his face when he found out I wasn't. I knew that he felt guilty for going with me that day after I had been drinking. The same way I saw guilt in Mia's eyes today, but this wasn't either of their faults in any way. It was mine. I was the one who drank myself into oblivion to alleviate my own guilt and now I had placed that same guilt onto the two people I cared about most.

I hated Mia seeing me this way. I felt like a half a man. Mia had the biggest heart out of anyone I knew and I was so grateful to her for wanting to support me through this, but at the same time, I didn't want to drag her down into a life that she didn't deserve. I loved and wanted to be with her more than anything in this world, but not this way. I knew that I had to get better for her, so we could live the life that I had intended, before my world fell apart. I closed my eyes and imagined that she was lying beside me in my arms, the way that she used to, the way that I hoped that she would be one day again.

***

After a two-month stay in the rehab center and a month of being home, I was starting to adjust as best as I could. I wasn't accepting it any better, but I was learning to deal with it. Mia was there for me more than anyone. She had completely let me back into that huge heart of hers. Just when I thought it wasn't possible to love her any more than I already did, she proved me wrong. She was running herself ragged with working and running over to my place after work. She spent a lot of her nights with me and it was comforting to have her lying beside me.

I was waiting for Jerome, my physical therapist, to get to my place for my daily regimen of therapy. Mia had just left to have breakfast with Juan. I was glad that she was still doing something that was in the norm of her old life. She felt the need to be here with me so much that she had been neglecting herself and all of the things that she once got enjoyment from and I hated it. I hated seeing her catering to my every whim and even though I knew she was doing it because she cared, it bothered me because it made me feel helpless. I was feeling lower than usual this morning as I thought about last night and what had happened or, should I say, didn't happen. My doctor had told me that sex may or may not be possible. We had discussed the whole sex thing and Mia was well aware that it just might not work.

Mia crawled into bed with me last night and nuzzled close to me. She smelled so good and everything inside of me wanted her after being so long without her. "Mia, you don't know how badly I wish I could make love to you right now."

She moved closer to me and kissed me softly on the chest. "Me too." A couple of months ago, that's all that it would take and I would be ready to go. She moved on top of me and began to kiss my neck. "Do you want to try?" she whispered as a strand of hair draped over her face.

"Mia, I don't think it's –

She lifted her nightgown over her head and placed my hands on her breasts. I took in the sight of her perfect body. I ran my fingers across her nipples like it was the very first time that I was touching them. She was so beautiful. She leaned down and kissed me. "Travis, I want you to be inside of me. I want to feel you again. I miss you so much," she whispered softly in my ear. Everything inside of me wanted her. I wanted to taste her skin, see the look of pleasure on her face, and most of all, feel the closeness of being one with her. Unfortunately, the one thing that wasn't responding the same way as the rest of my body was the one thing that I needed to respond the most.

After some time, I finally came to the realization that it wasn't going to happen.

"Damn it!"

"Travis, it's okay. Dr. Dey told you it's going to take time. Remember, practice makes perfect."

I couldn't even look at her, I felt like such a failure. She rested her head on my chest and ran her hand gently across my cheek. "Baby steps, Travis, we'll get there. I promise." She softly placed her lips on my chest. I didn't know what I did to deserve this woman, but whatever it was, I was eternally grateful.

Chapter 50

Mia...

I was nonstop, on the go; working during the day and spending all of my free time during the evening and the weekends with Travis. I realized now more than ever how much I loved him and I was willing to do anything to make sure he knew it.

In my effort to be there for Travis, I had realized I was neglecting other things, like my family and Juan. They were all very supportive with my decision to help Travis, but I didn't think any of them realized how much time I would be committing to him.

I was so glad finally to be sitting down to a long overdue breakfast with Juan that I couldn't wipe the smile from my face. It was a beautiful early summer day. We sat in the outdoor seating area as I sipped on my coffee and took in all of his pictures from his trip to Paris from which he and Brian had just returned. I laughed at the photos of Juan posing in front of the Eiffel Tower, while my mouth watered over the pictures of the delicious French pastries he had taken. It looked heavenly. I couldn't help but wish that someday Travis and I would get there.

"These are great, Juan." I tried to sound as upbeat as possible, but he must have still sensed a little sadness in my voice.

"Mia, what's the matter?"

I bit my lip and looked away. "Travis and I tried to have sex for the first time since his accident." The words were out before I could even stop them. I just felt like I needed to talk to someone about it.

"Mia, I'm not trying to be funny, but if he can't feel anything from the waist down, then how would that work?"

"His doctor said that there is a chance of it working." I went on to explain exactly what Travis' doctor had said. I couldn't believe I was having this conversation with him.

"So now, he's all upset over it."

"Well, what about you? Are you okay that it's not working?"

"Of course I am! I mean I want to make love to him more than anything, but it's just going to take some time."

Juan sighed. "Oh, Mia, you are such a great person, you know that?" I smiled, not used to Juan being so serious. "Well, you know what they say: a good man is hard to find and a hard one is good to find! And sometimes I have neither; at least you got one of the two." I nearly spit my coffee out at his words.

"You are too much, Juan."

"Well, it's the truth; at least yours has an excuse! I'll help you take care of that problem until he gets it working."

My jaw dropped down to my knees. "What!"

"Oh my God, girl, relax. I love you to death, but not in that way! I'll take you to this store that I know about that sells, you know, things that will help get you through until Travis gets over his problem."

"Um, no, that's okay! I never used one of those and I don't intend to do that now."

"Well, maybe you should, and this is coming from someone who spent a whole year around you when you weren't getting any. Trust me, you were no picnic, sweetheart."

"Well, you will just have to deal with my bitchiness until then, the same way I have to deal with yours – that's what friends are for." I giggled and took another sip of coffee as Juan rolled his eyes and shook his head at me.

***

I finished up with breakfast and headed back to Travis'. I nearly walked right into Jerome, Travis' physical therapist, as I was getting off the elevator. "Hey, Mia, how are you?"

Every time I looked at him, I couldn't help but see Apollo Creed from Rocky. He looked so much like him, it was scary. He told me that he had gotten that a lot from people when I mentioned it to him. "I'm good, thanks!"

"Travis had a great morning. Just please keep encouraging him. I think it's really helping with his therapy."

"I will." I smiled just before he stepped into the elevator and the doors closed.

"Hey, handsome!" I said as I entered Travis' apartment. I walked over to him and handed him a bag containing a peanut butter fudge brownie. "Got this just for you." I leaned down and kissed him on the cheek. "I ran into Jerome in the hall. He said you're doing really great! See, I told you –"

"Mia, just stop."

"What's the matter, Travis?"

"Nothing, I'm sorry. I'm just tired."

"Well, it's a beautiful day. Do you want to get out? We can go over to Central Park."

He shook his head. As much as I tried to be upbeat and put on a happy face, I knew Travis was anything but happy. He was depressed and no matter how much I tried to be his cheerleader, there was nothing that I could do to fix that. He had too much pride; he didn't want anyone to see him in a wheelchair. He wasn't ready to face the world.

I leaned down by him and ran my hand through his hair. "Travis, sweetie, I'm not even going to say that I know how you're feeling, because I don't. But you need to get out of this apartment and start living your life a little."

"Live my life, like this? This isn't living, Mia; it's just existing."

"Travis, it's only temporary."

He was unresponsive; he just rubbed his forehead and looked down at the ground.

I moved closer to him and kissed him on the lips. "So, what do you say? Let's go to the park and if you don't feel comfortable, we can come right back." I rubbed my fingers along his face.

"Fine," he finally answered half-halfheartedly. Central Park was right across the street from his apartment, so luckily we didn't have far to go. I could tell that he was self-conscious; this was the first time he had been out other than going to his doctor's appointments. I did what I did best; I talked nonstop as I stood behind him and pushed him. I finally stopped when I came to a bench.

"See, this isn't so bad, is it?" I asked.

"No, I guess not."

We sat in comfortable silence and people watched for some time before he began to speak. "Mia, you know that I wanted to make love to you more than anything last night, right?"

"I know. Dr. Dey told you, it's going to take time. I'm not going anywhere, Travis. You're worth the wait." I was suddenly realizing why he was in such a bad mood.

"Mia, you are the only thing that's keeping me going. I don't know what I would do without you. I love you so much."

"I love you too, Travis, always."

I told Travis all about Juan's trip to Paris and all of the beautiful pictures. I was happy to see him actually smiling a genuine smile for the first time in a very long time.

"I'm adding that to our bucket list."

"What's that?" he asked.

"Paris. Someday we will get to see the Eiffel Tower and walk along the Seine."

He looked away is if it pained him to hear me making plans for our future. "That's just one of many things I'm adding to that list." I kissed him softly on the lips and pressed my forehead to his. "I have great things planned for us, Travis Montgomery."

Chapter 51

Travis...

We spent most of the afternoon at the park. Mia was right; I did feel a little better after getting out. The only time that I was even remotely happy anymore was when I was with her. Although hearing all about her plans for the future for us had me a little disheartened. Not because I didn't want a future with her; I just knew that I couldn't offer her much of one right now. We got off the elevator and headed down the hall to my apartment.

"Hey, guys!" Mia exclaimed upon seeing Mike and Stacy with their three-week-old baby girl. I hadn't met the baby yet and neither had Mia, so to say she was excited was an understatement. Mia quickly unlocked the door and let everyone inside.

"We were just in the neighborhood and thought it was time for Brenna to meet her Uncle Travis," Stacy said she placed the baby in my arms. Mia knelt down next to me, taking everything about the baby in, unable to wipe the smile from her face.

"She's really beautiful, guys. Good thing she looks like you Stacy." I made my best effort at a joke.

Mike laughed, but I could see hurt in his eyes every time he looked at me. "Ah, you see that, Travis, you made her cry."

"No, you didn't, Travis, it's time for her bottle," Stacy said as she lightly smacked Mike on the arm.

"Oh, can I feed her?" Mia asked.

"Sure!" Stacy answered.

Mia went over to the kitchen sink and washed her hands while Stacy prepared the baby's bottle. She instantly stopped crying as soon as Mia took her from my arms. I had such mixed emotions as I sat there and watched her. She was beaming, never taking her eyes off the baby or the smile off her face.

"You're a natural, Mia," Mike said.

"I love babies. I could just watch them eat and sleep all day," Mia said.

"Yeah, somehow I don't think you would be saying that when she's screaming her head off at 3 a.m.," Mike joked.

"Wouldn't bother me one bit," Mia said as she gently placed the baby over her shoulder to burp her. "I love her name."

"Thanks, that was a name I had picked out from the time I was a little girl. I always knew that I wanted it if I had a girl," Stacy said.

"Oh, I have one of those too, but mine is for a boy. Jackson Samuel."

"Jackson Samuel Montgomery. Sounds perfect!" Stacy said.

Mia's smile became a mile wide while my heart felt like it was being ripped from my chest. As much as I wanted to give Mia that more than anything, I didn't know if that would ever be feasible. Mike looked at me, seemingly reading my thoughts as he quickly started up a new conversation with me about last night's baseball game. Mia and Stacy took the baby into the bedroom to change her diaper.

"How you doing, buddy?" Mike asked.

"Okay, I guess."

"Well, I'm glad to see that things are going so good between you and Mia. She's really a great girl, Travis."

"Yeah, I know," I said, sounding very emotionless.

"Well, don't sound so excited about it."

"Because I'm not, Mike. I can't give her what she deserves and I don't know if I ever will. Did you see her face when she was holding the baby? It's what she wants more than anything."

"Travis, man, it has only been a few months. Give it some time. You're getting more and more nerve sensation in your legs every day. I'm sure that it's only a matter of time before 'that' starts waking up too. She loves you, Travis. That is so apparent to everyone. Just be happy that you got her back for right now. Just deal with one thing at a time, man."

I had gotten her back. But this wasn't how I wanted her back. I wanted to be able to give her all of the same things that I was able to before we broke up and I hated myself for not being able to do so.

Chapter 52

Mia...

I sat on the edge of the bed, putting on my lotion before getting in. Travis was quiet for most of the night after Mike and Stacy left.

I got under the covers and rested my head on his chest. "Today was a good day," I said as I stretched my neck to kiss him on the cheek. He didn't answer. "Travis, what's the matter?"

"Mia, what if we can't have a baby together?"

"What? Travis, why are you even thinking that way?"

"Mia, I'm being realistic. I have to be. There is a good chance that if you stay with me, you may never have a child."

I didn't want to think about the prospect of that happening. Travis was going to get better; there was no doubt in my mind. "Travis, just stop." I went to kiss him on the lips and he moved his head away.

"Damn it, Mia, stop ignoring what's right in front of your eyes. I can't have sex with the woman I love."

"Travis, it's just –"

"Mia, stop! I get that you're trying to think positive and I really do appreciate that, but, baby, this may be it. This may be your life forever. Is this really what you want?"

I didn't hesitate, not for one second. "Yes, it is. I want you, Travis. Nothing else matters to me."

He shook his head as if he were still uncertain. I nuzzled closer to him and kissed him softly on the lips. He finally looked at me with sadness in his eyes. "I love you, Mia," he whispered.

My stomach fluttered. I closed my eyes and hugged him tightly. Travis was my everything; no matter what the future had in store, I couldn't imagine mine without him in it.

***

Another two weeks had passed and Travis seemed to be slipping into a deeper depression. I had attended his doctor's appointment and his doctor was very happy with the outcome of some recent testing that he had done, which made me overjoyed. Travis, on the other hand, seemed unaffected by the news. He was so impatient; he just wanted instant results. He was becoming so distant with me. So, I, in turn, just tried harder to get through to him.

I had spent the night at Travis' and was readying myself to go to my niece's birthday party. I had wanted Travis to come along with me more than anything, but after asking him three times and all three times being told "no," I finally gave up. I hated leaving him, especially with him being so down and out. I had secretly called his mother, who was going to pay him a *surprise* visit. I knew that he probably would have gotten angry with me for confiding in her about him, but I was concerned for him. I was hoping that maybe she could break him out of this slump that he was in.

I finished dressing and walked over to Travis, who was doing something on his laptop. I stood behind him, bent down, and wrapped my arms around him. "I'm going to get going. I made extra chicken last night. It's in the fridge; just stick in the oven to warm it up." I kissed him softly on the neck. He pulled away like he was annoyed with me. "What's the matter?" I asked.

He just shook his head. I sat down next to him. Clearly, something was bothering him and I didn't feel comfortable leaving until I knew what it was. "Travis, did I do something?"

"Mia, I'm not a baby. I can take care of myself when you're not around."

"I'm sorry. I didn't mean to upset you."

"It's okay, Mia, just go have a nice time. Enjoy yourself with your family."

"I would enjoy myself more if you were coming along." I made one last ditch effort.

His only response was a shake of his head. I got up and sat on his lap. I wrapped my arms around his neck and kissed him. "I'll see you tomorrow?" His smile was like the first rain after a long drought. He nodded and ran his hands up my back, kissing me again with much more intensity. It had been a while since he had shown this type of affection to me and it made my insides smile. I pressed my forehead up against his. "I love you."

"I love you too," he responded as if the words pained him to say. I walked out of his apartment, not quite knowing how to feel. I was getting such mixed emotions from him. It seemed like the more I tried to be there for him, the more he was pushing away.

***

It was hard to believe that it was the end of June already and that my little niece, Paige, was four years old. It seemed like her birthday had just crept up on me this year. I helped my sister out, keeping the fifteen kids at the party entertained; but my favorite part was playing with my little niece, Emily. She was nine months old and just starting to form her own personality. Her smile made me smile and her deep belly laughs melted my heart. I couldn't believe how much these two little girls had grown since the last time that I had seen them, making me realize that I really needed to make an effort to spend more time with them.

It was nice to finally relax after all of the kids had gone. Emily was down for a nap and Paige was passed out on the couch from all of the excitement of earlier.

I helped my mom and sister peel the corn on the cob. My mom got up to check on my niece when she heard her stirring over the baby monitor. "Mom, she's fine. She's just turning over in her crib," my sister said. My mother ignored her and ran up the stairs to check. My sister and I just looked at each other and laughed quietly. My mother was neurotic when it came to her grandkids.

"Travis didn't want to come?" My sister asked.

I shook my head. I was trying my best not to think about him today and just to enjoy the day. Being with my nieces helped, but I still couldn't help but wonder what he was doing.

"Well, you look exhausted."

"Thanks!" I said rather sarcastically, knowing that was code word for "you look like crap."

"I'm sorry, Mia, but you do."

I put the piece of corn that I was peeling down on the table and began to unload everything on my sister. I didn't leave anything out, including mine and Travis' failed attempt at sex.

"Mia, maybe he just wants to do this on his own. I mean, think about it; the world sees him as this strong, competitive man and now he can't even walk. That's got to be eating him up inside."

"I get that, but why is he pushing me away? I just want to be there for him."

"Okay, you're probably going to get really pissed at me for saying this, but I'm going to say it anyway."

I took a deep breath in preparation of her words.

"You couldn't save Eric, so now you feel this underlying need to run yourself ragged trying to save Travis, when clearly he doesn't want that."

She was right - I was pissed! "What! That's not true, Tressa! And how dare you throw Eric in my face. My relationship with Travis has nothing to do with my relationship with Eric."

She softened her voice, trying to calm me down a bit. "Mia, all I'm saying is at some point you have to stop placing guilt on yourself."

"What are you talking about?" I asked defensively.

"The way you just get over stuff and forgive people. I mean, look when our father came to see you. You just forgave him like it was nothing, after he abandoned us."

"Tressa, he was dying!"

"And do you think he would have cared if the situation were reversed? He wouldn't have even known if one of us was dying."

"What the hell are you trying to say, Tressa, that if the situation were reversed that Travis wouldn't be there for me?"

"No - I don't know what I'm trying to say. But, Mia, what Travis did to you was wrong. I stood by your decision to let it go and forgive him, but when I see you running yourself ragged because you feel that this was your fault that this happened to him, then I feel the need to open my mouth and say something. It's not your fault, Mia. Travis did this to himself. It was his own guilt over what he did to you that caused this."

"Oh well, then I guess I should be honored that the 'queen of unforgiving' stood by my side when I chose to forgive the man who matters most to me in this world. Do me a favor and mind your own damn business, Tressa!" I got up and pushed in my chair. I was on emotional overload as I fought to hold back the tears. I never fought with my sister, so this was very hard for me. My mom had just walked downstairs with the baby. She stood there speechless, trying to figure out what had just happened.

I walked out into the backyard where my brother-in-law and stepfather were deep in conversation.

"Gary, can you please take me to the train station?"

"Mia, I thought you were spending the night at our house," he responded.

I just shook my head. He didn't ask any more questions once he saw the tears in my eyes. He just got up and took my bag as we walked off to his car.

Chapter 53

Mia...

I submerged my body into the foamy bubbles of my tub and rested my head against my bathtub wall. It felt good to be alone and just relax in my own apartment. I ignored the phone calls from my mom and sister; I didn't want to deal with that just yet. I was emotionally drained after my little disagreement with my sister this afternoon. I knew that she only meant well, but I knew what I wanted in life and it was Travis. It had nothing to do with me feeling guilty. I was planning on calling her to talk things out, but not just yet. For the moment, I just wanted to let the bath bubbles envelop me and take away my troubles. I closed my eyes and my mind began to wander. I hadn't heard from Travis all day. I knew that he thought I was spending the night at my mom's, but I thought that he would have least called to say goodnight. As much as I didn't want to admit it, we were growing apart and I hated it. There was nothing I could say or do to make him feel better about himself. I reached my arm from the tub, grabbed my phone from the back of the toilet, and dialed his number. I wasn't going to let him drift away from me so easily. He finally picked up after the third ring.

"Hey, Mia."

"Hey, watchya doin', handsome?" I was trying to sound as upbeat as possible.

"Just got done running a marathon," he said with a sarcastic edge to his voice.

I hated how moody he was lately. Still, I tried to be my normal bubbly self. "Haha very funny. You just might be in a couple months from now."

He was silent.

"I miss you," I said, trying to keep up the conversation.

"What time will you be home tomorrow?" *Okay, not even an "I miss you too"? Ouch!*

"Actually, I am home."

"I thought you were staying –"

"Yeah, I was supposed to, but it's a long story."

"Oh, well, I'm really tired. I guess I'll just see you tomorrow."

"Okay. I love you, Travis."

"I love you too," he said as if it were an effort before hanging up the phone.

I hung up the phone and looked down at the fading bubbles around me. I couldn't help but compare them to mine and Travis' relationship. Was that all that was left of us, remnants of something that once was?

I awoke the next morning, feeling like I had been run over by a train. My throat was killing me and my head was pounding. I couldn't even bring myself to have a cup of coffee. I chose tea instead, hoping it would help soothe the fire in my throat. I finally decided to call my sister. The fact that I was arguing with her didn't make me feel any better, so I figured I would at least get that taken care of.

"Hey, Tress, I'm sorry," I said as she answered the phone, realizing that my voice sounded like a raspy seductress.

"I'm sorry too. I didn't mean to upset you, Mia. I'm just worried about you."

"I'm okay, I promise."

"What's wrong with your voice?"

"I don't know. I woke up with a horrible sore throat."

"Well, you better get a doctor's appointment if it gets much worse. When I had Paige at the doctor's last week, he said that summer strep is going around."

"I will, I promise."

We talked for a little while longer. I felt much better emotionally after hanging up with her. I didn't like being on the outs with her. She was my touchstone. I took a shower and dressed, trying to make myself look halfway decent. I looked sick and no amount of make-up was going to fix that. I finally gave up after applying half the bottle of concealer to the dark circles that were encompassing my eyes. I was just about to call Travis and tell him I was heading over, but then realized I couldn't take another chilly phone conversation with him, so I would have a chilly one with him in person. At least then I could sneak a hug in whether he wanted me to or not.

By the time I had arrived at Travis', I looked like a drowned rat. It was a hot, humid New York day with thunderstorms that came in downpours, just as I was getting in and out of the cab. I stopped and picked us up some soup for lunch along the way. Even though today was not soup weather, it was the only thing that I could even fathom getting down my throat. I took the elastic ponytail holder around my wrist and pulled my hair back into a ponytail before stepping off the elevator.

Travis looked at me strangely when I walked through the door. "Mia, what happened to you?"

"Well, let's see, my throat is killing me, it's about one hundred degrees with one hundred percent humidity and each time the sky would open up it was when I decided to get in and out of the cab."

"You sound horrible. Why aren't you home in bed?"

"Because I wanted to see you." I walked over and gave him a hug. He hugged me back tightly, making me glad that I ignored the fact that I felt like death and came to see him instead.

"I bought us some soup." He began to laugh. Not the full-fledged laugh that I used to get from him, but at least it was something. "What are you laughing at?"

"Your voice; you really shouldn't be talking."

"You know that's impossible for me." I smiled.

"Yeah, I do." He smiled back.

We sat down and ate our soup as I pried out of him how his physical therapy had gone this morning. I was elated when he told me that he had a meeting this week to talk about his business venture that he had put on the back burner since his accident.

"Travis, that is awesome."

"Yeah, well I don't know how awesome it will be since the owner of this potential swim school can't even swim himself."

I put my spoon down and stared at him. "What?" he asked as if he were annoyed.

"Can you please stop being so negative? It's not helping the situation any."

"Oh, okay maybe it will make things better if I just pretend that one day I'm going to wake up and everything is going to be the way it used to be. Live in a fuckin' fantasy world like you are, Mia."

My eyes began to burn with tears. "I'm not living in a fantasy world, Travis. I just happen to believe in you."

"Yeah, you believe in me so much that you had to call my mother and father over to babysit me yesterday? What do you guys think, that I'm that stupid and didn't see that was a whole set up? Or maybe, the fact that you stopped living your

Drowning in Love

life and are on the brink of physical exhaustion because you feel the need to be with me every second of your free time?"

"Travis, that's not true. I want to be with you all the time because I love you. Why can't you see that?" The tears began to flow down my face. "Why are you being so mean to me, Travis? What did I do?"

He shook his head and motioned for me to come over to him. He pulled me down on his lap and hugged me tightly. "I'm sorry, Mia, you didn't do anything. I just want you to stop worrying a little less about me and a little more about you."

"Well, that's hard when you love someone as much as I love you."

He kissed me on my forehead. "I love you too, baby. Did you take any aspirin? You're burning up."

"Yeah, I took two before I left."

He touched my forehead with his cool hand. "You need to go lie down."

I didn't really want to, but my body felt like it needed to, so I didn't argue. I walked into his bedroom as he followed me in. "I could just go home and –"

"Mia, just lie down."

I crawled into his bed. It felt like heaven when my head hit the pillow. It felt even better when Travis got in next to me.

"Travis, I don't want to get you sick."

"I'll be fine."

He hugged me tightly and kissed me on the head. I didn't need any medicine. The best medicine in the world was lying right beside me.

Chapter 54

Travis...

I held her tightly and listened to her labored, feverish breathing. She had no business being out today. She should have never gotten out of bed, but again her constant need to take care of me forced her here. I was feeling really bad for getting her so upset. I had so much on my mind. I pondered over what Jerome and I discussed during my physical therapy session today. I didn't know what to do. I knew it would kill me to have to leave her, but maybe it was for the best. She needed to move on with her life with someone who could give her everything. I got a sick feeling in my stomach just thinking about her with another man. But, I needed to do this if I ever wanted to walk again and I had to do it on my own. I looked at Mia, and immediately began to second guess myself. She was so beautiful; she was my angel and even though she wanted to save me, she couldn't. I had to save myself.

I moved a strand of her hair from her face. She was breaking out in a sweat as her fever was breaking. I smiled at her familiar sleep talking that she often did. I was going to miss that so much. I was going to miss everything about her so much. I pulled her to me and whispered in her ear, "Mia, baby, I love you so much. I just want you to be happy and as long as I'm in your life this way, you won't be. I am the luckiest man alive to have been loved by someone like you." I closed my eyes to fight the burning. "You will always be my girl."

Chapter 55

Mia...

It took almost a whole week before I was finally feeling one hundred percent. By Sunday morning, I was climbing the walls to see Travis. I hadn't seen him all week. I was so tired after work with not feeling well that I just came home every night and crashed. I was so glad that I was feeling much better today. I missed him so much. Juan and I met for a quick cup of coffee and a bagel and I was on my way. I looked down at my watch. Travis would just be wrapping up his physical therapy. When I entered his apartment, I was surprised not to see Jerome, but instead, a pretty brunette. The two seemed to be very entertained by each other as the sounds of their laughter filled the air. I bit my lip and tried to put on my best fake smile. Travis turned around when he heard me enter. "Oh hey, Mia, this is Christine."

"Hi, Mia." She walked over to shake my hand. "Travis was telling me all about you." *Okay, and would someone mind telling me just exactly who you are?* "I was just filling in for Jerome today." *Not only was she pretty, but she reads minds as well.* "Well, I have to run. It was great to meet you, Travis, and you too, Mia."

We said our goodbyes as I walked her to the door. I walked back over to Travis, sat down on his lap, and wrapped my arms around his neck. I kissed him softly on his lips and pressed my forehead against his. "Well, if that's all it takes to finally put a smile on your face, then why didn't you just say so," I said half joking and half serious. I was a little annoyed that he wasn't able to laugh like that with me anymore.

"What are you talking about?" he asked as if he were clueless.

"A pretty physical therapist." He rolled his eyes at me. "Well, at least she can make you smile, because Lord knows I can't anymore." I knew I probably shouldn't have said that, but I was feeling a little hurt.

"Mia, really, you're jealous over her? Well, you don't have to worry about anything, you know better than anyone – it doesn't work down there."

"Oh, so what are you saying, if it did, you might be tempted?"

"What, no! Mia, what the hell is your problem?"

I knew I had two choices: either shake my head and tell him nothing or chance getting into a knockdown, drag out fight and tell him how I was really feeling. I decided to go with the latter of the two and hope for the best.

"I don't know, Travis, I'm doing everything that I possibly can for you and I'm lucky to get a forced smile. She's here for an hour and you're laughing away like she's your best friend, like you used to do with me. Travis, what did I do that's made you so angry with me all the time?"

"Mia, you haven't done anything. It's me. I can't look at you without being reminded of all of the things I'm not able to give you, things that you deserve, and it makes me angry. I'm angry at myself and I take it out on you."

"Travis, don't be. Everything is going to –"

"Mia, I'm leaving," he blurted out of nowhere.

"What? Where are you going?"

"To Los Angeles. Jerome was telling me about a doctor out there who's supposed to be a miracle worker with my type of injury."

"That's great. When do you think you will be coming back?"

He looked away and was silent for a brief moment before facing me again. "I'm not coming back."

I shook my head in disbelief. "Wha –what are you saying?"

"Mia, I can't keep doing this to you. You don't deserve to be trapped, taking care of me. You need to be living your life."

My eyes were burning with the familiar sting of tears. "I'm not trapped, Travis. I want to be here."

He shook his head. "Mia, I have never met anyone like you before in my life. You have the biggest heart and give so much to everyone else. You have been given so much crap in your life, but you still give with all that you have. That's why I can't do this to you anymore. Why can't you see that you deserve happiness? You deserve to be with someone who can give you everything."

I was shaking with emotion. "Travis, I don't want to be with anyone else. I want to be with you. I love you."

"Mia, I have nothing to offer you but pain."

I shook my head as the tears rolled down my face. "No, Travis, that's not true."

"Mia, I look at you and think about what a great mother you're going to make someday. I'm not going to deny you of that."

I was sobbing. He looked away as if it pained him. "Travis, that doesn't matter to me. As long as I have you, that's all that matters. I'll wait for you, Travis, if that's what you need – time alone - I will wait for you, for however long it takes. Just please don't do this." I felt myself getting panicked over the thought of losing him.

"Mia, I don't want that. I want you to move on with your life!"

I stared at him, with tears rolling down my face. I knelt down next to him and took his face in my hands. "Travis, you are my entire world. I don't want a life without you in it." I wrapped my arms around him and hugged him tightly.

He rubbed my back and kissed me on the top of my head as I tried to catch my breath in between sobs. I raised my head from his shoulder. "Please, Travis, please tell me that you won't go. I can't lose you again – I'm begging you."

He ran his hand though his hair and looked at me with tears in his eyes one last time before putting his head down. "I can't, Mia."

"Travis, look at me!"

He slowly lifted his head up and gazed into my eyes.

"You will never know how much I love you and, I promise you, I will love you for the rest of my life."

He looked down again and placed his hand on his forehead. "Please just go, Mia."

I stood up on my shaking legs, staring at him one last time. I bit my lip and took a deep breath. I grabbed my purse and walked out the door with tears gushing from my eyes. I got into the elevator. Once the doors closed, I dropped to the ground and began to sob uncontrollably.

Chapter 56

Travis...

It felt like someone had just kicked me in the balls when she walked out that door. It was the hardest thing that I ever had to do. The look in her eyes crushed me. I felt like such an evil person for hurting her this way, but I knew in the long run she would be thanking me. I had to head to L.A. and get out this place as soon as possible. I needed to get away from the memories of her and just focus on getting myself better. I knew that this was going to be the hardest fight of my life, but I was determined. Learning to walk again was going to be the easy battle; getting over Mia - that was going to be the hard part.

Chapter 57

Mia...

I stepped out of Travis' apartment building and onto the busy New York City streets, oblivious to anyone around me. I didn't care that it was a sweltering hot summer day and that the sun was cooking the back of my neck like a fried egg - I was numb to everything. I began to walk, not headed to anywhere in particular. I couldn't believe this had happened. He broke my heart again and this time beyond repair. After walking about fifteen blocks, I finally stopped off and grabbed an iced tea. I sat in the outdoor seating area, sipping it down while wiping away my tears. I loved him so much, why couldn't he see that it didn't matter to me? I had never felt so alone. I was so tired of being "Woe is me Mia" and burdening my family and friends with my problems. My sadness was quickly turning to anger. I hated Travis for doubting my love for him. I hated him for thinking he knew what was best for me and, most of all, I hated him for leaving me all alone. I wiped the last teardrop away, vowing not to slip into the same damsel in distress mode that I gotten into the first time we had broken up. It was so clear to me now - I wasn't meant to fall in love. I would never give the shattered bits of what was once my heart to anyone ever again.

***

"Mia, why don't you come to dinner with me and Brian?" Juan coaxed. It had been two weeks since Travis and I broke up. I hadn't a clue if he was in Los Angeles or not and I really didn't care. I found that the more time that passed, the angrier I became at him. I kept my promise that I had made to myself and didn't shed any tears for him - at least not in front of my family and friends. But when I was alone, tucked away in the confines of my apartment, I would let it all out.

"No, I'm really tired. I want to go home and relax. I've got a busy Sunday planned with my nieces tomorrow."

"Well, would you mind locking up for me so I can run home and get changed?"

"Not a problem." He kissed me on the cheek before heading out the door. I sat in comfortable silence for some time looking out the window at the people going by, wondering if any of them felt as low as I did right now. I was in such trance that I didn't even see Travis' mother coming through the door. My eyes immediately filled with tears upon seeing her.

"Mia, I was hoping I could catch you before you left."

I got up as she walked over to me and took me in her arms. Strangely, I didn't feel funny about showing my feelings to her, maybe because she may have been feeling the same thing herself.

"It's okay, honey. You're going to be okay."

"Why didn't he have enough trust in me to see how much I love him?"

"Mia, he knows." It felt good finally to be able to break down to someone. "If you don't have any plans, I would love to take you to dinner," she said as she wiped away a tear from my face.

"Sure," I responded.

I locked up the salon and we took the short walk to the bistro-style restaurant up the street. After we placed our orders, she began to talk.

"He left today," she said gently. I bit my lip and looked out the window. "Mia, he did this because he loves you."

I shook my head. "If he loves me, then why doesn't he want me to wait for him?"

"Because he wants you to get on with your life."

"But I don't want to get on with my life if it doesn't include him. It doesn't matter to me that he can't walk. I always loved Travis for the person he was inside, not the gold medalist. Those things never mattered to me. All that mattered was us, not what he could give me."

I could see tears forming in her eyes. "Travis was right; you do have a beautiful heart. Mia, he always loved you, honey. When the two of you broke up the first time, he became this person that I no longer knew and it scared me."

"If I had only listened to him and gave him a second chance, this probably would have never happened. I just wish I had enough faith in him to have believed him when he told me that."

"Mia, you had every right to be upset with him for what he did. I was at a benefit the night that little witch Chloe concocted her whole plan. I never liked her from the beginning; the way she would hang all over Travis and make a spectacle of herself was just so unprofessional. I told Travis not to go along with it. Then when I found out that you were the girl and I had seen how much Travis had fallen for you, I wanted to choke her. I told Travis to tell you the truth, but he was too afraid of losing you."

I bit my lip and wiped a tear away. "And he did anyway and now he can't walk because of it."

"Oh, Mia, what happened to Travis has nothing to do with you. Don't blame yourself. But at the same time don't ever doubt the love that Travis has for you. This is something that he's got to get through on his own. He doesn't want help from anyone. Not even me or my husband. He's always been stubborn, ever since he was a little boy."

"I just don't want to imagine my life without him in it. Travis did something that I never thought was possible after I lost my fiancé; he showed me how to open my heart and love again."

"And you did something for Travis that I never thought was possible. You showed him how to love too. Mia, Travis was a totally different guy before he met you. I never thought he would settle down with one woman and then you came along and became his entire world."

"I will never give my heart to anyone ever again."

She looked at me sadly. "You never know, Mia, maybe someday you and Travis will be right where you both belong again – together."

***

I had left a few of my things at Travis'. In my haste to leave that day, I forgot to give him back his key and he still had mine. I smiled deep inside, just knowing that, hoping that one day I would come home and find him sitting on my couch. Travis was right; I was living in a fantasy world and I needed to snap out of it. I had asked his mother at dinner if she would mind if I went and picked my stuff up. It was funny, how just a few weeks ago I felt so comfortable just walking into Travis' apartment unannounced, and now I felt as if I needed permission to do so. I walked into the familiar place that now seemed so foreign. I could still feel his presence. I could still feel the love for him that was busting inside my heart. Standing here in his living room made me realize that he still had all of me completely, even though he was thousands of miles away. Time and distance would never erase the bittersweet memories. The more I tried to tell myself that it was over and that I was going to be okay, the more I found myself wanting him. I took a deep breath before walking into his bedroom, unable to fight the tears as I sat down on his side of the bed. I grabbed his pillow and hugged it tightly. *Why couldn't he just let me be there for him? Why didn't he see that I loved him, no matter what?* I thought about him on the other side of the country, all alone, and it broke my heart. I had a sinking feeling in my chest. I knew that I needed to get out of here. I had to get away from the place that held the most memories of us. I grabbed the few things that I had out of the dresser drawer and placed them in a box. I was halfway out the bedroom door when I remembered the two pairs of shoes that I had in the closet. I walked into the closet and turned on the light. I looked around at Travis' clothes, seeing him just as if he were standing in front of me wearing some of them. My attention was drawn to his black winter coat, the one that he had on that horrible night at my apartment when we had broken up. I closed my eyes and held back the tears, remembering the look in his eyes that night. *Why didn't I give him a chance? Why was I so quick to believe that bitch and let her ruin both of our lives?* I took the coat from the hanger, sat down on the floor, and hugged it. "I'm so sorry, Travis. I'm so sorry for not giving you another chance." I sat for some time, just clinging to his coat before I finally pulled it together; I stood up and placed it back on the hanger. I bent down to pick up the small black box that had fallen out of the pocket. My stomach dropped when I opened the lid. It was the most beautiful diamond ring I had ever laid my eyes on. My hands were shaking. I knew exactly for whom that ring was intended. He must have planned on giving it to me on the night I had last seen him wearing this coat, the night we had broken up. I quickly closed the lid; I couldn't look at it anymore. I cried even harder, thinking about how different both of our lives could be right now –

this was all my fault. I went out into the kitchen and found a piece of paper and a pen. My tears fell onto the paper as I began to write:

Dear Travis,

It's only been two weeks since you left, but it feels like eternity. It would have always been yes and it always will be. I told you that I would love you forever and I meant it.

Yours always ~
Mia

I went back into his room and placed the ring and note on his dresser, hoping that maybe someday he would come back and see it. Maybe then, he would realize that I meant it when I said – I would wait for him, forever.

Chapter 58

Mia...

One year later…

"Mia, it's your birthday, we have to celebrate!" Juan pleaded.

"No, that's okay."

"Brian and I will be picking you up at eight. We're going to meet Victor and you are going to get drunk!" He didn't give me any time to protest before walking out the door.

I wasn't up for celebrating turning another year older and another year lonelier. I felt as if my life had just frozen in time from the day that I had walked out of Travis' apartment. I was just going through the motions, feeling a lot like I had after I lost Eric. I hadn't heard anything about Travis. There were many times that I was tempted to ask Mrs. Montgomery while I was doing her hair, but I stopped myself. I was better off not knowing; it would only open up the wounds that were just starting to scab over. My mom was on my case more than ever to move back home and I was now seriously considering it. I spent most of my free time commuting back and forth there on my days off anyway. Funny how most people head to a big city to start over again and I was contemplating leaving one for my new beginning.

I finished up with the last of my clients and headed home. The last thing I felt like doing was going out tonight, but I knew there was no way I was going to get out of it, so I reluctantly texted Juan to ask him where he planned on taking me against my will - so that I could be dressed appropriately.

I rolled my eyes at his text back: *Dinner and a club so make sure you wear your hooker heels.*

I was dressed and ready to go by the time Juan and Brian had arrived to pick me up. I had decided on my black mini skirt and my black and gray polka dot shirt with my cute silver sandals - no hooker heels!

By the time the taxi pulled up to my favorite Italian restaurant, I was glad that I had let Juan force me into going. My stomach muscles were sore from laughter after listening to him and Brian bantering back and forth on the ride there. We walked in and the hostess led us to the back room.

"Surprise!" I jumped when she turned on the lights, to find a dozen or so of my co-workers seated around a large table to celebrate my birthday.

I couldn't contain my smile. I hugged Juan tightly and walked over to greet everyone. Dinner was delicious and by the time it was over, I had far exceeded my one-drink limit. So, when Juan announced that we were all meeting up at Cielo, a nightclub in the meatpacking district, I was totally game.

The loud music and scant lighting in the club was only adding to my dizziness, but that didn't stop me from drinking the Malibu bay breeze that Juan handed me. "You do realize if you make me late for meeting my mom and sister tomorrow, they will kill you!"

"Oh, Mia, have fun for once!"

I didn't put up much of a fight as I sipped my drink down. I was having a great time and feeling totally relaxed. "Mia, you want to dance?" Victor asked over the blaring music.

"Sure!" I answered without hesitation. The two of us went out on the dance floor. I was having such a great time, making me very happy that I decided to come out of my shell a little tonight. I couldn't control my laughter as the music changed and we began to our best attempt at dirty dancing. By the time we were done, I had broken out in a sweat and needed more to drink - something non-alcoholic. I knew my limit and I had well surpassed it tonight.

"Victor, do you want something to drink?" I asked as he took the empty seat next to Juan.

"Oh yeah, rum and coke."

I made my way through the people to get to the bar and order our drinks. I was just heading back to the table when I heard someone shouting over the music. "Mia!" I turned around and was unable to feign any form of excitement when I saw Chloe approaching me. I was speechless. Even though I knew what I wanted to say to her, I remained silent. "I thought that was you out there on the dance floor. You're quite the little dancer, aren't you?"

"You know what; I have nothing to say to you."

"Oh, Mia, you're still upset over that whole Travis thing? You should be glad I told you, it's not like he's of any use to you now anyway. Although I did hear he moved to California just to get away from you."

It was taking everything in me not to throw one of the drinks that I was holding in her face. Juan must have been watching and sensed that I needed him as he came over to where I was standing.

"You make me sick, Chloe."

"Well, I don't know why, seems like you've moved on to someone just as nice looking," she said as she looked over at Victor. "I have to say, I don't know what was more pathetic; him crippling himself over you or you running back into his arms after his accident. Too bad his arms were the only thing he was able to wrap around you." She raised eyebrows and flashed me a devious grin.

I turned around and quickly handed Juan the drinks before following her back where she had just sat down.

"You go, girl!" Juan shouted.

She looked surprised when she looked up to see me in front of her. I looked over at the man she was seated with. "Are you her boyfriend?" I asked, feeling my adrenaline pumping through my veins.

"No, she's my agent," he clarified.

"Oh, so that means you're fucking her as well."

She pursed her lips and shook her head at me.

He began to chuckle, making me think that I was completely accurate in my assessment of the situation.

"Well, just a warning. Don't reject her or she'll ruin you."

I felt complete satisfaction just seeing the look on her face. I started to walk away before stopping myself and turning back around.

"Oh, and Chloe, why don't you take some of that money that you made off of Travis and get yourself some good hair extensions because those look just as fake as your boobs." I realized that I was still shouting to talk over the sound of the music that had just paused, causing a bunch of people to turn around and stare.

I could tell that the man she was with was trying to hold back his laughter while Chloe sat there, speechless. She just stared at me coldly as she mouthed the word "bitch" to me.

I smiled a genuine smile. "Thank you. Coming from you, I will consider that a compliment."

Juan was frozen, still standing in the same spot that I had left him in, holding the drinks. "Oh, Mia, I trained you well!" He laughed. "I'm guessing that was the bitchy agent?"

I nodded. I felt totally sobered up; it was if that altercation had flushed all of the alcohol out of my system. I was still fuming, wishing I could just rip that fake hair right out of her head. She was just a very painful reminder of my failed life and why I needed to move away from all of the old ghosts that still continued to haunt me.

Chapter 59

Mia...

After two very action packed, fun-filled days with my nieces and the rest of my family, I was looking forward to spending a quiet afternoon at home, unwinding before going back to work in the morning. That was until I received a text on the way home from Eric's partner, Ian, asking me to meet him for lunch. Besides being Eric's partner, he and Eric were great friends. He had been there the day the Eric was shot and he took his death very hard. Ian was there for me a lot after Eric's death. Then life began to get in the way and his every other day visits turned into once a week, then once a month to a Christmas card. I was saddened when I drifted apart from him and his wife, Amy. The four of us would go out together all of the time. I knew that part of it was my fault too. They were a painful reminder of my life with Eric and how I wished my life could have turned out. We had decided on meeting at Stand4, a burger restaurant. I had just stepped out of the taxi and onto the street when I heard Ian calling my name. I used my hands as a visor to block the afternoon sunlight out of my eyes. My smile was a mile wide when I saw him approaching me.

"Ian, how are you?" I hugged him tightly. I hadn't seen him or even talked to him in such a long while. I looked inside the stroller that he was pushing to find the most angelic little baby sound asleep, sucking on his pacifier. I could tell it was a little boy because he was dressed in all blue. "When did this happen?" I asked with a huge smile on my face.

"Six weeks ago," he said proudly.

I bent down to get a closer look at him. "He is beautiful! What's his name?"

He looked at me as if he was nervous to tell me. "Jackson – Jackson Eric." I stood up and fought the tears that were filling my eyes. Ian's wife, Amy, loved the name Jackson too, after I had mentioned it to her. She would always joke around and tell me we would be in a race to have the first boy to get the name – she won.

We settled into the outside seating area. It was a gorgeous day with no humidity, which was a rarity for a July afternoon in New York City. We gave the waitress our order and began to catch up. He had told me that Amy was spending a much-needed day to herself and he agreed to take the baby to give her a break. I looked down at the baby, still sound asleep and smiled. How I yearned to have one someday and with another birthday just passing, I was really beginning to feel my biological clock ticking.

"So, Mia, what's been going on with you?"

"Nothing much, same ole same ole."

He looked at me sadly. "I still think about him every day, Mia."

"Yeah, me too," I said, feeling the instant burn of tears.

He looked at me like he wanted to ask me something but was afraid. "I heard you were dating Travis Montgomery."

I quickly smiled. "Boy, you cops sure do know everything." He nodded and smiled. "Yeah, well, that's ancient history." It had been a whole year and it still pained me to say.

"That was really a shame, what happened to him."

I felt my eyes instantly filling up with tears. I bit my lip and tried my best to hold them back. I couldn't believe that I still got myself this emotional just thinking about Travis. When was it going to stop? "Oh, Mia, I'm sorry."

"No, it's okay. It's my fault. I should be over it by now."

He looked at me sympathetically. "I'm a good listener." I smiled and told him the whole story of Travis and me right from the beginning. By the time I was done, I felt much better. I wasn't sure if it was from unloading what I had bottled up for the past year, the Smores milkshake that I was sipping on, or the fact that the baby was beginning to stir and I was finally going to get to hold him.

"He's like an alarm clock, every three hours for his bottle." Ian laughed. He grabbed the diaper bag and took out his bottle.

"Can I feed him?" I asked.

"Sure!"

I carefully picked him up from the stroller as he cooed. He was so tiny, so perfect, that I felt myself becoming emotional just holding him. I couldn't take my eyes from him as he eagerly took the bottle. "He's so beautiful; you and Amy are so lucky."

He looked at me with a sympathetic smile. "Thanks, Mia, we really are."

I took the bottle from his mouth, wiped his lips with his burp cloth, and carefully sat him up to burp him. I felt a ping of triumph as I got a teeny tiny burp from him before feeding him some more. I was so engrossed in watching him that I didn't even see Stacy approaching me. "Mia! Oh my God. How are you?" She bent down to give me a kiss.

There was so much that I wanted to say to her. Like, *how is Travis? Does he know that I still love him and think about him every day?* But instead, I just went with, "Hey, Stacy, how are you?" She looked down at the baby and then at Ian. "Oh, Stacy, this is Ian, and this beautiful boy is Jackson."

She was silent for a brief moment before a smile appeared on her face.

"Stacy, come on, we have to get going!" I looked over to see a woman that was just about to enter a taxi calling her.

"I'm sorry, I have to run! I would love to get together and catch up."

"Yeah, sure, that would be great."

I watched as she walked off and jumped into the cab. I turned my attention back to the baby and Ian. "Just another reminder of a painful memory and why I need to move from this city."

Ian and I finished up our lunch and said our goodbyes. He made me promise that I would keep in touch. I assured him that I would. The memories wouldn't be so painful, now that I had had a new ghost that I was running from.

Chapter 60

Mia...

Summer had come and gone, along with my mind. I don't know what I was thinking. I must have seriously lost it, but I was going out on a blind date arranged by Juan. I couldn't believe I was doing this. I trusted his judgment with choosing the perfect dress, but choosing a man was a different story. He had made several failed attempts at playing Cupid. First, there was Renzo, a client of his who was about five feet tall, two of those inches was his hair alone. He was a miniature "Don Juan," or so he thought. He was under the impression that every woman's name was "Yo, babe!" Then there was Allan the nerdy UPS man who would gawk at all of the women clients like a pervert when he would make his daily deliveries. The lucky guy who had won a date with me this evening was Keith Bradford, a friend of Brian's brother. Juan had gone on and on about what a nice guy he was and what a good job he had, but was unable to answer one simple question: what did he look like? I found out after the date was all set up, that Juan had never even met the guy. He was going solely on the word of Brian's brother, who was a little strange himself.

I agreed to meet him for a drink. The only thing I knew was that I was looking for a guy with dirty blond hair. So I was hoping that there weren't too many guys that fit that vague description at the restaurant. Since he was a personal trainer, I was assuming that he would have a halfway decent body, giving me another clue of what I should be looking for. When I stepped out of the taxi into the cool October air, I surprisingly wasn't nervous in the least. I was looking at this as my "getting back in the game" date. Funny, that was how I viewed my first date with Travis and look what ended up happening. I walked into the restaurant and looked around, trying to act as if I really knew who I was looking for. "Hi, can I help you?" the hostess asked.

I decided to drop my "play it cool" façade and be honest. "Actually, I'm supposed to be meeting a blind date here. I have no clue who I'm looking for and I don't even want to be here, to tell you the truth."

She flashed a caring smile. "Been there, done that. I think the gentleman you are looking for is sitting right over there at the bar." She pointed to a surprisingly very handsome man with dirty blond wavy hair. As I approached him, I could tell that I was correct in my nice body theory. "Hey, Keith?" I asked.

He stood up and smiled. He wasn't very tall, only a few inches over my 5'4", making me regret wearing my higher heeled boots. He extended his hand to me. "Hi, Mia, it's really nice to meet you." I took the empty seat next to him at the bar. He ordered me a Malibu Bay Breeze and wasted no time jumping into conversation. I heard all about his job and how he had met Brian's brother, nothing that really interested me. Nonetheless, I shook my head and smiled, trying to act like I was somewhat interested. He was rambling on so much that my mind began to wander. I so wasn't ready for this dating thing. Was this my life now, date a million frogs before I find my Prince Charming? Deep down inside, I knew I had already found two Prince Charmings. Both of which were now out of my life. Was I asking too much in trying to find a third?

"So, Mia, Brian said that you went out with Travis Montgomery?"

Ouch, I think I would rather still be listening to his one-sided conversation instead of bringing up this topic. "Yeah, I did," I said in a very dismissing tone.

"Wow, what was that like? That guy was amazing in the Olympics."

"I don't know; he was just like any other guy, I guess." *Boy, was that a full blown lie.*

"Yeah, well that really was awful, what happened to him."

I nodded and looked away. Why couldn't he get that I didn't want to talk about this?

"I wonder if he's going to try and compete any more, now that he's walking again."

Suddenly my ears perked up as I choked on the sip of my drink I had just taken. "What? Who told you that?"

"One of the trainers that just started working at my gym used to work at Travis' gym. He still keeps in touch with him from time to time."

I felt like I had been kicked in the face. I had been the one that was there for Travis the most. I had been the one who was willing to wait for him. I had been the one that loved him more than anything and this was how I had to find out that he was walking again. Okay, maybe he didn't want to rekindle what we once had, maybe he had gotten over me a lot better than I had gotten over him, but I still thought that I deserved to hear that news from him. Even if it was just to wish him well. I sipped down my drink a little too fast, and quickly ordered another. Keith continued to ramble on as I continued to put away the drinks. "Mia, are you sure you don't want anything to eat?"

"No, no, I'm good." I wasn't good. I hadn't eaten since breakfast, the room was spinning, and I felt like I was going to throw up. But somehow, I didn't think that alcohol had anything to do with the nausea. I had basically put my entire life on hold for the past fifteen months, holding a secret vigil for some guy who could care less about me. *I hated him.* I rubbed my hand over the stubble on Keith's face. "Let's go back to your place." He raised his eyebrow at me and smiled. He stood up quickly and took my hand. I made a loud commotion, causing everyone to turn around and look when I walked into the bar stool and knocked it over. "Oops, sorry." I giggled as the busboy rushed over to pick it up. "I'm so sorry..." I squinted to read the name from the tag on his shirt. "Roger?" I said as if I were sounding out the words. "Is that your name - Roger?" I slurred. He just smiled and nodded. "You're pretty cute." He smiled again, this time turning a little red. Keith took me by the hand and led me out of the restaurant, making sure that I kept my balance along the way. The maître d' opened the door for us as we exited. I placed my hand on his shoulder. "Thank you, the drinks were really yummy."

"You're welcome, miss, I'm so glad you enjoyed them."

"I did, very much, and now I'm going to have sex for the first time in over a year, all because I sat around waiting for some stupid guy who didn't love me. Do you believe that?"

"Oh, I'm so sorry," The maître d' said, looking very uncomfortable.

"Mia-" Keith was pulling on my hand, trying to get me to stop.

"What! I'm talking to my new friend here."

I turned my attention back to the maître d'. "Travis Montgomery, do you know him?"

"Yes, the Olympic swimmer. Yes, I know who he is."

I got close to his ear and whispered, "He's a bad, bad man."

"Mia, come on." Keith gently wrapped his arm around me as he apologized to the maître d'.

We got into the taxi and Keith immediately asked for my address. I blurted it out as he repeated to the driver. "Oh, okay, so you'd rather go back to my place. Well, I say 'fuck it.' Let's be adventurous and do it right here." I moved closer and shoved my tongue down his throat.

He gently pushed me away. "Mia, believe me, you are a beautiful girl and I'm sure sex with you is amazing, but not in the condition you're in."

"Nobody loves me." I began to cry. He pulled me to him as I rested my head on his shoulder.

"Mia, I don't know what he did to you, but it's okay."

"No, it's not. I love him. I waited for him for over a year. Why doesn't he love me?" He gently rubbed my back as the tears flowed down my face and a huge snot bubble formed in my nose. *Thank God I really hadn't been into this guy.*

The taxi pulled up to my apartment and he walked me inside. He helped me take my coat off and walked me in the bedroom. I lay down on the bed while he took my shoes off. "Just go to bed and sleep it off, Mia. Everything will be better in the morning."

Chapter 61

Mia...

I rolled over in bed and placed the pillow over my head to ignore my ringing cell phone. "Shut up, shut up, shut up!" I shouted. My head was pounding, my mouth felt like it was stuffed with cotton, and my body felt like it just wanted to curl up and die. I closed my eyes and drifted back to sleep.

"Mia, wake up!" Juan's voice was like nails on a chalkboard.

My head felt like a lead weight as I tried to lift it from the pillow. Juan walked over to the window and opened the blinds. I quickly hid my eyes back into the pillow. "Close them!" I snapped.

He quickly abided by my wishes and closed them back up. "What the hell is the matter with you? I just tried calling you to see what kind of bagel that you wanted. They were out of egg, so –"

I put my hand up for him to stop talking. "Please don't talk about food."

"Are you hung over, Mia? Well, I would ask if you got lucky last night, but since you're still wearing your jeans, I'm guessing no!"

I covered my face with my hands and rubbed my eyes. Juan sat down on my bed and took my hand. "Mia, what happened?" I told him what I had learned about Travis last night, trying my best not to cry, but it was useless.

"Why didn't he tell me, Juan? I loved him so much. I would have done anything for him. This is such a slap in the face to everything I thought we had."

"I don't know, Mia." Juan looked at me sympathetically.

"Why can't I just get over him? It's been over a year and I still miss him like crazy."

Juan lay down next to me and hugged me until my cries subsided. "Mia, it's going to be okay. You've been through worse than this and you moved on. You of all people should know that this takes time." He pulled me to him and kissed me on the forehead.

"Yes, but with Eric it was so final. Travis is still here and I want him to be with him. He just doesn't want to be with me. I just feel like we never had any closure." I began to cry again.

"Mia, you've got to pull it together. It's like these past few years you've been in a fog. It lifted for a while when Travis came into your life and now you've just fallen deeper into it."

I knew he was right. I was a complete mess. I knew more than ever now that I had to get away. As much as I would miss Juan and my life here, I had to start fresh, leaving behind all of the memories this place had held.

"I know. I'm going to get it together, I promise."

He smiled at me and gave me a hug. "Good girl, now go wash your face and come have a bagel." I smiled and kissed him on the cheek as I slowly got out of bed.

"Oh and Mia - brush those teeth!" He always managed to make me laugh. I threw the pillow at his head and went into the bathroom to pull it together.

I headed out into the kitchen. Juan had a steaming hot cup of coffee waiting for me. It was heaven to my eyes. "If only you were straight, we would make the perfect couple." I giggled.

"Oh please, girl, if I were straight, we wouldn't get along this well. We would be fighting with the same set of problems most couples have."

"True." I sighed.

I grabbed my laptop from the counter and opened it.

"What are you doing?" Juan asked.

"Freeing myself from my ghost." I had been a social media and news outcast since Travis had left. I didn't want to know anything that was going on his life. Since I was going to start over, I felt that it was important for me face my past so I could move onto the future. I typed his name into the search bar. The butterflies began to flap around when I saw his name appearing on all of the different websites. Juan moved his chair around so he could look with me. I clicked on the first website. It was a video of a press conference with the various newscasters regarding his rehabilitation. I looked at the date; it was from September, one month ago.

I hit the arrow, feeling a wave of nausea as I waited for it to finish buffering. Juan took my hand, seemingly sensing my nervousness. The video began to play, starting somewhere in the middle. I felt the tears building up at the sight of him, looking exactly the same as when I last saw him.

"Mr. Montgomery, do you think you will compete again?" one of the reporters asked.

"I'm hoping that maybe….." I wasn't even comprehending his words. All I could focus on was the sound of his voice. I missed it so much, telling me he loved me, whispering in my ear. I bit my lip and continued to watch.

"Mr. Montgomery, I'm going to ask the question that the entire female population wants to know. Is there someone special holding the key to your heart?" one of the female reporters asked.

"Yes, there is." *Hit in the face like a ton of bricks.* I couldn't listen to it anymore. I quickly closed my laptop and pushed it away. Thank God, Juan was there to grab it or it would have been in a million pieces all over my kitchen. I took a deep breath, wishing I had never watched it.

Juan took my hand. "Mia, that right there, is your closure, baby cakes."

I nodded as I wiped away a tear. As much as I hated to admit it, he was right. Travis had clearly moved on; now it was my turn to do the same.

***

I called my mother later that afternoon and told her everything. I had made the decision to move back home and be closer to my family. I had a few job prospects already. I knew that I wouldn't be making nearly as much money as I was making now, but since the rent on an apartment would be half the price, it kind of equaled itself out. I looked around my tiny little apartment, thinking about how much I was going to miss it. I had happy memories here of me and Eric. If only he weren't taken away from me, my life would be happy right now. I would have been protected from the constant pain that came along with knowing Travis. I pulled out my laptop and began to type out an email to my landlord. *Subject: Termination of Lease.* Yes, it was finally time for me to break free from my self-pity mode and move forward, even though I didn't know exactly what I was headed for; I knew that it could only get better.

Chapter 62

Mia...

According to my lease agreement, I had to give two months' notice before I could vacate and get my security deposit back. I had gotten a job at a salon close by my mother's and sister's houses and would be starting there as soon as I moved back. With less than one month to go, I was becoming very anxious. I had signed a lease on an adorable apartment that was three times the size of the one that I had now and one-third of the price. Yes, I was finally starting to get excited over something. Ever since I had half watched that video of Travis, he seemed to be popping up all over my TV. The newscasters would gush over his recovery and his potential comeback into the Olympics, making me want to throw my remote right at my television. The final straw was when I had caught a glimpse of him with a woman on the entertainment channel, making me actually throw the remote. Instead of hitting the TV, it broke my little owl statue that Eric had given me for my sixteenth birthday. I carefully glued it back together and proudly displayed it once again, even with the crack running down his little nose.

It was a crazy Tuesday, one week before Thanksgiving and the holiday madness was just beginning. Mrs. Montgomery was my first client of the day. I hadn't broken the news to her yet that I was leaving and that she would have to find a new hairdresser. I knew that I should probably tell her soon, so she could start shopping around for a new one.

"Good morning, Mrs. Montgomery," I said with a smile.

"Good morning, Mia dear."

I was amazed with the rapport that I had with her; it was if I had never known her grandson at all. We never mentioned his name.

"How are things with you, dear?"

"Very well. I… um, have some news that I wanted to share with you."

"What's that, dear?"

"My last day at the salon will be December sixteenth. I'm moving back home."

"Oh." She looked at me sadly.

"It's going to be a good thing for me," I reassured her.

She smiled and nodded as if she didn't really believe me.

"So we're just doing your color today, right?" I said, quickly changing the subject.

She nodded.

"Okay, let me go mix that and I'll be right back."

I walked into the back to prepare the color. Juan was downing one last sip of his coffee.

"Did you tell the Ice Queen that you aren't going to be her personal stylist anymore?"

"Yes, I did and will you please stop referring to her as that. She's really a nice lady."

"Well, whatever. I don't know how you can even want to still do her hair after everything her grandson put you through."

"She has nothing to do with Travis' actions."

"Oh, Mia, if everyone could be as loving and forgiving as you, the world would be a much happier place."

I smiled. "Just remember that the next time you call me a bitch!"

"What am I going to do without you, baby cakes?"

"You won't be without me. I'll be taking up residency in your spare bedroom a lot, when I need to get my city fix."

"It's yours! Let's go pick out a comforter set and curtains," he joked. "Seriously, Mia, you know that you will always have a place to stay and a job, if you ever decide to come back."

"I know." I began to feel myself tearing up. "You'll always be my best bud."

"That's right and don't you ever forget that; especially when some other wannabe queen tries to steal you away from that Dolly Parton Steel Magnolia's salon that you're going to be working at."

"You are too much!" I shook my head and laughed as I walked back out to Mrs. Montgomery, who was just finishing up a conversation with my assistant Abby.

"Yes, my grandson is coming home for the first time in over a year. I'm very excited."

I stopped dead in my tracks and gripped the bowl of color tightly in my shaking hand. Abby must have seen the look on my face at the mention or indirect mention of his name. She hurried up and took the color from me and placed it at my station. I tried to pull it together and not appear how I was actually feeling – flustered. *Mia, stop it! It's over and you shouldn't be acting this way.* I pulled it together as best as I could and applied her color. I was so happy when I finished up with her. I wanted to grill Abby on the information that Mrs. Montgomery had shared with her.

I waited patiently for Abby to finish up with rinsing out a client. I took her hand and pulled her into the break room. "What did Mrs. Montgomery say about Travis?"

"Mia!" Juan shouted, startling me as he walked in the room.

"What!"

"Why the hell do you even care what she has to say about him? Remember your closure?"

"Yes, I know, but I'm just curious."

Juan looked at me and shook his head in disapproval. "Okay, Abby, what did –"

"Don't tell her, Abby." Juan demanded.

"Will you just shut up? Don't you have someone else that you can be harassing?"

"Mia, I'm not going to be an enabler and let you listen to anything about him."

"Good, then leave and you won't have to hear what she says and then you won't be an enabler." I raised my eyebrows at him.

"Suit yourself," he said as he exited the room.

I waved my hand at Juan, dismissing anything he had to say. I listened closely as Abby began to speak. "She just said that he's coming back."

"She didn't say when or for how long?"

"She said he was coming back in a few weeks. I think she was going to say more and then you came walking out."

"Darn!"

"Abby, can you go rinse out Tammy?" Juan interrupted.

"Yeah, no problem." Abby left the room as Juan stood there staring at me.

"What!"

"Mia, watching that video did nothing for you; you're still not over him, are you?"

"Yes, I am."

He looked at me and smiled as if he didn't believe me.

"You know, he's probably bringing his new girlfriend home to meet his parents. I wonder if he tells her that she means the world to him and that he loves her more than anything...." I was rambling on while Juan just shook his head and laughed at me.

"What's so funny?"

"Yeah, you are *so* over him," Juan said as he rolled his eyes.

Okay, maybe he was right. Maybe I wasn't over Travis. I didn't think that I would ever be. Travis Montgomery had a hold on me and even though he had moved on, my feelings for him were just as strong as they had been when I had first met him.

Chapter 63

Travis...

I was excited and at the same time nervous to be returning back to New York. Los Angeles was great, but it wasn't home. I felt as if I was finally able to return and live my life the way that I had always intended, minus the one person that I wanted to live that life with most. I had a lot of exciting things on the horizon, with a ton of meetings scheduled as soon as I got back to New York. First of which was meeting with Carol Reicher, a commercial real estate agent at one of the top agencies in the city. I knew now more than ever, after everything I had been through, that this swim school for handicapped children was a venture that I was made to take on. I was really excited to be finally getting it underway after all these years. I only wished that the one person who had been so supportive and cheering me on to do it could be by my side to see it happen. I was still considering competing for a shot in the next Olympics, even though the media already had me in it and taking home every medal possible, I was still a little unsure. I had planned on putting any more Olympic aspirations behind me once I met Mia. I had wanted to focus on other things, mainly being her husband and having a family together. But now since that was out of the question, the Olympics just might be a nice distraction. I concentrated on the luggage spinning around on the conveyer belt. It had only been seventeen months and twelve days since I told her goodbye. So much had happened in that short time, but one thing would remain the same no matter what - she would always have the biggest piece of my heart.

I finally grabbed my bag and stepped out of the airport. The cold December air hit me in the face, making me realize the stark difference in temperature between New York and L.A. My flight had been delayed and it was well after midnight when the taxi finally pulled up to my apartment building. I was greeted immediately by Charlie, my doorman. "Travis, welcome home!" His smile was a mile wide as he extended his hand to me.

I walked into my apartment for the very first time in over a year. I looked around and was filled with memories. Memories of the time spent here with Mia. I walked into my bedroom and stared at the picture of the two of us on my dresser. I needed to get her out of my head, but I just didn't know how. I thought about her every single minute that I was away, but being in this place that held so many memories of the two of us was even harder to bear. I could still see her lying in my bed. I could still hear her contagious laugh and I could still feel her tender touch. I put the picture down and I couldn't help but notice the little black box sitting on my dresser. My stomach clenched when I opened it up; it was a painful reminder of what should have been. I placed it back down, almost missing the envelope with my name on it that was sitting right beside it. It was no doubt Mia's handwriting. I took a deep breath as I opened it up

Dear Travis:

It's only been two weeks since you left, but it feels like eternity. It would have always been yes and it always will be. I told you that I would love you forever and I meant it.

Yours always ~

Mia

"Forever was too long, baby," I whispered to myself. I read the piece of paper over and over again, wishing that it wasn't too late, wishing that things were different between us. Most of all, wishing that Mia were mine again.

***

I awoke in the morning, feeling like I had finally gotten a good night's sleep for the first time in over a year. It amazed me how my body somehow knew it was finally home. I was headed to the gym and then to sign the papers to finalize the business deal at Carol's office; she had made special arrangements to meet up with me on a Sunday so that I could get it started right away.

I made a quick cup of coffee, changed, and was just about to head out the door when I suddenly remembered something else I needed to do today. I grabbed the ring box from my dresser. I needed to get rid of it. It was just a painful reminder of how my life could have been. I stuck the box in my gym bag, hoping that I would have time to stop off at the jeweler at some point in the day.

I had been keeping up on my fitness routine while in Los Angeles and was almost back to where I had been before my accident. I knew once I started working with my old trainer, Dave, I would be back to where I wanted to be in no time. He had moved to a new gym, but I didn't care; he was the best there was, so I was willing follow him anywhere.

I took the taxi ride across town to the gym. I walked into the lobby and was greeted by an over enthusiastic red-headed girl.

"Oh, Mr. Montgomery, it's so nice to meet you," she said, extending her hand to me and eyeing me up and down. I wanted to make it clear that I wasn't the least bit interested. I just nodded and smiled. She picked up the phone. "Dave, Mr.

Montgomery is here." Within seconds, the door flew open and Dave appeared. "Travis, my man!" He shook my hand and quickly wrapped his arm around me. "You look great, man," he said.

"Thanks, I'm still not feeling where I should be at physically."

"Oh, don't you worry about that, bro, I will have your ass whipped back in shape in no time!"

"I'm depending on that, man."

After an intense two-hour workout, we were finally wrapping up. My body was sore, but it felt great.

"So will you be coming back tomorrow for some more torture?" Dave asked.

"Definitely."

"Oh, Travis, I wanted to introduce you to Keith." I extended my hand to the short stocky guy who had just entered the weight room.

"Wow, Travis Montgomery, this is an honor, man!" he said.

"Thanks, great meeting you too."

"You know, we have a mutual acquaintance," he said.

"Oh yeah, who's that?" I asked.

"Cute little blonde girl. What was her name? Oh, Mia."

Suddenly my ears perked up at the sound of her name. "How do you know Mia?" I demanded.

"She's a friend of a friend. Beautiful girl, but man, is she messed up. What the heck did you do to her?"

"What the hell are you talking about?" I was losing my patience, fast.

"Well, when I bought up your name, she just lost it; got totally wrecked, I mean drunk off her ass wrecked. She is one fine-looking piece of ass. You're a lucky guy to have been hittin' that. I'm going to be honest, I wouldn't have minded fucking her myself."

I could feel the anger coursing through my veins over the way he was talking about Mia. I grabbed him by the shirt. "You are so lucky that you didn't tell me that you did, because I swear to God I would have had to kick your ass right now."

He held up his hands in defeat. "Bro, calm down, nothing happened. Sorry, man."

I took a deep breath. I was still raging inside. "I'll see you tomorrow, Dave."

"Yeah, okay." Dave was looking a little shocked over my abrupt reaction.

I took a deep breath, trying to calm myself down before walking out to shower. The thought of him touching Mia in any way made me want to kill him.

I stepped into the shower and tried my best to figure everything out. Why the hell would Mia even be associating with that guy? The only thing that I could think of was that he was full of shit and making everything up. He could have easily read about my relationship with Mia and used it in a conversation. It wasn't like it wasn't plastered all over the internet. Little did he know, that was a topic of my life that was totally off limits.

Chapter 64

Mia...

I had made a huge dent in the packing process, but still had a long way to go. My mother and stepfather were a godsend; they had spent the last two weekends at my place, helping me out. It made me wonder: how the heck did I fit all of this stuff into this tiny little apartment? I had to stop and pull myself together, the few times that I had come across some of Eric's items. I made sure that I tucked those things safely away, never wanting to part with them. It made me think about how different my life would be right now if only he were here. I would have been married, probably with my two kids that I had always dreamed about having. I would have been happy, instead of running away and trying to rebuild a life for myself.

I had enticed Juan and Victor into giving up their Sunday morning to help me out, by promising to take them out to dinner later in the week. I was hoping that they could help me get my bedroom closet at least a quarter of the way packed. Although I think Juan was having more fun picking apart my wardrobe, making a comment about every article of clothing that he would place in the box.

"Could you just shut up and pack?"

He shook his head and laughed. "Just wait until she moves back to the boondocks, Victor. She'll be dressing in muumuus."

"Haha….you are so funny! Just for that, maybe I'll find a new friend to be my shopping buddy."

"Oh, Mia, you know I'm just kidding with you! Besides, you will never find another friend with my fashion sense."

"Less talking and more packing!" I yelled. "I have to be at Mrs. Montgomery's by one!"

Mrs. Montgomery hadn't been feeling well and hadn't been in the salon in two weeks. She had asked me if I would mind stopping over to do her hair for her. Since I was only going to be at the salon for one more week, I agreed to go over, also to allow me to say my goodbyes to her.

"Really, Mia, why the heck are you giving up your Sunday to go over there?" Juan asked.

"Because she asked me to and I feel bad. Besides, I want to say goodbye to her before I move."

Juan rolled his eyes and shook his head at me. "Whatever, Mia! She's just a painful reminder of the one person that you're trying to forget."

I walked over to my jewelry box. I wanted to go through it and get rid of some of the old costume jewelry that I no longer wore. I began to throw away some of the old mismatched earrings that I knew I would never wear again into the trash. I briefly closed my eyes and took a deep breath when I pulled out the gold heart necklace that Travis had given me a few Christmases ago. I had buried it in the bottom of the jewelry box so that I wouldn't have to look at it; this was now another very painful reminder of what could have been. I turned it over and read the inscription. "Yeah, okay," I said sarcastically.

"What?" Juan asked in confusion. He walked over to see what I had in my hand. "Mia, put it away! Get rid of it! Remember your closure?" He went to take it from my hand, but I wouldn't let him.

I lifted my hair and clasped it on my neck. "It's okay, I want to wear this so I can always look down and be reminded of what a sucker I was for him and never fall into that trap with any other man."

"Oh, Mia, what am I going to do with you?"

I shook my head and smiled. "Nothing, I am a hopeless fool – don't you know that?" I sure was hopeless, still hopelessly still in love with a man who didn't love me back.

***

The elevator doors closed as I made my way up to Mrs. Montgomery's apartment. I was in such a good mood, thinking about the progress that we had made this morning with my closet. I was another step closer to my new life. I was immediately greeted by Bernice, Mrs. Montgomery's maid.

"Mia, it's so nice to see you again. It's a shame that we only get to see one another when Charlotte is under the weather."

"Yes, I know. Is she feeling any better?"

She shrugged her shoulders. "She says she is, but who knows? Maybe once she gets her hair done, that will help."

I smiled as I made my way into the living room where Mrs. Montgomery had her nose buried in a book. She finally looked up at me and a smile appeared on her face. "Mia, dear, how are you?" She stood up and wrapped her arms around me.

"I'm good. How are you feeling?"

"Much better, dear, but the doctor said he still wants me taking it easy."

"Well, let's get you beautiful so you'll be all ready to go out when the time is right."

She smiled and patted my shoulder as we made our way to her kitchen to work on her hair.

I was feeling myself getting upset by the time I was done and getting ready to say my goodbyes to her. I was truly going to miss her. She had become a very special part of my life. She walked me to the door and wrapped her arms around me. "I will never find another stylist as good as you."

"Aw, thank you, Mrs. Montgomery."

"Please make sure you come and see me when you come back into the city."

"I definitely will."

"Oh, wait one second, dear." She walked back into the living room and came out with an envelope.

"What's this?" I asked.

"It's just a little something to get you started with your new life and to say thank you for always being so accommodating to me."

I gasped when I opened up the envelope to find a check for three thousand dollars. "Mrs. Montgomery, this is so very kind, but I can't accept this."

"Mia, I will be insulted if you don't. You are very special to me. You're like the granddaughter that I never had. You have been through so much, first with your fiancé, then with Travis. Please, dear, take it. No one deserves it more than you."

"Mrs. Mont –" She waved her hand at me to stop me from talking.

"Thank you so much. You have no idea how much I appreciate it."

I hugged her tightly and began to cry. "Just be happy, Mia. You deserve nothing but happiness, dear."

"Well, that's my plan. Hopefully I'll succeed," I said as I wiped the tears from my face.

She took my hands in hers and I could see tears forming in her eyes. "I have a good feeling that you will." I gave her a smile before heading out the door. The tears rolled down my face as I waited for the elevator. I wiped my face and tried pulling it together as I heard the dinging of the elevator. My stomach dropped along with my jaw when the elevator door opened and I was staring into Travis' eyes.

Chapter 65

Travis...

I was speechless. I had to do a double take to make sure I was seeing right. But there was no doubt, it was her, even more beautiful than I remembered. "Mia, how are you?"

She stared at me coldly; the look in her eyes was so different from the Mia I used to know; the Mia that I loved and still loved with all my heart. She bit her lip and shook her head. She was silent, staring at me coldly. "Why didn't you tell me?" she finally shouted.

"Mia, what are you talking about?"

I could see the tears building in her eyes. "I was your biggest supporter. I tried to be there for you every step of the way and I had to find out that you're walking again from a virtual stranger. Regardless if you wanted to be with me or not, I think you could have least picked up a phone and told me that news yourself."

"Mia, I'm sorry. I just didn't want to intrude in your life."

"Oh yeah, because my life has been so exciting since the day you left. Well, I'm glad to see that you did it, Travis, but other than that, I have nothing else to say to you."

She pushed past me and got into the elevator. I grabbed her by the arm and pulled her back out. "Ouch, Travis -stop it!" she yelled.

"Listen to me, Mia, I did what I had to do for you because I loved you. I still fuckin' love you so much that it hurts. You have everything that you want now and even though I'm not happy, I know that you are and that's all that matters - that's all that ever mattered." I couldn't resist kissing her softly on the cheek. I had to catch my breath as my lips grazed her velvety soft skin. My eyes widened when I focused my attention on the gold heart hanging around her neck. She quickly placed her hand over it, almost as if she was embarrassed for me to see it. I stared into her eyes, looking for some kind of warmth, but there was none, only sadness.

"You will always own my heart, Mia, forever," I whispered in her ear.

"Really? I'm sure your girlfriend wouldn't be too happy to hear that," she said as she stepped into the elevator. She looked at me one last time before putting her head down, just as the elevator door closed.

I hadn't a clue what she was talking about or why the hell she was so angry with me. I stood in the hallway just outside my grandmother's door, trying to pull it together. I finally felt composed enough to enter and was greeted immediately by my grandmother's maid, Bernice.

"Travis!" She smiled and wrapped her arms around me. I smiled back and kissed her on the cheek. "Your grandmother is going to be so happy to see you!"

I walked into the living room, where my grandmother was sitting on the couch, wiping her eyes with a tissue and finally looked up. "Travis, you have just made my day!" She got up and hugged me tightly. She looked me over, up and down, as more tears formed in her eyes. "I knew that you could do it, Travis. Oh, my goodness, I'm going to go through a whole box of tissues today, between you and Mia."

"Mia?" *Why was she crying with Mia?*

"Yes, dear, she was just here doing my hair for me. She's moving in a week and we both had a good cry when we said our goodbyes."

"Oh," I said, trying to play it off like the mere sound of her name didn't pain me.

We both took a seat on the couch and began to catch up. She listened closely as I told her all about California.

"Well, I'm just glad you're home now."

"Yeah, I am too."

"Why don't you stay for dinner?"

"Oh, I can't. I have to get to the jeweler before they close."

"Oh?" She raised her eyebrow at me.

"Yeah, I need to get rid of a painful memory." I opened my gym bag that I had been carrying around all day and pulled out the box. I opened the lid and my grandmother's eyes widened. "This was meant for Mia, a long time ago, before I messed everything up."

She looked at me sadly. "Oh, Travis, dear. Have you tried talking to her since you've gotten back?"

"I actually just ran into her in the hallway, would you believe that?"

"And?"

"Nothing. It's too late now anyway."

"Why is it too late? She's only moving an hour away, Travis, and who knows; maybe you could talk her out of it."

"Yeah, well somehow, I don't think her husband would appreciate that."

My grandmother looked at me strangely. "Her husband?"

"Yeah, it's okay, I'm slowly getting over it. Stacy told me all about her husband and her baby. It's what I wanted for her, so I can't complain about it."

My grandmother furrowed her brows and looked at me in confusion. "What are you talking about, Travis? Mia's not married and she certainly doesn't have a baby."

"But Stacy ran into her a few months ago. She said she was having lunch with some guy and she was holding a baby – Jackson."

"Jackson?" my grandmother asked.

"That was Mia's name that she had picked out if she ever had a son. She told Stacy that the baby's name was Jackson."

"Well, I don't know whose baby it was, but I can tell you for certain, it wasn't Mia's. I have been going to her faithfully to get my hair done and I know for a fact that she has *never* been pregnant!"

Now, I was more confused than ever. I snapped the lid on the box and shoved it in my coat pocket. "I have to get going." I gave my grandmother a kiss on the cheek and sprinted out the door.

"Travis," my grandmother shouted just as I reached the door. "Good luck!" Her smile was a mile wide.

I nearly got run over trying to flag down a taxi. I jumped in the back and gave the driver the address to Mia's apartment.

I hadn't a clue what I was going to say to her, but I didn't care. I needed to see if she really meant it when she said she would wait for me forever.

Chapter 66

Mia...

I arrived home and jumped into the shower. I was more confused than ever by Travis' bizarre behavior. *I had everything that I wanted now? Was he serious?* Little did he know that the one and only thing I wanted was him! And, how dare he say that he still loved me when he was going to press conferences professing his love for someone else. I wrapped myself in a towel and sat on the toilet, trying to clear my mind. If I ever wanted closure, I had to watch the rest of that video and hear it with my own ears, just exactly who the "lucky girl" was in Travis' life. I quickly threw on my sweats and scoured through the boxes on my kitchen table for my laptop. I typed Travis' name in the search engine and found the video that Juan and I had watched a few months ago. But this time, as much as it hurt, I was going to watch the entire thing. My stomach clenched when I listened to the reporter ask the question:

"Mr. Montgomery, I'm going to ask the question that the entire female population wants to know, is there someone special holding the key to your heart?"

"Yes, there is."

"Do you mind me asking who she is?"

"She's actually no longer in my life. But she will always remain the number one person in my heart. She believed in me when I didn't believe in myself and I will always love and appreciate her for that. And I truly believe that she is the only reason that I'm walking

right now." His voice turned almost into a whisper and his eyes became much more emotional. *"Thank you, Mia."*

I covered my mouth in shock. "Oh my God!" None of this was making sense to me. If Travis didn't have someone new in his life, then why didn't he call me and tell about his good news? I was more confused than ever. I was done playing guessing games. I needed to confront him immediately to find out exactly what was going on inside that head of his. I quickly changed into my jeans and threw on my coat. I opened the door and gasped when I saw Travis standing on the other side.

The sight of him standing in my doorway stirred every emotion possible inside of me. His stare was intense as if he were looking at me for the very first time with those beautiful chameleon eyes that I missed so much. We were both silent as I opened the door further and he entered. All of my emotions that I had been holding in for the past year and a half were coming to the surface. I was speechless. All I could do was grab his face and kiss him. His lips on mine and his arms wrapped around me were like an instant adhesive, quickly mending the pieces of my broken heart. He held my face in his hand and looked at me intently. "I missed you so much, Mia. I thought about you every single day."

"Why didn't you tell me Travis?"

"Mia, there was no one that I wanted to share that news with more than you, but I thought you were married and had a baby."

"What? Why would you think that?"

"Stacy said that she ran into you a while back with some guy and a baby and the baby's name was Jackson."

I quickly thought back to the day that I had run into Stacy. Never in a million years did I expect her to make that assumption. I took a deep breath and shook my head. "That was Eric's partner and his baby - not mine!"

"I didn't know. I thought you were happy and I didn't want to do anything to interfere with that happiness."

"You stupid, stupid man. Did you really think that I would have gotten over you that quickly? Do you really think that I would have gotten over you at all?"

He looked down at me with such passion in his eyes that my insides screamed for him. He kissed me vigorously as he moved his tongue around my mouth. "You have no clue how much I want you right now," he said.

"It can't be any more than I want you."

I smiled and took his hand, leading him through the maze of boxes and into my bedroom. I took off my coat and threw it on the floor. He quickly lifted my shirt over my head and removed my bra as he leaned down and began to tease my breasts with his tongue. He unbuttoned my jeans and removed them along with my underwear. I took off his jacket and his shirt and moved my hands up and down his bare back, reacquainting myself with every inch of his perfect body. He had his hands on my waist and stared at my naked body as if he were looking at it for the very first time. "I missed this beautiful body so much," he whispered in my ear as his tongue cascaded over my neck. I let out a cry of pleasure when he inserted his fingers inside of me. I wanted him so badly. "Travis, why are your pants still on? I need you now."

He pushed me down on the bed and kissed me hard. He trailed his tongue down my stomach, stopping between my legs. I gripped my hands tightly to the sheets to control my quivering body from his pleasurable assault. I tried to catch my breath as I allowed his tongue to have total control of my body. My entire body quivered as I let out a loud scream.

"Travis, please, I need to feel you inside of me." He looked up at me as I continued breathing heavily. I watched in anticipation as he took off his pants and boxers. *God, I missed him so much.* I wrapped my legs around his waist as he entered me, letting out a loud pleasurable groan. I pulled him closer to me as he moved around, meeting him with each move that he made. He began to slow down a little. "Mia, I have to take this slow; you feel too good and it's been too long."

He ran his tongue down my neck. "Travis, please don't stop. I need you inside of me. I need to feel all of you tonight, every last bit of you."

I raised my hips to meet him as his thrusts became more urgent. I ran my hands up and down his back. I pulled him closer to me as he continued to move. I was feeling every emotion imaginable. "Travis, I love you so much," I whispered in his ear.

He lifted his head and tried to catch his breath. "I love you too, baby." He rolled over on his side and pulled me toward him with my back up against him. He gently kissed my back, reached his hands around me, and caressed my breast. I let out a pleasurable cry when I felt the fullness of him inside of me once again. "I missed you so much, Mia," he whispered in my ear. The sound of his voice and the feel of his thrusts were all too much. "Oh my God, Travis!" I screamed. My whole body completely melted around him. He continued to move in and out of me while I tried to come back from the state of ecstasy that he had just put my body in. "I want you to do it again, Mia. I want to know that I'm the only one that could ever make you feel this way." He turned me on my back and hovered over top of me. I was breathless as I looked up at him. He had never looked sexier as he stared down at me like he was looking at me for the very first time.

He entered me once again. His movements were quick and hard. I placed my hands on his shoulders and met him with each eager thrust. My insides began to awaken once again. I let out another scream just as I felt the warmth of him filling me up at the same exact time. He buried his face into my hair and tried to catch his breath.

He rolled over on his back and pulled me towards him. "Mia, that was the best sex I ever had."

I rested my head on his chest and looked up at him. "Why, thank you!" I giggled.

"Come here, you." He pulled me on top of him and pushed my hair out of my face. "I missed that laugh so much. I missed everything about you." I rested my head on his chest, unable to wipe the smile from my face. *Yes, it was really happening. I wasn't dreaming. Travis was here and he was all mine.* I kissed him gently on the lips, knowing this was right where I wanted to be, in Travis' arms -forever.

Chapter 67

Travis...

I wanted to give her the ring so badly tonight. We had wasted too much time. I didn't want to waste any more.

I played with her hair while she laid her head on my chest.

"Are you hungry?" I asked.

"A little, but I don't want to leave your arms," she said as she nuzzled closer to me.

I kissed her on the head and got up to dress. She looked surprised. "Hey, where are you going?"

"We're going out to dinner. Get dressed," I said.

"Well, I will sacrifice food for more sex," she said as she sat up and kissed my back.

I turned around and smiled at her. "Who says you have to sacrifice anything? There will be plenty of time for sex later."

"Okay, fine." She got up and dressed. We headed out into the cold December air. I grabbed her hand and we began to walk. "Travis, where are we going? It's freezing!"

"I'll warm you up." I wrapped my arm around her. She leaned her head into my chest and we took the short walk to the place of our very first date, the Italian restaurant up the street from her apartment.

She smiled when we reached the door. "Hey, I remember this place."

We walked in and the hostess' smile was a mile wide. "Travis Montgomery, wow!" She led us back through the maze of tables. I looked over to find that the table that Mia and I had sat at the last time we were here was empty. "Can we sit over there?" I asked.

"Sure, not a problem," she said as she led us over to the out of the way table by the fireplace.

"I think I'll be daring and have a glass of wine," Mia joked as we sat down.

"Go for it." I couldn't stop staring at her. I couldn't believe she was here with me. I thought I had lost her forever.

The waitress came over and took our order. "I ordered the same exact thing that I did the last time we were here," Mia said.

"Well, hopefully you will be able to keep it down this time."

"Haha, you are so funny," she joked.

"So, Mia Taylor, what have you been up to this past year and a half?"

"Hmm...let's see. I've been missing someone like crazy. Other than that, not very much."

I smiled. "That's funny because I was missing someone like crazy too."

"Oh yeah, is it that girl that I saw you with on the entertainment channel a few months ago?"

"Who?"

She went on to explain to me about what she had seen and how she ended up throwing her remote at the TV because of it.

"I have no clue who that was. For all I know, that picture could have been from years ago." I hadn't been with anyone since Mia. I didn't want anyone else. "Mia, I swear there has been no one since you."

She smiled. "So I was your first, since...."

I smiled and nodded. "Well, I am honored, Travis." She giggled.

"Okay, my turn. How do you know that roid head at the gym?"

"Who?"

"Some asshole guy at the gym that says he knows you."

She began to blush and was unable to control her laughter. She went on to tell me about her blind date with him and how she lost it when he had told her that I was walking again. "It was the second most embarrassing night of my life."

"Oh yeah, what was the first?"

"Our first date. The only difference was I didn't care about what he thought of me."

We had finished up with eating and I still hadn't asked her yet. I didn't want to do it here in front of all these people. I had to find the perfect moment.

We walked out of the restaurant and headed back to her apartment. "It's snowing!" Mia exclaimed. She looked up at the sky and smiled.

I waited until we were walking up the stairs to the front porch of her apartment building, when it struck me that now was the perfect moment. "Hey, Mia, a lot of stuff went down on this porch, you know?"

She turned around and looked at me strangely. "What do you mean?"

"Well, you threw up in front of me for the very first time. I do believe that I got my first kiss on the cheek from you right on this very step. So, I thought it would only be fitting if I did this here." She pushed her hair behind her ear and stared at me intently as the snow continued to fall. "You have no clue how hard these past few months have been for me, thinking that someone else had given you the one thing that I know you want the most. I want to be that guy. I want to be the one who makes all your dreams come true. And now, I can give you everything that you deserve. Mia, I love you so much and I want to spend the rest of my life with you. I don't want to waste any more time, so I was wondering, would it still be yes?" I pulled out the box from my pocket and opened the lid.

She covered her mouth with her hand and began to cry. "Oh my God, Travis. Yes, yes, yes!" she shouted as tears streamed down her face.

I slid the ring on her finger. "This should have been on your finger a long time ago, but now it's finally right. Now I know it's forever. There are no more obstacles in our way."

"I can't believe this is really happening," she said as she looked down at the ring.

"Well, it is and I'm not ever going to let you go again, even if you want to."

She shook her head and smiled. "Well, you don't ever have to worry about that because I will *never* want to."

I hugged her tightly. "You are the love of my life, Mia Taylor. From the day that you cut my neck, I knew there was something special about you."

She laughed. "Out of all of the salons in the city, you had to come walking into mine, Travis Montgomery."

"Really? Casablanca, Mia?"

"Hey, you knew where I got that line from? And here I wanted you to think I was being original." She laughed. "But you know, I'm so happy that you did, even if you were a complete jerk to me."

"Yeah, well, what can I say? That was the old Travis. You changed me. You turned me into a better person and I'm so grateful to you for that."

"I can't wait to be your wife, Travis."

"Me neither, baby." Mia Montgomery; just hearing that name in my head made me smile.

Chapter 68

Mia...

I was happy once again. In fact, the happiest I had ever been and something deep inside told me that this time it wouldn't be fleeting; it was forever. Travis and I were planning our wedding in June or should I say my mother, Travis' mother, and Tressa were planning it. They were so excited about putting together a big fancy wedding. If it were up to Travis and me, we would have gotten married right away. I decided to let them have their fun, chiming in from time to time, when one of them would get a little too over the top with their ideas. I had put my plans to move back home on hold temporarily and had moved in with Travis. We had planned on revisiting that plan once we were married and began to start a family. Travis' Christmas present to me was another trip to Saint Lucia for Valentine's Day and unlike last time, this time we actually went. Travis was right; it was like heaven on earth. We were staying at one of the nicest resorts on the island. We had a beautiful suite with its own very private pool overlooking the beautiful aquamarine ocean.

I rolled over in the bed to reach for him, only he wasn't there. I opened my eyes to the bright sunlight coming in and saw him, standing on the balcony in just his shorts. I smiled at the sight of his perfect form. I found that I never tired of staring at his flawless body. I stretched out before hopping out of bed to join him.

"Good morning," I said as I stood behind him and wrapped my arms around him.

"Good morning, beautiful girl." I closed my eyes and rested my head on his back, taking in the warm ocean breeze.

"Do you want to go for a morning swim?"

"Sure," I said as I grazed my lips over his bare back.

He turned around to hug me. "Go get your bathing suit on."

"Really?" I didn't see a point in putting on my bathing suit when it was probably going to be taken off in just a matter of minutes anyway.

He pressed his forehead against mine. "Well, unless you want to skinny dip in front of all of those people on the beach."

"You mean swim in the ocean?" I felt my nerves getting the best of me.

"Yeah!"

"Um, no, that's okay, I'll pass."

He pulled me closer. "Aw, come on, you can't come all the way here and not swim in that beautiful water."

"Travis, I draw the line with the pool."

"Please, do it for me." He had the most adorable look on his face, making me unable to say "no."

"Fine!"

I washed my face, brushed my teeth, and reluctantly put on my bathing suit and headed down to the beach with him. It was still pretty early, so there weren't many people on the beach yet.

"I'm going in and getting out. Two minutes, that's it!"

He smiled and shook his head at my reluctance. We walked into the crystal clear water and I had to admit, I was in awe over its beauty. I stopped once the water reached my knees. He yanked on my hand to get me to come in further. I shook my head and didn't budge.

"Travis, no!" I protested when he picked me up and carried me in further. He ignored my objection and continued walking in deeper.

We finally stopped just at where the waves were cascading over my shoulders. I could feel myself shaking and he must have noticed too. "Mia, just relax and enjoy it."

"Well, I can't enjoy it. Who knows what's swimming around us."

He laughed at my edginess and wrapped his arms around my waist. "I love you so much, Mia."

"I love you too," I said, kissing the saltwater that was on his lips. I was finally relaxing a bit, taking in the warm sunshine and the gentle waves. "I guess you were right; it is beautiful," I said, looking around at the turquoise water surrounding me.

My arms were wrapped around him and my head was leaning on his shoulder. "This should have been our honeymoon."

"Nope, Paris. Remember your bucket list?"

"You spoil me, Travis."

"You deserve to be spoiled. And you just allowed me to check something off mine."

"What's that?"

"Getting you into the ocean."

"It was done under protest," I joked.

"Mia?"

"Hmm…" I was so relaxed I didn't want to lift my head from his shoulder.

"Thank you."

I finally lifted my head from his shoulder and looked at him. "For what?"

"For being my everything, for always believing in me, and for always keeping me in that big heart of yours. I can't wait to spend the rest of my life with you."

"Travis, this is the rest of our life. We are living out our happily ever after, right now. We don't have to wait for anything. I am yours forever. The only thing that is going to change in a few months is you will be my husband and I will be your wife and I can't wait for that day. But if there's one thing that I've learned over these past few years, it's to live for today and appreciate every single second, so you never have any regrets. And I have none, Travis. I'm right where I want to be with the person I most want to be with."

He kissed me softly on the lips. "You're right where you want to be?" he joked as he looked around at the water surrounding us.

"Yes, I am. As long as it's with you, I don't care where I am."

"You are my girl forever, Mia."

"Forever," I repeated.

He pressed his lips to mine and kissed me deeply. "I think we should continue this back in the room. What do you think?" he asked with a sexy grin.

I shook my head and smiled. "I couldn't agree with you more." I looked off into the horizon and saw a big wave beginning to form. I gasped and wrapped my arms around him.

He laughed at my edginess. "Oh, come on, Mia, we've been through worse than that little stinkin' wave." He smiled.

"Yeah, I guess we have." I watched as it moved closer.

"It's okay; I'm never going to let anything happen to you. You trust me, right?"

I smiled and held onto him tightly as the wave came closer. "Always."

Beth Rinyu

***

One month had passed since our trip to Saint Lucia, which meant we were one month closer to our wedding. Travis' birthday was tomorrow and I still had to figure out what to do to make it extra special for him; but for the moment, I couldn't focus on anything; my nerves had gotten the best of me. I sat on the bed, rocking back and forth as I stared at the clock; this had been the longest five minutes of my life. I jumped when I saw Travis standing in the doorway.

"Hey, what are you doing home? I thought you had that meeting?"

"I did and it got done early, so I thought that maybe I would spend the rest of the day with you."

I smiled through my edginess, which he picked up on right away. "What's the matter, Mia?"

I took a deep breath and decided to spill it. "Travis, when we went to Saint Lucia, I forgot to bring my birth control pills and - "

"Oh my God, Mia. You're pregnant?"

"I don't know." I looked at the clock. "I'm about to find out in about two minutes, though." His smile was a mile wide. He pulled me close and hugged me tightly. "You're not upset?"

He pressed his forehead against mine. "Mia, why would I be upset? The woman that I love more than anything is going to have my baby. I'm the happiest man in the world right now."

"Well, it's not one hundred percent yet. But I'm late and I threw up this morning." I looked at the clock. I stood up from the bed and grabbed his hand. "Are you ready to find out with me?"

He smiled and nodded. I stopped just before we entered the bathroom. "Travis, you won't be upset if *I'm not,* will you?"

He was still smiling as he shook his head. "Remember, Mia, practice makes perfect and if you're not, we'll just have to keep practicing until you are."

"I love you so much, Travis."

"I love you too."

I took a deep breath "Are you ready to find out?" I asked.

"Never been readier...."

Epilogue

Mia...

I semi-permanently retired my role as hairstylist to take on the new roles of wife and mother. These were the most rewarding titles that I could have ever imagined. I had given birth to Jackson Samuel Montgomery eight months ago and I couldn't imagine how I had ever lived without him. Despite being three months pregnant on my wedding day, it was perfect. It was the type of wedding that I had dreamed of ever since I was a little girl. We honeymooned in Paris and even though I was throwing up every morning with morning sickness, I wouldn't have traded it for anything.

Travis had given up any further aspirations of Olympic medals and was focusing his time on running his swim school and being the best husband and father that anyone could ask for. We moved into our new home when I was seven months pregnant. It was a beautiful four-bedroom colonial, with a built-in swimming pool, of course. But the best part all - it was only minutes away from my mother and sister. Travis commuted every day into the city, but he didn't mind; he loved being away from the city, especially now that we had Jackson.

It was the picture perfect Fourth of July. My backyard was filled with everyone that I loved. I watched as my niece Paige carefully sat down and held Jackson; with my other niece Emily sitting beside her as my mother snapped a picture of the three of them. I couldn't believe that Paige was already six and Emily would be three in a few months. It made me realize just how quickly time passed and to enjoy every single second of Jackson's childhood. "Paige and Emily come in the pool," my sister shouted as she floated around.

"You girls are the best big cousins," I said as I took Jackson from Paige's arms.

"I think someone is sleepy," my mom said as she walked over and kissed Jackson on the forehead. He let out a deep belly laugh at the sight of her, causing her to go into baby talk mode. "You're Mom-Mom's baby boy, yes you are!" He smiled at her again before burying his face in my shoulder. I placed his sun hat over the little bit of platinum blond hair that was just beginning to grow in. He was always such a happy baby, even when he was tired or hungry. I trailed little kisses on his cheek and sucked in his baby scent. I didn't think it was possible to love another human being as much as I loved this little boy.

I looked around the backyard and smiled. My world was finally happy. I focused my eyes on the man who was responsible for that happiness – Travis. He was playing a game of quoits with his father, my brother-in-law, and stepdad. He looked over at me and gave me that deep dimpled smile that still made my insides turn to mush.

I walked over to Travis' grandmother, who was sitting under the umbrella, and sat down next to her. "Are you too hot out here?" I asked.

"Oh no, dear, it's a beautiful day."

I placed Jackson on her lap and a smile stretched across her face. "Do you know how much I adore this little boy, Mia?"

I nodded. "I do. And if it weren't for you, he probably wouldn't be here right now."

She placed her hand on mine. "You and Travis were meant to be together, dear. It had nothing to do with me."

"Well, maybe next time, you will finally get a granddaughter. Not for a few more years though," I joked.

"Oh, Mia, I already have a granddaughter and she's the best granddaughter that a grandmother could ask for." She looked at me and smiled.

"Thanks," I whispered. "Hey, would you mind holding Jackson while I go make his bottle?"

"I would love to!"

I went inside to prepare the bottle. Travis came in behind me and wrapped his muscular arms around me. He moved my hair and whispered in my ear, "You are driving me crazy in that sexy bathing suit. Tonight, after everyone leaves and Jackson is asleep, we have a date in that pool." My stomach tingled just thinking about it.

"Umm, Travis, there's just one thing."

"What's that?"

"I told your grandmother and parents to spend the night."

"Oh, Mia what are you doing to me?"

I laughed and smacked him lightly on the arm. "It's a long drive for them. Plus, they love spending all the time they can with Jackson."

"Well then, I guess you will have to be a lot quieter than usual."

I laughed and shook my head at him. "You're crazy, you know that?"

"I'm not crazy, just in love with my beautiful wife."

"You are too sweet." I turned around and placed a soft kiss on his lips that immediately turned passionate. He pushed me up against the counter and ran his hands up my body.

"Travis, this isn't the time or place for this." I gave him a sympathetic smile. Truth was, I wanted him just as bad, but with twenty plus people out in the backyard, something told me that it wasn't a very good idea. His arms were still wrapped tightly around me. "Good things come to those who wait." I laughed as I ran my fingers along his face.

"Why do you have to be so damn beautiful?" He still knew how to unleash the butterflies in my stomach.

"Excuse me…." Juan cleared his throat loudly as the back door slammed. "This little boy is a little stinky." He was holding Jackson out at arm's length. "And Auntie Juan draws the line at changing diapers."

Travis took him from Juan's arms. "Aw, man," Travis said, referring to Jackson's diaper situation.

"Told ya," Juan said.

I laughed as Travis took Jackson upstairs to change him.

I smiled at Juan. "You are a very good auntie, you know that?"

"And you are a very good mommy," he responded.

"Thanks; it's my most favorite job in the world."

"I could see that." Juan smiled.

"Juan?"

"Hmm?"

"Thanks for being the 'best' best friend that anyone could ask for."

"You're welcome and thank you too, Mia. Now stop with all this mush. I have to get back out there to my fans and I won't be looking all sexy in my bathing suit with tears rolling down my face."

"Who the heck are your fans?" I laughed.

"Your mom and sister. I just came in to grab some hamburger rolls and save Mrs. Montgomery from your stinky little baby."

I shook my head and handed him the rolls to take outside. I looked up at the clock, noticing that it was just about time for Jackson's nap. I quickly finished warming up his bottle and brought it upstairs. I stood in the doorway, unable to wipe the smile from my face as I listened to Travis' conversation that he was having with Jackson.

He was sitting in the rocking chair while Jackson looked up at him as if he understood every word that he was saying. "I bet you don't even know how special you are? I'm going to make sure you know every day of your life. Your daddy loves you so much and you have the best mommy in the whole world, but I'm sure you already know that." He kissed him on the forehead. Jackson always seemed so content in Travis' arms.

I walked into the bedroom and handed Travis the bottle. "It's nap time." I knelt down alongside Travis as Jackson immediately sucked down the bottle. It amazed me how I had gotten so much enjoyment out of just watching him taking his bottle.

"We did make a beautiful baby together, didn't we, Travis?"

"Of course we did. With you as his mother, I never expected otherwise."

I leaned my head on Travis' shoulder and watched as Jackson's eyes slowly closed.

Travis had allowed me to check off two more things on my bucket list – the two most important things; him as my husband and the beautiful baby in his arms. Sometimes life isn't fair and takes us in a direction that we least expect. But as long as the outcome is sweet, it makes all of the heartache and roadblocks that we have to endure worthwhile. I couldn't have asked for a better ending to my journey. I had never been happier, being an *ordinary* girl, living an *ordinary* life, making me realize that Travis was right - sometimes ordinary is better; in fact, it's the very best there is.

The End

For an excerpt of Beth Rinyu's The Exception to the Rule, *turn the page.*

Excerpt from *The Exception to the Rule*, available on Amazon and Barnes & Noble. Visit Beth Rinyu on Facebook, at: www.facebook.com/BethRinyu

We walked into the large windowless meeting room that was already filled with people. We hurried, finding two seats together in the second row. The seminar was to give a brief overview of the current statistics of outbreaks, the area's most in need, and to answer any questions that we might have. The guest speaker was Dr. Julian Kiron, a pediatric oncologist. He had been over here several times to assist in pediatric cancer outbreaks that had been occurring recently. He was well known in the medical world as one of the most up-and-coming doctors in his field. I had read many articles about him and was curious to see the face behind the name. Although I had heard he was a dynamic speaker, I really wasn't very interested in hearing anything he had to say today – my mind was a million miles away.

Tricia read over the agenda for the seminar. I used mine to fan myself and shoo away the bugs. I wanted to get this over so I could go and check on Akin. I looked around at the other attendees. I focused my attention on a strikingly handsome man making his way across the room as everyone stopped him to talk. He was well over six feet tall with a perfect body. He looked like he was in his early thirties, with very strong features and perfectly pitched lips. His hair was jet black and cut very short around his ears with a little more length on top, showing off a very slight wave. He had a boyish smile that exposed two perfectly placed dimples. He was either born with perfect teeth or his parents spent a lot of money on braces. The intensity of his eyes could be seen from across the room. I had never seen eyes that blue; they almost didn't look real. Tricia mumbled something to me but I wasn't paying attention to her. I was too focused on this stranger who had just entered the room.

The room became silent as a short, stout woman approached the podium and introduced herself as Dr. Courtney Jones. I got butterflies in my stomach when the handsome blue-eyed stranger took the empty seat next to me. I tried to focus as best I could on what was being said as I checked off every item on the agenda in anticipation of it being over. I rested my head against the back of the chair and rolled my eyes whenever someone would slow down the process and ask a question.

"Bored?" the handsome, blue-eyed man sitting next to me leaned over and whispered.

My stomach fluttered – the color of his eyes was so intense. "Huh?" I said, taken off guard. "Oh well, I just have a ton of other things I could be doing right now," I answered quietly as I finally regained my composure.

His smile made me melt and I felt myself instantly smiling back. "Well, it's almost over," he said.

"Yeah, just one more stuffy doctor's boring speech to sit through. I'm sure he's so full of himself that he'll probably drag it out forever, talking about how great he is," I whispered.

His smile turned into a huge grin as he chuckled. I really didn't think it was that funny, but obviously he found some humor in it. Tricia slapped me lightly on the arm to pay attention. But it was of no use—I was much more interested in this beautiful man sitting next to me. I caught myself glancing at him once more – suddenly this seminar wasn't so boring after all.

Dr. Jones gave a brief history of Dr. Kiron's achievements, which most of us already knew. I was daydreaming and wishing that she would just get on with it.

"It gives me great pleasure to introduce Dr. Kiron." Dr. Jones said.

I was shocked when I saw the handsome blue-eyed man sitting next to me approach the podium. My face became heated and I knew I was probably turning beet red. I sank in my chair a little lower, wanting to find a way to escape from my humiliation as he gave me a quick smile before he began to speak.

"He's gorgeous!" Tricia said with her jaw nearly dropping.

Dr. Kiron's voice was just as lovely to listen to as his face was to look at. He seemed poised and confident. I couldn't stop staring at his eyes and a few times I felt like he had noticed as he glanced over my way. His speech finally ended and I had no clue what it was even about. I was still in awe over Dr. Kiron.

www.ingramcontent.com/pod-product-compliance
Lightning Source LLC
Chambersburg PA
CBHW070737180626
46818CB00007B/2882